The Girl's Guide To The Apocalypse

John Murray McKay

ISBN 978-1-7343341-9-7

Corvus Quill Press LLC
901 S. 2nd St. Ste. 201
Springfield, Illinois 62704

www.corvusquillpress.com

To Zakia. Thank you for the coffee and for the friendship. Jazak Allahu Khair.

When sleeping women wake, mountains move — Chinese Proverb

CHAPTER 1

I sat back on the battered old lawn chair, feeling the cold plastic through my torn gray shirt. Closing my eyes, I listened to the world around me. It was quiet now, and the only noise was the rustling of the far-off trees and the erratic fluttering of broken flags before me. A drop of scarlet blood hung precariously from my lips, seemingly undecided if it should stay or go before dropping sadly to the ground. With mortally tired eyes, I looked over the battlefield; only the myriad damaged traps, the broken heaps of bones and the slightest twitching and moaning of the odd orc indicated the epic ass-kicking fiesta that took place here only a few minutes ago.

I'd always had that feeling, hidden deep inside me, that this day would eventually come, though the amount of destruction brought a sobering calm over me. I never wanted this burden, nor did I wish to carry the cross he'd left me, but I had no choice. Someone had to take his place on the wall and stand watch. The distant lights twinkling behind me; I could almost imagine the townspeople sleeping blissfully unaware and safe in their beds.

They must never find out what happens around here when the sun goes down.

And how the hell would I ever even explain it to them?

"Orcs and lycans and skeletons and all sorts of things that go bump in the night are real, but don't worry; I'll keep you safe."

Only fifteen years old, I would've been carted off to the nuthouse long ago. I couldn't even get a driver's license yet, but here I was, the last line of defense against every sort of messed up nightmare that poked its collective snout from the underworld.

'You read too many comic books, Michaela,' I chided myself gently. I sat there for a moment, studying the bruises on my arms intently and feeling all the pockmarks and scars where it had taken damage. We had been through a lot of really screwed up things and seen stuff that could make any jock cry like a bitch into his low-alcohol beer. I glanced down to the off-pink teddy bear stuffed into my belt, seeing its missing arm and two black crosses where its eyes used to be. As the soft rain started to drizzle down and mingle with the creatures' spilled blood, I thought of her again. I missed my little friend and partner in crime terribly. She would have loved being here, right by my side, kicking the ass of any nasty that was stupid enough to get through our defenses.

Wiping away a tear and silently cursing myself for showing weakness, I looked up to the grove of darkened trees in the distance. The wind picked up slightly, rustling my long blonde hair. The rain grew subtly colder as I felt him approach. Both material and never really there, the shadow drifted across the battlefield, its eyes looking down in disdain at the carnage I had caused. Carefully stepping past a still functioning spring-loaded trap and shaking his skeletal head at me, the demon approached. We had been at it so long that a sort of mutual respect had formed between us. He threw everything he had in his arsenal at me, sent the rank and file and the elite of his army, but somehow I'd clung on and driven them back time and time again. Sometimes it was sheer luck, and the stupidity of the grunts he commanded; other times it was pure desperation and knowing that if I failed, there would be nothing stopping them tearing the townspeople to shreds.

Just a girl, her best friend, a ratty and torn engineering handbook, and the know-how to build the best traps and defenses you could imagine. It was weird, but I sometimes felt like the last gunslinger, the unnamed cowboy making his final stand; the sort Nazmirah and I used to watch on her parent's old TV in their basement. I could almost hear the Ennio Morricone score of *The Good, The Bad, and The Ugly* playing in my head as the shadow walked up to me and stared out from under his black cape. It had gone so well for him, destroying any who dared stand in his way with callous ease, spreading his darkness subtly through the land and gathering power as he went, and yet he could not get the better of a little girl somewhere deep in the heart of America. To be frank, it was pissing off Death terribly. He cleaned his fingernails with his scythe and looked down at the woman below him, raising his bony eyebrow at the sight of the teddy bear on my belt and shaking his head in disbelief. I stood up, looking the Horseman straight in the face, fire dancing in my black eyes; I smiled crookedly and spat out a blood-stained tooth.

"Bitch." Death said in a gravely, demonic voice. So there we were, as if frozen in time, two foes standing face to skull, neither of us willing to give an inch. The skeleton in the black robe and the girl with what was left of the engineering book floating around her. All while the cold rain came down, somewhere in a little town in America.

Away from this the scene, another figure emerged from behind the tree line. A curious creature in shades of red with a large soup-strainer mustache and a pronounced belly, squeezing the belt that was keeping his pants up. He tapped his chubby fingers on his belly and smiled deeply at the two figures in the distance.

"That's my girl." He said softly, stepping behind a tree and fading from view, the only sign of his presence the deep red, lingering glow of his eyes.

Six months earlier, in a little town somewhere in Middle America

"Jones? Miss Jones, are you even listening to me?" The elegant voice rose a notch as I slowly came to, lifting the engineering manual off my face and staring at the teacher with dark shadowed eyes. I blinked a few times, shaking my head and pulling my feet off the table. Must have fallen asleep in class again. Another late night, keeping watch on the wall, and it was starting to catch up to me.

"I doubt there are textbooks on American geography inside your eyelids, Miss Jones." I usually appreciated Mister Perry's sarcasm, but not this morning. I smiled sheepishly at the forty-something teacher and reached for my bag. He didn't have to say anything; the simple act of opening the door and showing me out was a clear sign of the often-repeated act of sending me to the principal. The others had an ungodly fear of the old man, but we had an unspoken bond deep down. We have both suffered in life, he with his messy divorce and me…well that's obvious. I think he recognized the scars of war in my eyes. I kinda liked him, though I never showed it.

"And what do we say, Miss Jones?" Mister Perry asked, a devilish glint in his eyes.

"Suck my dick?" I knew I was playing with fire, but I didn't care. When you'd faced the worst the underworld had to offer, then a trip to the principal's office and a bit of detention really didn't scare you.

"Suck my dick is the correct answer. We have a winner." I did not look back, merely heard the door close behind me. In case it isn't obvious yet, I was the girl who never fit in. The Dolls and Jocks thought I was nothing short of the Antichrist, and even the Goths steered well clear of me. It didn't matter to me, though; my only goal was to get out of this dump and back to the things that really mattered to me, like keeping the town safe from the monsters. I would have quit school a long time ago, but I'd promised my father, and the thought of disappointing his memory…no, I couldn't do that.

The halls were empty and quiet; the only sounds were the voices of the teachers inside their classrooms. I could find my way to the principal's office blindfolded. As I walked the well-worn path, I thought about the insane asylum they called a school. It could not be more middle-America and clichéd if they'd tried. It had the usual assortment of freaks and losers inside its prison walls: the Dolls, the Jocks, the Band Geeks (which I had a soft spot for. I would often listen to them practice when I was stuck in detention), the LGBTs, the Atheists, the Goths and all sorts of other denizens trying to survive this dump. Life was pretty standard for all of them, well, as much as can be expected. It would be best if they never found out what exactly was going on outside the town and how I was involved in it. I had barely made it around the corner near the cafeteria when I heard a banging from the nearby lockers.

'Not again,' I sighed, shaking my head. Reaching for a hairclip in my bag, I quickly picked the poorly made lock and waited the obligatory three seconds. A small figure burst from the locker. I caught her by the hijab, pulling her back.

"Where are those fucking clowns? I will stick my hand up their asses and work their vocal cords like a puppet," the irate figure screamed, clawing at the air. I pulled her slowly back, careful not to get bitten. She turned around in anger, then saw it was me. She immediately calmed down and smiled broadly in my direction.

"Why, Naz, why?" I asked, already knowing the answer.

"As-Salaam-Alaikum, Michaela." She beamed at me, fixing the scarf around her neck. I raised an eyebrow at her, and she fell quiet. "The Dolls again. You make one crack about how they plaster their faces with a cement trough, and you get stuffed into a locker."

"Sweetie, how many times has it been now?" Nazmirah was two years behind me and was the closest thing I had to friend in this godless place. She came to my rescue a few years ago as the Jocks were beating me up. We left a lot of bruises and bite marks that day, even though we both spent considerable time in the nurses' office. I was the guardian on the wall, but I was never a fighter. The whole Buffy-badass persona never applied to me, but I did what I had to do to survive. I admired Naz's spirit, even though she was only five foot something. Her heart was much bigger than that.

"It's all good, baby; it was worth getting a shot in on those stuck-up bitches." She paused for a moment, then smiled slyly at me. "You got the stuff I asked for?"

I rolled my eyes good-naturedly and reached into my bag. "You know this is ridiculous, right?"

Nazmirah took the USB drive from my fingers, looking at it like it was some sort of magnificent treasure. I had downloaded all the weekly American and Japanese wrestling shows for her. "We all got our vices, sweetheart; don't deny a woman this." Naz was utterly, hopelessly addicted to professional wrestling and she would often show me the collection of wrestling t-shirts she kept hidden in her school locker. Once or twice, I'd had to pull her off some unfortunate Jock she was trying a wrestling move on, often with unfortunate consequences.

"Why can't you just watch it on a TV like a normal human being?"

"Are you kidding me? My parents think Road Runner is too violent. Between them and Madrasa, do you think I have any chance of sitting down and watching my shows in peace? No, I gots to get my freak on here at break time."

I laughed softly to myself and walked away. "Stay classy, you nut."

"They can't touch me, baby!" Naz knew I was on my way to the principal's office but said nothing about it, just staring after me as I disappeared down the hallway. Maybe she knew I was hurting inside, but I wouldn't allow anyone near me.

'*Here we go again,*' I thought glumly to myself as I pushed open the office door, seeing the secretary sitting by her computer. She was supposed to be working, but I knew she was secretly writing an erotic novel, one that would make management sweat bullets if they ever found out.

"Moneypenny," I said casually, tapping on the counter.

"Bond. Back for our usual engagement, are we?" She didn't bother looking up at me, already knowing the drill.

"Thought you guys were lonely without me," I quipped back, smiling resignedly.

"Just wait over there, and he'll see you in a bit." The secretary pointed with a pencil, not taking her eyes off the screen. With a deep and palpable sigh, I sat down on the hard wooden bench and closed my eyes, thinking back on everything that has happened to me in the past, pulling the sleeves down low over the scars on my arms.

My name is Michaela Jones, and this is my story.

I am the girl on the wall.

CHAPTER 2

A few months earlier

I was never anyone special. Never the head cheerleader or the top academic student in school. Just above the wallpaper in this dump I called a school, that's where my little niche was. My goal was always to survive this place as quickly and safely as possible before moving on to an Ivy League university and putting this little town in my rearview mirror. I had bigger dreams than this place could ever give me. I would often sit afternoons daydreaming with the sun on my face, thinking of my life in a university. I was not sure which direction I wanted to take, but I always had a love for building things. Maybe engineering—but we'll see when the time comes. Guess I got my knack from my father. Henry Jones, my dad, ran a local shop where he fixed everything and anything. The place usually looked like a herd of elephants had waltzed through it, but he insisted there was a system in place. It used to drive my mother insane, but she adored him nonetheless. I smiled and looked down at the lunch tray before me, still trying to figure out precisely what the unidentifiable blob was before my eyes. It might have been food, but only for the briefest of moments in the distant past.

Tying my long blonde hair up in a ponytail, I glanced over at the Muslim girl sitting next to me. She was deeply engrossed with her tablet, watching some wrestling show. I barely knew her, and we never spoke. All I knew was that her parents were immigrants from Malaysia or somewhere thereabouts. She glanced over at me and bared her teeth. I wasn't in the mood for drama, so I took my tray and headed for the cafeteria exit. I'd barely made it a few steps when I caught the unmistakable smell of the Jocks. Jack Mathis and his crew of inbred paste eaters had taken up position behind the girl and started to push her in the back. They laughed and pulled her hijab. I watched in mute fascination as she lowered the tablet, fire flashing in her eyes. Like a pitbull whose favorite squeaky toy had been stepped on, she went for the Jocks, grabbing the nearest one around the neck. Hanging on for dear life, she tried to do an ill-fated half-nelson, but she was no match for the brutes. Wincing, I watched as Jack picked her up and threw her across the table, the poor girl landing with a thud on the sticky cafeteria floor. Then, to add insult to injury, he took out the comb he always carried with him and combed his hair back before stepping on her tablet and smashing it with his foot. Their laughter was hyena-like as they walked away, leaving her in tears on the floor. Nobody lifted a finger to help her.

I paused and looked at the door, then shook my head and turned to walk back to her. I saw that the tablet was toast and the screen was destroyed; I bent down and started picking up the pieces.

"What are you doing?" she asked, trying to wipe away the

tears. A blue welt was rapidly forming on her cheek.

"What does it look like?" I replied testily, suddenly feeling guilty for not saying something earlier. Don't know what difference it would have made to those Neanderthals, in any case. They weren't used to their authority being questioned, and anyone who did try standing up to them they made pay.

"I didn't ask for your help," she said softly, wiping a thin strand of blood from her mouth.

"Oh yes, you had the situation perfectly in hand." I smiled and reached out a hand. "Michaela."

"Nazmirah, but you can call me Naz if you want." She hesitated, looking down despondently at the crushed tablet. "You're not worried about hanging with the Muslim girl? I'm not exactly good for your social standing."

"The Band Geeks have more chance of getting laid than me, so don't worry about it. And sorry about Jake and the pack of drooling perverts he calls friends. That gorilla has been running riot on the school for years now, and yeah, he's an asshole."

"Really? I would never have known," Naz replied sarcastically, smiling grimly and turning to leave.

"Wait, let me have a look at your tablet. My father has a way of bringing things back to life. Don't know how, but the man has a touch. I'll ask him when I see him this afternoon."

Naz thought about it for a moment then nodded appreciatively.

"*Shukran*, Michaela, I would really appreciate that."

"Cool, now let's get you to the nurse and let her have a look at that bruise for you." Ignoring the piercing eyes of the other students, I headed to the exit with Naz in tow. '*Way to keep a low profile*,' I thought bitterly, really not wanting to be on the Jocks' or the Dolls' radar. Just do my time and get the hell out of this dump. As irony would have it, I spotted Bethany and her two handbag accessories down the corridor, posing for selfies as usual. Rolling my eyes, I kept my head down and motored past them. I really didn't need that particularly unwanted bit of nonsense today.

"*Cough* whore *cough*," Naz said just loud enough to be heard in passing.

"Was that needed?" I asked, looking down at the little figure and noticing the wrestling t-shirt she had on.

"I have no filter; it's a character flaw," she replied sweetly. I had to admit the girl had guts, though it wasn't always to her benefit. I laughed and shook my head, not bothering to turn around. I could already hear the Dolls hissing behind me. I didn't like how they had been looking at me lately, but I pushed the thought to the back of my mind. Eventually we reached the nurse's office and I bid farewell to Naz, bumping fists with her before turning and heading back down the corridor. I didn't have the luxury of friends, but it was nice to know I wasn't completely alone during my prison sentence. Knowing I was late for class and due for a tardy, I hurried down the corridors. I spotted Mr. Perry in passing. He was fighting with his wife, a fellow teacher in the teacher's lounge. He might have been a bit of a stick in the mud, but he was cool; he tried his best to get history into my head but failed most of the time. We all knew he was going through a rough time and that he deserved better than the harpy he called a wife; but we said nothing, preferring to keep our silence.

'*You are so dead.*' I knew exactly where I would be next period:

Helga, the Horrible, our nickname for Miss Hammersmith, the fearsome custodian of the English department. Some claimed she was a direct descendant of Attila the Hun, others that she'd worked a border post in Germany, circa 1980, either way, she was not a woman to screw around with.

'*Into darkness, I go.*' Trying to open the door as quietly as possible and sneak in, I may have made it two steps before the familiar grunt sounded in the classroom.

"So delighted you could join us, Miss Jones, maybe pop in to see some old friends," Der Rottweiler barked out as I froze in place. The behemoth (three hundred and fifty pounds, perhaps more) turned around and gave me her patented death stare. I twittered nervously, desperately seeking the sanctuary of my desk.

"Your lateness has been noted. The tardy slip will be on my desk after class," she stated matter-of-factly. I looked with muted horror at her huge bosoms and how the brown flower-print dress kept them at bay. Sighing, I settled into my seat and tried to pay attention to her class. She might have been nothing short of an SS stormtrooper, but I had to admit she was good at her job. Nobody explained English Grammatica better than her. The hour slipped by without any undue incident, and it was soon home time. Grabbing the tardy slip off her desk, I felt Helga's eyes boring into my skull from the back.

'*Do not look back and don't make eye contact.*' Quickly, I slipped out into the hall and out of reach of the Rottweiler. Unbeknownst to me, a slight smile formed on her face. She reached for an apple on her desk, turning it into ash and watching as it crumbled before her eyes.

It was only a quick bike ride from the school to the shop, and soon I had pulled up to the front curb. "Things and Times by Wayne Alexander Jones": My father took great pride in the name, having made the ornate copper metal board himself by hand, and I always took a moment to appreciate it. He was old school, and even though it would drive me insane some days, I still loved him for it.

"Dad? I'm home!" I shouted, peering past the piles of broken electronics and gadgets on the floor. The place was in a catastrophic mess, and one could easily get lost in the chaos. *'Wouldn't surprise me if they found Hoffa under all this junk,'* I thought sarcastically to myself, kicking the parts of a broken clock out of the way. "Dad?" I called out again, putting down my backpack.

"Right here, sweetie," I heard him yelling out. He was hunched over a desk with a welding mask pulled low over his face. I kissed him on the forehead and shook my head playfully at the mess in front of him. "I want to be put up for adoption."

"Humour. I recognize it. Very nice." He held up a perfectly working toaster and turned it over in his hands, marveling at his work. "How was school?"

"The usual delight, rainbows, and unicorns," I replied, digging into the fridge.

"That bad, eh? Oh, that reminds me, the school social is tomorrow night. I hope you haven't forgotten about that." He carefully studied me as I froze in place, my nose still stuck in the fridge.

"What? No, please! I have homework to do. Please don't make me go." I protested in vain, already knowing I was screwed.

14

"Social interaction builds character, and besides, it will be good for you. Maybe meet a nice boy. I would love to be a grandfather one day, you know." He ducked as a tomato flew past his head. I looked on in glum resignation as he smiled sweetly back at me. Throwing my hands up in mock defeat, I headed upstairs to my room. Glancing over my shoulder, I saw the door that led to the basement. It was always locked, and my father had forbidden me from a young age to go down there. He said it had some boilers and it was dangerous. Though I was curious, I respected his decision and never pressed him about it.

My father sat quietly by his bench, savoring the workshop's quiet. It was immediately interrupted by an errant fly. With a flick of the fingers, he sent a tiny fireball in the direction of the hapless insect, frying it instantly. He watched with distant detachment as the burnt-out body twitched on the countertop before becoming still.

The fires of war raged in his eyes.

CHAPTER 3

Somewhere in Middle America

A couple of bleary and bloodshot eyes stared back at me in the mirror. I had the enthusiasm of roadkill for the evening's school social, and I was less than delicate with my feelings about it. I would have given anything to just pass out on my bed and sleep until Monday morning. I still had a ton of homework to do and had barely had the chance to make a dent during the school day. There had been more dodging the knuckle-dragging members of Mensa all day long—and why could I not shake the feeling that Helga was watching me? I swear she'd been around every corner, but it must have been my paranoia taking over. It was weird, but even old Perry had seemed nervous today—and not in the usual way, as though his wife had used his balls for rearview-mirror ornaments again. No, there'd been an unmistakable vibe going around, one I just could not place my finger on.

'*What? Strange things going on? At your school with the most level headed and socially normal people on the planet?*' I thought to myself, looking at the inviting mess of my bed and trying to sigh loudly enough for my father to hear. After a few moments of silence, I shook my head and closed the closet door a bit too loudly.

'*Thank mercy I talked him out of the dress idea.*' I sometimes thought that my father didn't realize I wasn't his little girl anymore; I was only a few years away from college. But I guess Mom's passing hit him harder than anyone could ever understand. He didn't have anyone else but me; I understood that, but sometimes he got on my nerves a bit. Instantly feeling selfish, I grabbed my bag and pepper spray and headed out. I marched through the still settling chaos of the shop and paused at the door; looking back in a desperate, last-ditch attempt, I gave my father a fake death stare. He didn't bother looking up from his workbench. He was trying to coax a spring into some gadget whose purpose eluded everyone but him.

"Back before ten, dear, and if you meet a cute boy, I'd love to meet the young man before he asks your hand in marriage." He knew exactly how to get under my skin; a grin formed on his face as my howl of anguish erupted from the door. He listened carefully as the sounds of my bicycle faded down the street, then he sat back and opened the drawer by his right knee, carefully peering inside. Satisfied that all was well, he locked it again and placed the key around his neck again. Time dragged by, the hands on the antique black cat clock moving ever so slowly as he sat back and folded his hands, deep in thought.

What was there really to say about the town where I was born and raised? As American and middle class as anyone could think of, but without the apple-pie southern charm of other towns. It was a gray, drab place where the biggest event was the annual homecoming dance. It had the usual sights: the community hall, the just-too-small library, and the football field near the school. We were never a championship school, nor were we one of the bottom feeders. No, just lovely and comfortably depressing in the middle. I weaved my bike around the local mailman and watched with detached interest as the Mexican shopkeeper down the block stood in his doorway waiting for customers. He claimed he got robbed back in '83, but nobody believed him. As I said, nothing ever happens in this dump.

'Just a little bit more, and you are out of here.' I could almost taste the seawater of California and feel the warm sun on my skin. *'Michaela Jones, Brown graduate.'* It sounded pretty damned good to me. Pulling the bike up on the curb by the lights, I felt the fresh evening air through my long blonde hair. It was slowly inching towards winter and the yearly darkening of my mood. This girl did not do winter; I needed sun and lots of it, dammit. As I waited for the light to change, a shudder ran down my spine. I looked over my shoulder: the southern end of the city. No one sane ever went there. I had heard so many stories about this part of town, everything from sinkholes that could swallow a man whole to children that went missing, never to be found again. They said a drifter would lure them in, then strangle them before eating their intestines. There were also rumors that military experiments took place inside the darkened forest, but I took that with a pinch of salt. I remember how we kids would dare each other to go there, but we always chickened out at the last moment. Even the town's adults were wary of the mist-covered dark part of town where there'd been no development or building. My father told me once that in the 1970s, a man tried

his luck there. He barely made it a week before the construction site burned down, and his burnt body was found. No, the place was bad luck, and I knew it was best to keep my ass as far away as possible.

'*Get a move on Michaela; you do not want to be late.*' The sarcasm was sharp as I pushed on to the school, putting the southern reaches and its mysteries in the back of my mind. The sun was setting, and soon it was just me on the roads, all alone in a town somewhere in Middle America. Long blonde hair trailed in the wind as a skeletal hand reached over the crumbling ruins hidden deep inside the forbidding forest. Unholy energy pulsated beneath its feet, beating like a blackened heart.

Energy worth destroying the world for.

My mind was not with the work tonight, and I could feel myself getting more agitated with each passing minute. The workshop's silence was starting to affect me, and I would often find myself looking at the clock. You would think I'd be used to the tomblike atmosphere since Clair's passing, but it was never quite the same. I would often imagine hearing her voice or smelling her cooking again. She smelled of coffee and home, and I missed it so damn much every single day. I tried being strong for Michaela's sake, but it wasn't easy. She didn't need it, though; my girl had her mother's stubbornness and willpower and was one of the most influential people I knew. I knew she sometimes cried herself to sleep in her room, thinking I couldn't hear her, but every morning she got back up again and carried on. We had no choice; we couldn't let the cancer demon get the best of us. Lifting a picture of Claire, I ran a tear-soaked finger over her face, remembering the short time we'd had together. It was three years ago, on a family trip to Disneyland, and she hated getting her picture taken. I managed to sneak one in with her and Michaela. It seemed like just yesterday that we were together.

Sighing and putting the frame down, I paused as the shop door creaked open.

"Took you longer than expected, brother." I sat back in my chair and watched the dark-suited figure ease himself into the chair opposite me.

"Well, you know me, I'm a busy man. I had to mediate some sectarian violence in Northern Ireland, and you know how much of my time the Israelis and Palestinians take. Nevertheless, I managed to open my schedule just for you."

"Delighted," I replied acidly, seeing two hulking green demons appear at his shoulders. The little prick was never one to get his own hands dirty. "I see you've gone for a new wardrobe."

"Got to change with the times, brother of mine. The black cloak was a bit too Hollywood cliché for me, and besides, Armani suits me just fine." His voice was like an ice cube scraping over freshly lain gravel. I tapped the ornate worktable a few times, seeing the leftover parts for the upcoming week's work schedule before me. I thought I'd have more time to get it done.

"So how close are you?" It was a question I had replayed in my head over millennia, since Cain first struck his brother down all those years ago.

"It's the final roll of the dice, and, ironically, it all has to end here in Hicksville, USA. I expected it to be on some glorious battlefield with a million souls teeming towards me, but one can't be picky, I guess." He straightened his slick black hair and sat back in deep contemplation. The most minuscule of smiles formed on my face as I looked at him across the table. "Kept you busy for long enough, though."

"Irritatingly so. From Thermopylae to the Battle of the Bulge, you were always a thorn in my side, but I fear your time has run out. There is no guardian left, and I can retrieve the crystals at my leisure. You have put up a sterling resistance, you and the mongrels that fought for you, but you always knew I'd come out on top."

"Had to be a pain in the ass; it made life interesting, at least." I felt a green claw folding over my shoulder, the demon's breath both massive and shallow on my back. I stared Death straight in the eyes and nodded. It was an understanding that only siblings had, over eons of battle. "Last call?"

"Last call."

In a flash, I grabbed the demon's claw and pulled down with all my might. Throwing the beast off balance, I launched a fireball straight in his face. The demon howled in agony, clawing at his burnt face and tripping over a pile of springs. I couldn't allow them to recover; I grabbed a wrench and swung with all my might. The other brute grunted in dull pain as the massive brass tool clipped him behind the ear, knocking him to the floor. My brother had stepped back into the shadows, leaving the dirty work to his minions.

'Got to get out of here...got to get clear.' I couldn't take the chance of them finding Michaela here. Moving catlike between the heaping piles of metal, I worked my way to the exit. I didn't want to leave the manual behind, but my daughter's safety was more important. I was just a split second too late. A pair of leathery wings swooped down from the roof—and a set of wickedly sharp claws were embedded deep into my shoulder. Fighting with everything I had in me, I managed to wrench the imp off me, sending it hurtling into a standing clock in the corner. Black blood seeped from my wound, but I had to ignore the pain. I had to keep moving. I could feel the room starting to vibrate with movement, as more and more creatures appeared. Skeletons climbed down the piles of scrap metal, lifeless fingers clawing at the void, looking for another soul to tear apart.

'*Can't let them box me in.*' Through the gloom of the poorly lit workshop, I dodged from side to side, working my way to the far side of the room. I had set up the place precisely for a time like this, each pile and pathway perfectly conceptualized. One on one, I could take these sons of bitches, with one hand tied behind my back, but I had to think of Michaela. If they found her here…

'*Stick to the plan…get them away from the shop.*' I pulled out a rusty lever, sending a pile of gears crashing down on an incoming orc. He barely had time to squeak before being engulfed by the avalanche. '*Almost there…oh shit.*' A stone golem had planted himself squarely by the door, pounding his gray rock fists against each other—no way out but through him. I steeled myself and dropped my shoulder, hitting the behemoth squarely in the midriff and lifting him off his feet. With a sickening shatter of wooden splinters, we crashed through the door and into the outside alley. It had barely knocked the wind from the Golem, but it was enough to make my escape.

Or so I thought.

I never saw him coming, but then again whoever does?

Turning right into the jarring metal knife, I gasped for air and clutched my stomach. A river of black blood flowed from my belly as Death held me tightly. Unable to move, I locked eyes with him for what felt like an eternity.

"In the end, dear brother, you always had to know it would be me."

I laughed softly, lurching in pain while the life flowed from me. "Last roll of the dice." Death stared at me with widening eyes, then casually let my limp body slip from his grasp. "Should we set fire to the place?" The golem asked, nursing an aching shoulder.

"Why bother? Without him, the resistance is over. The stubborn fool should have seen the light centuries ago. Come, there is still much to do before we can claim the last crystal cache," Death stated coldly, turning and fading into the alley's settling gray mist, leaving behind only a body splayed out in a pool of black blood.

I made it to the social just before six and parked my bike in its usual place. Already I could hear the thumping sounds of something that once resembled music coming from the hall.

'*And cue the Jocks smoking behind the bleachers in three…two… one.*' I rolled my eyes at the hopeless clichés and marched on through the parking lot.

'*Just get this over with. Nice and easy with as few casualties as possible.*' I froze in the doorframe and looked out over the pathetic mass of humanity inside. A couple of seniors were trying to spike the punch bowl; one or two future divorce cases were sucking face behind the curtains; a few nerds from the chess club were hoping to sweep vulture-like on any leftover scraps with mascara running down her eyes. Gaudy and overly bright decorations littered the room, and the music sounded like something that would have best stayed behind in the 90s. My left eye started twitching as I saw one of the obviously drunk seniors ambling towards me—Mister Latin Lover thinking he saw a quick hit it and quit it.

'*Hell no. Michaela, exit stage left.*' I had overstayed my welcome; I turned to leave. I'd barely made it two steps when I heard the annoying, high-pitched voice of Bethany. She wiped something from her lips; no doubt she had sucked the soul from some poor bastard again.

"Didn't you see the sign outside? No dogs allowed on school property." She laughed over dramatically at her tired joke, reaching for a mirror in her bag. I leaned back and sniffed the air a few times. "Scraping the bottom of the barrel again, are we? I detect the usual smell of Jock and maintenance worker, but the third aroma escapes me. Is that…nerd on your breath? Prepping early this year for exams, I see. Not that it would help, but I am so glad you are making an effort."

"Whatever." She rolled her eyes and snapped her fingers as one of her handbag pets handed her a bright red chapstick. "Who invited you anyway? Nobody wants you here, you freak."

"Hey, finally something we can agree on. One side, skank, I need to get to a place where the discourse is somewhat of a higher level."

"Huh?" The beach blonde bimbo looked down at me in disgust.

"I said…oh, never mind. The solitary peanut in your skull

wouldn't understand anyway." I pushed past the Dolls, eager to be rid of them.

"It's a long walk home," Bethany said, cackling like a hyena and throwing a nail against my chest. Before I could say anything, they had already turned around and disappeared into the crowd inside. Fuming in silence, I decided it wasn't worth getting into a fight with them. True to form, I found three nail-sized holes in my front bicycle tire. I had no choice but to leave it here and walk home. I would have to fix it in the morning. Using every curse word I had in my admittedly impressive arsenal, I stuffed my hands into my jacket pockets and started the long walk home. Luckily, it was safe outside, and the only thing I had to worry about was the odd idiot out tagging a building. Like I said, middle America, Snoresville, USA.

The lonely evening hours gave me time to think again, plan stuff out in my head. Though I was furious at the Dolls, I had great company to keep myself busy. I had mentally written out the application letter to Brown a million times in my head, getting it down just right. I was so caught up in my thoughts that it took me a while to notice the flashing blue and red lights down the block. I wondered if it wasn't old Missus Harrison who lived nearby. She was a frequent flyer with the local ambulance service.

Freezing in my tracks, I realized it wasn't just the emergency services. There were also a few police cars. Paramedics were running around.

'What...no...no...' An icy hand clenched my heart as I started running. I was running till my lungs burnt inside my chest. Bursting onto the scene, my worst fears came true. Something had happened at the shop. I looked at the small brownstone building, not believing my eyes. I had to see what was going on inside. Ducking under the bright yellow police tape, I ran for the door, tears already flowing from my eyes. A paramedic grabbed me and pulled me to the side.

"Let me go! That's my father in there!" I struggled violently to free myself.

"Listen to me." He tried desperately to calm me down. "Michaela, you got to listen to me." Thunder flashed in my eyes as I looked at the EMT and saw the blood on his crisp white shirt. "Your daddy has been stabbed. He's lost a lot of blood, but he is still alive. You hear me? He's clinging on with everything he has, but you need to be strong now." It felt like my whole world was caving in on itself as the paramedic pulled me to the side, and I saw the gurney roll past me. He looked so quiet, lying deadly still with the plastic oxygen mask over his face. I broke free and rushed to his side.

"Daddy? I'm here… I'm so sorry…Daddy!" Eyes wide as he stared at the heavens, face splattered with blood. I could never have imagined seeing him like this, so vulnerable, so broken.

"Michaela…" He hissed inaudibly, struggling for breath.

"I'm here. Everything's going to be all right, you hear me? I'm not going to lose you." My composure broke as he reached out and gripped my hand tightly.

"Take this, and do not lose it." He blacked out, his head slumping back as the emergency workers wheeled him away. Head bowed in grief, I stood in silence, watching the ambulance roar away into the night. My mind was a maelstrom of jumbled thoughts and broken emotions. Only a few moments later did I realize that my father had given me something.

A red copper key lay in my hand.

CHAPTER 4

Somewhere in Middle America.

Truth be told, I couldn't remember much of those few days. It was a blur in my mind. Between numerous visits to the local police station, making statements and answering questions, I kind of lost my grip on reality a bit. Our local P.D. wasn't the brightest at the best of times, and I wasn't really sure what they could do. They kept me asking me questions I had no answers to, no matter how hard I tried. My father didn't have enemies; he was a mechanic, for Christ's sake, and would not hurt a fly. The whole town was abuzz about the attack, and I could feel people staring at me and whispering behind their hands. They treated me like I was some sort of endangered zoo animal, kept asking me if I was okay. The point was, I had to lift my chin and carry on, no matter how much it hurt. I went through hell when my mother passed on, and now it was being played out all over again.

'*Michaela Jones, badass.*' More like Michaela Jones, alone and scared out of her mind. However, I kept my mask on, saving the tears until I was alone. Simply smiling and thanking everyone who brought food and kind words. Nevertheless, as with all things, time passes and people start to forget. The yellow police tape faded away, and I was left alone again in the shop. The place was a complete mess, but I didn't care; all that mattered now were the daily trips to the hospital. The same old route, past the same old buildings, sitting by the same old bed with nothing to do but pray and wait for any signs of movement. I had never seen my father so quiet, so lifeless before. He could never sit still, was always busy tinkering with something, his hands moving like a blur. It was one of the many reasons my mother adored him; his restless soul spoke deeply to her.

Mom.

I didn't want to think about it, especially after everything that had happened, but this was where I had said goodbye to her. I was very young, barely six, and the memories of the long corridors, the smell of the disinfectant, it was all burnt into my subconscious. I could still feel my father's rough hands as he led me to her room for the final time. There were no tears left in me; my throat was raw from crying. I just stood there, suspended in time, my bare feet on the cold tiles, watching the frail body breathing heavily under the off-white bedsheets. She could barely talk, the mere act of moving her lips straining her beyond her limits. She simply whispered, "I love you," her deep blue eyes twinkling. And then she was gone, just like that. The heart monitors faded away into a cold monotone, and I was alone again.

'*Michaela Jones, badass.*'

There was nothing to do but sit by his side and make sure he was comfortable. I even set a tablet on repeat for him. He always adored the old John Wayne movies, and it might not have been much, but maybe deep down, he could hear the Duke again.

It was one rainy Thursday afternoon, and I was on my usual chair, eyes semi-closed and feeling the air conditioning on my skin. I had not been to school in over a week, and it was the last thought on my mind. I didn't have the energy to deal with those assholes, seeing their plastered smiles and fake words. No, I'd go back when I was ready. At least I knew I had a friend out there. Naz's mother sent over some Beef Rendang, and my little buddy would pop in now and again. Usually with wrestling shows in hand. We sat watching in silence, but it was enough. She carried me through those dark days and did more than she could ever realize.

My thoughts were interrupted by a nurse checking the charts, the squeaky sound of her cart jarring me back to reality. I was just about to get up and head home—it was getting late and I hadn't eaten—when I felt a slight vibration around my neck. It was the red copper key my father had given me. It was pulsating as if it had a mind of its own. Carefully peering at it under my jacket, I saw the copper glowing brightly, almost unearthly in my hands. I looked up quickly to check if the nurse had noticed anything. I need not have worried; she was way too occupied with changing Dad's I.V. to notice anything unusual. Amid all the chaos, the key had slipped my mind. I'd thought little of it since putting it on a lanyard around my neck for safekeeping. But here it was, glowing and vibrating, almost calling out to me. I looked up at my father; deep frown lines were etched on my face. What dark secrets did he hide? He was the most gentle and caring man I had ever known. It disturbed me so much because

I had no answers—just his still body and the mysterious glowing metal in my hands.

'*What does it all mean?*' I thought glumly, sighing and kissing my father on the forehead. With a heavy heart, I pulled my hoodie tight, turned and left the grave-like hospital room. The ride back home was hazy at best, my mind a million miles away. The first gray flecks of winter were coming down, making this already miserable place somehow worse. People were rushing to get home all around me, pulling up their collars against the sudden onset of cold, and even the shops were closing early for the evening. It didn't matter; it was just the lonely girl on her bike, caught up in the mess she called a mind. It was strange coming back home with everything so quiet. Flecks of yellow police tape littered the ground, and all the neighbors' windows were shut tight; most likely they were afraid to stick their noses out. I climbed off my bike and pushed open the door, feeling the sudden chill inside the shop. The warmth had left the place, and it felt empty. Folding my hands behind my head and rocking back and forth on my heels, I pondered for a second if I should just leave things as they were.

'*And what would your father say if he saw this mess?*' I knew I could not let him down now, that everything had to be in tiptop shape when he got back. So with renewed gusto, I jumped into the work. I threw a ready meal into the microwave, tied a bandana around my head, and got down to it. The first order of business was to clear a path to the back door and get it barricaded. I did not want more unwelcome guests in here. A pile of gears scattered across the floor caught my eye, and I started heaving the heavy pieces of metal back into a somewhat organized pile. I had to force myself not to think of what had taken place here.

'*Keep it together, Michaela.*' With the eggplant parm's smell filling the corners of the workshop, I worked fastidiously, only stopping to take a quick bite of the cheesy deliciousness before carrying on. Slowly but surely, I started conquering the mess, never throwing things out, even though I desperately wanted to. Little drops of red and black blood littered the floor, but I pushed them to the back of my mind, scrubbing away any signs of the fight. Just before two in the morning, I finished boarding up the back door and lugging a nearby cabinet in front of it. It was exhausting and backbreaking work, but it was something I had to do. Throwing myself into the work helped me forget my sorrow, even if it only was for a little while.

'*One more pile, then you can rest,*' I thought to myself, downing my umpteenth cup of coffee for the evening. A pile of old stove parts in the far corner of the store caught my eye.

'*Why the hell does the man keep these things? It saw its best days in the Nixon administration.*' I grabbed a set of coils, pulling it free and placing it behind me. I was almost to the bottom of the pile when I noticed something twitching there. A rat? No, it looked like...an arm?

"The fuck is that..." Bending down, I grabbed the bony appendage and yanked at it. I thought it might have been a leftover Halloween prop or something. To my horror, the arm suddenly yanked back, sending me flying over a pile of scrap metal and landing with a dull thud that knocked the air out of me. I turned in amazement as the arm broke free and made an escape for the door.

"Come back here!" I shouted, scrambling off the pile and grabbing a broom as I ran. The arm flat out ignored me, barrelling through the workshop at breakneck speed, sending spare parts flying in all directions. Not pausing to think how utterly insane this all was, I gave chase. The damn thing was quick, its bony fingers scurrying over the tiled floor. I could hear it bashing against the front door, trying desperately to turn the knob and escape.

"Come on, you…whatever you are. Show yourself." It had gone quiet in the workshop; I sneaked past the piles of scrap metal, listening intently for any sounds. A roll of nuts ran down a pile of junk a few paces before me. I tightened my grip on the broom.

"Where…" I never got to finish the sentence. The arm burst free just above my head. In an instant it was on me, trying to dig its bony white fingers into my skull. Falling backward, I fought mightily to keep it off me and slammed it to the ground. Back and forth we tussled, sending pieces of metal clattering to the ground. We were making enough noise to wake the devil himself, but nobody came to my aid. It was just me and this…thing. In the struggle, I caught sight of the microwave behind me. It was a crazy attempt but the best I could do. Grabbing the arm and smacking it a few times hard on the tabletop, temporarily stunning it, I then yanked the microwave door open and shoved the thing inside. The arm went crazy in there, cracking the glass, but it soon fell silent. I stepped back and tried to figure out exactly what was going on.

'*You're losing it, Michaela, you are losing it.*' The past few days must have caught up with me, and I was on the edge of a nervous breakdown. It was the only explanation for this insanity—but there it was, prowling like a caged lion inside the microwave. Scratching my head and confused beyond words, I stumbled back and sank into the deep comfy chair at my father's desk. I barely had time to think when the key around my neck started vibrating again. '*Not you as well.*' Pulling it off, I stared at the red copper key and felt it pulling towards the drawer. Almost like it had a mind of its own. Biting my lip, I turned the key and pulled open the drawer.

Empty.

Not a scrap of paper or anything. My tired mind struggled to comprehend matters, wondering why my father would give me a key to a drawer with nothing in it. '*Why would you do this?*' I thought, with my heart sinking into my shoes. Placing my tired head on the desk, I sat in glum silence. Slowly, ever so slowly, the key wiggled loose. It landed with a soft thud inside the drawer. I watched it scooting over to the side of the drawer. Nothing surprised me anymore. Leaning over, I saw for the first time a thumb-like indentation appearing in the metal. It wasn't there before; I would have noticed it, surely.

Shrugging, I leaned over and placed my thumb on the key. At first, nothing happened, then I could hear tiny gears turning inside the desk. I watched as the key sank away. A false bottom effortlessly slid open. With trembling hands, I reached into the dark and pulled out a book.

Wilson's Book of Practical Occult Engineering. First edition. It was a curious tome, dusty with age and covered in black material, with a skull and wrench embossed on the front cover. There was a strange and dark aura around it, almost an unearthly power radiating from the ragged pages. Why exactly it had to be kept hidden away remained a mystery to me, however. '*All this nonsense and secrecy for a book? Old man, you must be losing it.*' As I picked it up, a small yellow envelope slipped out and fell to the ground. Gently, I picked it up and opened it. The writing was spiderlike and elegant, and I would recognize it anywhere in the world. With eyes shooting full of tears, I read the first few words.

"*Hello, Pumpkin.*"

CHAPTER 5

Pumpkin. It's been years since my father had called me that. It was only when things got completely screwed up that he used that name. Like when Mom passed on. Wiping the tears from my eyes, I looked down at the letter again.

I really had hoped that you would never get the chance to read this. It seems my luck has run out, and the day that I always dreaded has finally arrived. I hate myself for lying to you all these years, but the hope was always there that you would never have to walk the dark path. Many have gone before you, but I so wanted you to be spared, live a normal life, and grow old peacefully. I hope you can forgive me one day.

I leaned forward, trying to make sense of the rambling words. It was so unlike my father, who was usually always direct and to the point. Something terrible must have been bothering him.

There is a darkness that haunts the world; an unspeakable evil kept at bay for thousands of years. We have been clinging on by the skins of our teeth, waiting for a worthy champion to appear again. We are Paladins, vanguards of the fight against the darkness, keeping watch over humanity since the dawn of time. We held the line at Thermopylae, and we were there at Orléans, fighting side by side with Joan of Arc. Countless times when humanity needed us the most, the defeat of the Spanish Armada, or in the mud at the Battle of the Bulge, we were there. I've always told you to think for yourself, and I am going to ask one more time, okay? You need to open your mind and realize that there are monsters out there in the dark— werewolves, ogres, shadowmen, things that go screaming into the night, and they are hellbent on the destruction of humanity. It's up to us to make sure that line is never crossed, holding them back, no matter the cost.

I lowered the letter and gazed at the skeletal hand lying prone inside the microwave. This was madness, pure madness, yet I knew my father would never lie to me. He was the most honest man I knew. I felt the shadows around the shop closing in on me and shuddered involuntarily. Could it have been one of these so-called monsters that caused all this? Put my father in a coma? It seemed ludicrous, yet it all added up. With my mind awash in thought, I focused back on the letter.

There are always two of us on duty, the Paladin and his engineer. This bond has never been broken for millennia, till now. The last Paladin fell nearly twenty years ago in Desert Storm. I was his engineer till the end, making weapons and traps for him. This is where you come in, Michaela. You will have to hold the fort and start preparations for the arrival of the next Paladin. His arrival could be tomorrow, or in ten years; nobody is really sure. I am placing a terrible burden on you, but there is no one else. You will have to be the engineer and make sure everything is ready for his arrival. I know you are young and know very little, but you learned from the best, right?

I grinned and wiped a tear away. I had been watching my father at work since I could walk. Learning and absorbing information. Little did I know he was preparing me for this seemingly impossible task. As I sat hunched over the letter, pouring over its contents, a pile of broken wires at the back of the shop started rustling. A skull wormed its way clear, its eyes glowing bright red in the dim light. Should have paid more attention, should have noticed the skeleton putting itself together again, reaching out and screwing legs and torso together.

You can access all my tools and parts in the shop, whatever you need you can use. There is an attachment to this letter showing you exactly where to set up your defenses.

I studied the accompanying map; my father had been meticulous in his drawing of the town. To my surprise, I saw that he had picked the southern end of town to install the defenses. He must have lost his mind; everyone knew that place was haunted and that no sane person would ever go there.

What? You think I chose to live in this town? It intersects perfectly with magical lay lines, carefully calculated by mathematicians over the centuries. This is where you and your Paladin will make your stand. Should you fall, then, simply put, it's the end of us all. Humanity will perish, and darkness will rule the planet. Kind of ironic, isn't it? After all the great battles, from Hastings to El Alamein, that the final battle should be fought in a tiny little town somewhere in Middle America.

I nodded, slowly starting to understand my father's brilliance. Nothing he ever did was without reason. He had picked this spot perfectly, just biding his time. The skeleton cricked its neck and straightened its jaw. Already it smelled human flesh; it could sense the figure sitting by the table. It reached out with a bony hand, picking up a piece of jagged steel.

But now I need you to listen to me, Michaela. I know you are a stubborn child; you got that from your mother, but please heed my words. You are not to take up the mantle of Paladin. You are to stay in the shadows and support the Paladin in every way you can. His role has been predetermined, since the dawn of time, and it cannot be changed under any circumstance. Your mother would slap me for saying this, but no woman has been a Paladin since the days of Joan of Arc, so leave the fighting to the warriors, okay?

My father always knew precisely how to get a rise out of me, but the enormity of the task began to dawn on me. All of fifteen years old and I was being asked to prepare for the end of the world. It was utterly ridiculous; it should have been some engineering professor at MIT or the like. Not little Michaela Jones, resident of God-knows-where, USA, trying her best to survive high school and make something of herself in life. I couldn't believe the faith my father had put in me. There was nothing to do but laugh morbidly and try to wrap my head around it all. The skeleton dragged its lame leg across the polished floor, its hand gripping the steel ever tighter.

But just so you don't think I am a completely heartless jackass, I left you a little present. Included with this letter is The Manual. It will help and guide you in your preparations. Included inside are my schematics, drawings, and concepts for weapons and traps, and notes on all the monsters and demons you are likely to face. I tried to simplify them as best as possible, but I know you are a clever girl and will work out the rest.

I peered past the letter at the dark and weighty tome lying on the table before me. I couldn't put my finger on it, but something was off about the book. It was a feeling I couldn't shake, but the engineering manual sent shivers down my spine.

The Manual has been with me since the beginning; we have seen many wars and battles together, and it's saved my ass more times than I can count. It's a temperamental thing when it wants to be, full of nonsense, but when you need it the most, the Manual will be there for you. I've included a care guide, just to help you along. I'm trusting you with my best friend; take good care of him, please. Oh, by the way, he might be a bit cranky at the moment. He's been sleeping in my desk for the better part of twenty years.

I wish I could tell you more, but you will have to stand on your own two feet now. There is nobody else on earth I can trust with this. Go get 'em, tiger.

I love you.

Dad

My eyes were locked on the letter, reading the last few words over and over. A slight rustling of papers caught my attention, so I lowered the letter suspiciously, peering over the edge.

The Manual was staring at me.

And what exactly was going through my mind at that moment? My eyes were locked on a book standing bolt upright, its pages rustling in the breeze. The impulse was there to turn and run screaming into the night, never to be seen again, or failing that, fall to the floor foaming at the mouth, convinced that I had finally lost my mind. The Manual leaned back, almost as though it were studying me. Its cover started to change. The skull and wrench faded away into a set of horrifyingly sharp teeth.

"Easy now, I'm not going to hurt you." I was talking to a book. Table for one at the funny farm, please. The Manual growled as best a book could, and before I could react, it pounced, flying past me, its jaws snapping through the air. It connected with the skeleton that had appeared behind me with a sickening cracking of bone. Falling from the chair, I watched in horror as the Manual tore the hapless skeleton to pieces. Bones were flying in all directions as the creature tried to crawl away. A final, brutal snap of The Manual's mighty jaws ended the proceedings. He had torn a gaping hole in the skeleton's skull, silencing it immediately. The remaining bones quickly disappeared down the maw of the Manual as it ruffled its pages in contentment. I got to my feet and dusted myself off.

'*Okay, this is where it gets weird.*' I bent down and opened my hand, knowing I was risking life and limb in doing so. "Hey buddy, you still hungry?" Reaching into my pocket, I fished around for a leftover bar of chocolate. Hands shaking ever so slightly, I held it out to the book. The Manual's cover changed again, this time to a question mark as it sniffed the candy bar. Ever so carefully, it leaned forward and pulled the chocolate from my hands. Just as I was about to touch it, the book scampered off into the darkness, peering out from behind a broken oven.

'*Keep it together now; it's just a demonically enchanted book. Normal Saturday here.*' Unsure of what to do, I gingerly reached behind me and pulled a framed picture closer. It was my father and me at Comic-Con. He had insisted we go dressed as Trekkies. Christ. I placed the picture on the floor, moving a leftover leg out of the way. The Manual crept ever so slowly forward, ready to run at the first sign of trouble. Leaning forward, it studied the picture carefully, its pages ruffling in thought. The cover changed, as it was prone to do, into a set of tears. I think it knew my father, his best friend, had been terribly hurt. Shuffling closer, the Manual looked up at me before leaning against my leg. I could feel it shaking in pain. It was almost human in its emotions. I hugged it tightly.

The strange scene—a girl with the world on her shoulders and her newly adopted partner in crime—faded out as I held the book safely against me. By some weird, cosmic coincidence, two lost souls had come together at exactly the right time. They were going to need each other more in the coming days than even they realized.

Far away, deep below the earth, Death was sitting on his throne of broken souls. An iron scythe in one hand, he twirled a shard of red crystal in the fingers of his other hand as he looked out over his kingdom. Legions of the damned, of orcs, goblins, and ghosts, stood ready at his command. Score upon score of night's creatures stood and chanted the Lord of Darkness' name. All against a scared little girl and her enchanted Manual.

The impossible battle had begun.

CHAPTER 6

Not much sleep for me that night. I rolled around for what was left of the morning, staring at the ceiling or sitting upright and thinking deeply. So much had happened in such a short while that I struggled to come to terms with it all. I must have read my father's letter a hundred times over, pouring over the contents and trying to make sense of it all. He must have been off his rocker, but then again, after tonight's events, my doubts were beginning to grow. The skeleton hand in the microwave did not last long—a brief yet disturbing midnight snack for The Manual. I did a thorough sweep of the shop before going to bed, but there was nothing else for him to munch on. I glanced over at the now still Manual sleeping on a nearby chair. It had made itself comfortable, tucking its pages in as a picture of a sleeping mask appeared on the cover.

'*Where do you fit in?*' I thought to myself, hearing the possessed book snoring. Well, as best a book can, I guess. It was no coincidence that it crossed my path at this exact moment. No, father had taken care of every detail, and now he had left me with all this. '*I am not ready.*' The words wandered through my head all night long, fueling my doubts with each passing moment. He could not expect all of this of me; it wasn't fair. I thought of all the paladins and engineers who'd kept the darkness back through the centuries; that the line could end with me seemed absolutely ridiculous. It was a mistake and one that I needed to fix very quickly.

'*And how, pray tell, will you do that? March on over to the nearest university and declare: "I have been chosen by a crazy old man to be the protector of all humanity against a vast army of darkness, and I need someone more qualified to take over this role, and by the way, this is my pet/bodyguard/possessed manual, but watch out for your fingers."*' Oh, very good, Michaela, that is a brilliant idea. I rolled my eyes heavenwards and softly swore at myself. The lack of sleep was affecting me, and nothing made sense anyway. Carefully, so as not to wake The Manual, I crept out of bed and headed to the roof of the brownstone. This was my private space, and I liked going up there when things got too much for me. Fishing out a bag of chips I kept hidden away, I sat on the ledge of the building and tried to clear my mind.

'*Maybe it'll still be a while before this so-called darkness comes knocking. With a bit of luck, I can get skipped over, and someone else can do it.*' I instantly felt ashamed, wondering what my father would have thought of me if he could hear me now. My hands were rhythmically diving into the bag; I could feel the burden already on my shoulders. It wasn't fair, it just wasn't fair.

The first morning rays played softly on my skin, and I could feel the cool touch of winter's air; it was always comforting in a way. Sitting on the ledge, I could see the edge of town.

The Southern Reaches.

The winter sun echoed on the piles of scrap metal and broken ruins dotting the landscape. It was amazing to think that such a barren and forgotten stretch of earth would play such an important role. It was almost beyond belief. Right then and there, the early morning wind whipping through my long blonde hair, I made up my mind:

'*You're going to get your life back to normal as quickly as possible. Father will come around soon, and then you will put your head down, finish school, and get your ass to college as quickly as possible.*' Pigheadedly, I chose to ignore many facts, not least of all the thing that was catching forty winks in my room at the moment. It might have sounded selfish, but I didn't care. This was not my responsibility, and they couldn't expect it of me. I was fifteen, for God's sake.

Realizing that I would have to get to school before the county officers came looking for me, I crumpled up the bag of chips and hid it away for next time. Taking one last look over the town and soaking in a last bit of golden sunlight, I headed downstairs for breakfast. The Manual was already up, doing some sort of weird yoga stretches on the carpet. Eyeing it suspiciously, I headed to the fridge.

"So, what do you eat?" I asked, rummaging in the fridge. Fishing out a frozen chicken, I looked back at the Manual and saw it nod in approval. He (it?) made short work of the meal, swallowing it whole. The only evidence of the meal was the solitary bone it spat out in the end. Burping loudly, the Manual settled back on the carpet, licking its chops and watching me get ready for school. I grabbed my backpack a few minutes later and paused before leaving. The Manual was staring at me again, fluttering its pages like some sort of demented puppy.

"What? Oh no, you have no chance!" I scolded it, to little effect. "You will stay right here, and I'll figure out what to do with you when I get back." '*Oh, nice one, Michaela, you are arguing with a book now. How interesting has your life become?*' The Manual looked at me dejectedly, two tears forming on its cover. It was trying to be cute, well, as much as a possessed book of arcane knowledge could be.

"Stay. You hear me?" I stated in my sternest possible voice, unlocking the shop's door. This was not a conversation I was keen on having: '*Oh hi, Michaela, is this your book, and why is it chewing on my leg?*' Hell no.

I'd barely made it ten yards when I heard a mighty cracking of wood behind me. My bike tires screeching, I looked back in horror. The Manual wasn't very receptive to orders: it had chewed its way through the front door with one mighty snap of its jaws. Seemingly unperturbed, it gave me the cute, butter-wouldn't-melt-in-its jaws look again. '*Well, this complicates matters, doesn't it?*' It would destroy the workshop if left unattended…and what if it got out? I could already see it chasing after the townspeople, mistakenly thinking they were some monster's afternoon nibble. I had only one choice left, and I hated myself for it already.

"Get in the bag, but if you so much as move a page, I swear I will turn you into a coloring book." The Manual hugged my leg and then happily hopped in my backpack, snuggling between the Geography and Calculus textbooks.

'*I must be crazy,*' I thought glumly, picking up my bicycle and heading down the road. The ride over to school was tense. I could feel the Manual stirring on my back, wondering for one demented moment if it was having a conversation with the other books. Soon school came into view. It was not something I was looking forward to. I didn't have the energy to be dealing with these chuckleheads.

'*Remember the plan. Get everything back to normal and try to stay out of the spotlight. Going to take it nice and easy and nobody will get hurt.*' With an already growing feeling of dread, I parked my bike and headed inside. '*You can do this, girly.*' The entire corridor full of students fell silent as I walked through, my head bowed. I could feel them looking at me, judging and whispering to each other. The whole town had been abuzz with the strange happenings at the shop. Many people claimed to have heard weird noises the night of the attack. I was the lonely girl, adrift in this ocean of suck while the sharks circled.

'*Just ignore them. Stick to the plan.*' I hadn't even thought about how I was going to get Dad on board with all this, to convince him to ignore all the tidings of doom and just carry on as nothing had happened. The Dolls were standing around by the girls' bathroom, preening like ridiculous parrots, squawking at some highly intellectual joke.

"Freak," Bethany coughed behind her hand as I passed by, the rest of the slime roaring with laughter. I paused in midstride, hands clenched in anger, staring straight ahead.

'*Let it go. Remember the plan.*' Lowering my head, I marched on. A cigarette butt cartwheeled through the air, striking me behind the neck. Gasping in pain, I sank to my knees on the pale green floor. I wanted more than anything in the world to stand up and hit her with everything I had left. See the blood splattering on the wall, hear her howling, clutching a shattered nose. I felt my backpack stirring. The Manual must have sensed what was going on.

'*Get out of here, Michaela, quickly.*' Scrambling to my feet, I clutched the bag and headed down the corridor. My neck hurt like a bitch, but I could not let them see that.

I finally made it to the lockers. Naz was standing nearby, flipping through a wrestling app. We didn't have to say much, a simple bumping of fists was enough. "Nice to have you back, comrade," she whispered conspiratorially under her breath. Noticing me favoring the burn on my neck, she became red in the face with anger and turned to have a go at the Dolls, but I gently caught her by the arm, shaking my head.

"This is my fight." Naz nodded, but I could see she was still upset. I wouldn't bank on her not trying to get Bethany in a headlock later on. "Catch you later, and I wouldn't mind checking out some of your wrestling vids, too." Anything to feel normal again.

"Got some nice new Lucha Libre yesterday. I have been dying to try out a Package Pile driver on one of these *al' abalah* (idiots)." I simply smiled and headed for class. It was nice to know I had someone to watch my back in this zoo. The rest of the day went smoothly, and I soon got back into the daily routine. I just had to keep my head down and all would be well.

Well, that was the plan until I got to Mr. Perry's class.

I sleepwalked through most of his class, something or other about tectonic plate movement and volcanoes. It didn't matter; I knew my work anyway. He was busy with a worksheet, concentrating as he walked among the students. Perry slowed down as he approached me. What did he want? I really didn't need any fake sympathy at this moment in my life. The lanky teacher paused and craned his neck over.

'*What the...oh shit...*' I'd forgotten to zip up my backpack. I looked back in horror to see Perry noticing the black cover of the Manual sticking out. '*No...no...no,*' I kept thinking, already picturing the hapless educator being mangled by the book.

"Interesting reading you have here, Miss Jones. I didn't know the library stocked such exotic materials." He said this in his calm-as-Sunday-afternoon voice, while flicking through the pages. To my utter astonishment, the Manual did absolutely nothing, lying as still as a baby while Perry perused its contents. No gnashing of teeth, or blood spurting, or screams of horror. It might have been the lack of sleep or the overabundance of strange happenings in my life, but I could swear I saw Perry's fingers glow a deep blue—just for a split second before disappearing.

"Every adventurer needs a good book," he said, smiling and placing the book on my table. Trying to stop my jaw from landing on the floor, I watched him walk away with all his limbs intact. I could swear the Manual was purring in happiness. What in the actual fuck was going on?

Thanking whatever god was looking over me, I heard the bell for the end of the day.

'*Just make it home in one piece and then get the squirrels in your head in line.*' Stuck in Weirdsville, USA, my life was getting nuttier by the moment, and I didn't like it one little bit. I streaked past the other students and did my best not to make eye contact—no time for after school activities today, not with this little bundle of destruction in my backpack. Nearly breaking into a run, I sped around the far building's corner and headed for the bike racks.

'*Come on…come on,*' I swore at myself, fumbling with the chains. My frantic thoughts were interrupted by a meaty foot stepping on the bike's bumper.

Jack Mathis towered over me, wearing his usual dumbass look and drooling ever so slightly. "Hey, freak. What the hell you doing back here?" he snarled at me in a slightly fake deep voice. His other nut clearly hadn't dropped yet.

"Please, I don't want any trouble. Just let me go." I tried shoving past him, but he was built like a brick shit house.

"We don't want your kind here, freak." His eyes grew cold as he shoved me hard, sending me flying over the other bikes. With blood streaming from my knee, I tried to get to my feet again.

"You don't understand," I said, desperately trying to buy time. I saw the zip on my backpack slowly opening. "*Oh fuck…*"

"I know exactly who you and your old man are. Bunch of fuckups that nobody wants around here. Can't wait for your dearest daddy to die so his screwed-up daughter can get the hell out of here." His words were like daggers, but I was paying little attention to them. The Manual was standing behind him, pages flickering red in fury.

The Jock heard the growling behind him and turned around. In a second, the Manual was on him, tearing clothing and snarling viciously in his face. Staring in wonderment, I watched the book go apeshit on the Jock, sinking its fangs into his leg. By some miracle, Jake managed to free himself, his hands flailing in the air. Blood streamed down his leg. He turned and ran—the book giving chase across the schoolyard.

Dusting myself off, I ran after them. "*Oh, please don't let anyone see them.*" It would be an absolute disaster if someone saw the possessed book. My luck held for the moment: most of the remaining students were busy on the football field; the rest had gone home already.

Things were going from bad to FUBAR, and I had to catch them before the Manual took the Jock to Squealtown and back. After a frantic chase across the yard and down the corridors, I finally caught up with them in a quiet corner near the science lab. Jake's clothes were in tatters, and the book had him up against the wall, licking its chops in anticipation of a quick meal.

"No! Sit, heal. Come on, you'll get bad indigestion." I dragged the ravenous Manual away from the Jock, smiling at him half apologetically. "Education. It's a killer."

Mathis did not stick around, but ran down the corridor and out the gate. I knew we had opened a whole new can of worms—but good luck trying to get anyone to believe him. I calmly picked up the Manual and cradled it gently. "What are we going to do with you, hmm?" It didn't respond, but promptly fell asleep in my arms. It had saved my ass from a terrible beating, but I still didn't know what to make of it. Only time would tell, I guessed. Shaking my head in disbelief, I took it back to the bike shed and placed it snugly back in the bag. Ignoring the searing bruise on my leg, I gingerly got on my bike and headed home.

Unbeknownst to me, Naz stepped out from behind a wall and looked at me intently as I left the schoolyard. She said nothing, but she tried to make sense of what she had just seen.

'*It's nothing but trouble. Lock it away before someone else gets hurt,*' I kept thinking as I pedaled home. Yet my little guardian had kept me safe today, and who knows what else was coming down the road? My head was hurting; it was all too much to take in. I pulled up to a red light. Deep in thought, I watched the afternoon traffic flowing by; everyone was carrying on as if it were just a typical day. My gaze drifted down the street, far into the distance to the Southern Reaches, the forbidden zone. I was feeling the Manual vibrate violently behind me. An evil vibe flowed down Main Street, washing over me. It was like I was losing control of my body; I turned the bike around in a trance and my feet started moving as I pedaled down the street.

Into darkness, I went.

CHAPTER 7

Somewhere in Middle America

'*What are you doing?*' The fateful words were ringing through my head as I kept pedaling, entranced by the ever-expanding sight before me. Should have stuck to the plan, and nothing would have happened, but something kept drawing me to the Reaches. I couldn't explain it, but there was an overpowering force pulling me towards it. Everything in me was screaming to turn around and ignore the siren song.

'*Don't do it, Michaela, don't do it.*' Shivering involuntarily, I zipped my jacket up and pedaled on. A strange tunnel-vision occurred. Everything faded into a blur; there was nothing but the thumping call of the unknown before me. Before I knew it, I had reached the last line of abandoned warehouses at the end of Main Street. All children knew it was the line that should never be crossed: to there and no further. I looked up at the broken windows, the last glint of sunlight fading away against rusted brown metal. Craggy weeds crept up the sides of buildings. It had become eerily quiet, and I soon realized that I was utterly alone. The winter's chill had driven everyone inside.

'*And now you're going there in the dark. Oh yes, this was a brilliant idea.*' Ignoring common sense, I carefully rode past the warehouses, stopping when I came to the train tracks. Involuntarily, I glanced from side to side. '*Stupid. The last train came past here in the forties.*' I saw flecks of rusts flapping on the cold train track as I eased past the once brightly painted boom gate. Darkness was building in the corner of my eyes, folding itself like material around me. Any sane human would have turned around and fled, like the devil himself was chasing her. Then again, when have I ever been normal? Grimacing at that last thought, I guided the bicycle on the dirt road, the town behind me fading away into an afterthought. The Manual peeked its cover out from the backpack and surveyed the surroundings. I could sense it was feeling nervous, but it stayed resolute, sitting behind me like some general going into battle.

"We are going to have a long and complicated talk when we get home," I said. Then my attention was diverted by a wall of shimmering energy appearing before me. Too late to hit the brakes, I crashed hard into it, toppling off my bike. "What the hell…" I whispered through clenched teeth, a dust cloud forming around me. It was the second time I'd been sent sprawling over my bike, and I was fed up with it. The Manual shook its pages in an annoyed fashion and pushed me upwards. I studied the anomaly carefully. It shimmered in a faint, nearly invisible glow that would never have been detected from town. It would take a lunatic to get close enough.

'*That would be you, dear.*' Ignoring my own sarcasm, I stepped back to get a better look. The ghostly wall ran for miles in both directions, but it didn't seem to affect anything around it. The ruins of old buildings and piles of leftover scrap metal stood stoically in the late afternoon sun. I hammered on the wall, watching it ripple with energy but not opening to let me through.

"Now what, genius?" I asked the Manual as it stood for a moment, thinking deeply. A light bulb formed on its black cover. Flicking its pages open, it prodded my leg, eager to show me something. I saw a picture of a big, brave warrior and an assistant trailing behind him; they were accompanied by the words 'Paladin' and 'Engineer' embossed in bright red letters on the ancient-looking pages.

"Worth a shot," I mused to myself, leaning forward and touching the wall. "Paladin," I said in a brash, confident voice, but nothing happened. The wall simply carried on shimmering, unperturbed by my actions. "Paladin," I screamed, willing the wall to listen to me through sheer force. Still nothing happened, and it was starting to piss me off. I was tired, hungry, and my legs were hurting like a bitch. The book coughed and raised itself so that I could have a better look.

"What?" I snapped at it. The Manual stood dead quiet, its pages open to the same illustration. I looked at the second word as it shifted slightly around on the page. Sighing deeply, I then looked up at the wall again and placed my hand on it. "Engineer." My voice was calm. The earlier brashness had faded from it. The wall relented, almost as if it were alive, and a door swung open, just big enough for the Manual and me. Picking the book up, I stared into the black void, all rational sense telling me to turn and run, telling me that this was the point of no return. Nothing would ever be the same once I stepped through that doorway.

'*Going to have to make a choice here, girly. It's all or nothing.*' I felt the power calling me inside growing stronger with each passing moment. The once quiet invitation had turned into a raging chant. The Manual nodded at me, sagely, touching my hand with its cover. I was being pulled headfirst into the impossible, into the darkest of unknowns. I didn't know what to do. All of fifteen and faced with this massive choice: I was scared and alone.

'*This is what your father would have wanted for you.*'

My eyes still shut, I took a deep breath and stepped over the threshold. A brisk wind greeted me as I looked up in wonder.

The battlefield lay before me.

A vast field—patches of green grass and swathes of dark soil—ran for miles. It was broken up here and there by the ruins of old brick buildings, dotted like little specks across the vista. They made a long but sporadic wall, standing against the gloom. In the distance, a dark and eerie forest rounded it all off. An evil aura radiated in black swathes from the forest, and I knew instantly that it was where the attack would come from. The darkness only had one path to the wall behind me, and it ran straight through the battlefield.

"Unbelievable," I said in awe, trying to take in the sheer size of it all. It would take an entire army to defend it, not just one warrior. To expect more was madness. A sudden urge took over: I had to see more. I started walking, pushing the bike next to me. The sun began to set behind the horizon and long shadows swept over the ground. Enthralled by everything around me, I pushed my fears to the side and began to explore.

"Hand me my flashlight, please?" The Manual ducked into

my backpack and rummaged around inside. Soon the yellow light was sweeping across the brick wall, dancing between missing bricks and craggy holes. Carefully placing my feet on crumbling steps, I climbed to the top, hearing the forest's rustling in the distance.

"It's too big to cover alone; the only way of evening the odds is to create a funnel and bring them inside," I said to the book. "Did my father leave a map or something with you?" The Manual nodded and produced a tattered piece of paper from deep inside its covers. I sat intently poring over the map in the beam of my flashlight.

"According to this, there is hill country all along this line, here. It won't be easy to cross, and it will force them to the plains in front of us. The problem is the far left: too much ground to cover." Tapping my fingers on the parchment, I pondered this newest obstacle. The Manual leaned over and tapped on the top left corner of the map, trying to get my attention.

"What is it?" I looked intently at the faded blue line before realizing it was a dam of some sort. Must have been leftover from whoever lived here once. I thought about blasting the dam and trying to wash the monsters away in one go.

'Stop thinking like a Paladin and more like an engineer.' I had to plan long term and think laterally.

"What if I make a hole in the dam and then flooded that section of the battlefield? Turn it into a mud pit. Anything heavy would get stuck instantly, making them vulnerable to gunfire." The Manual nodded, though a bit hesitantly. The spark of madness inside me was growing by the second, and I could almost see everything unfold before me. "But that will have to

wait for another day. It's getting late, and we need to get home."
Shelving my plans, I turned to head home. But a glimmer of light
caught my eye, barely a hundred yards ahead of us on the
battlefield.

"Get down!" I hissed at The Manual, grabbing the book and
sinking behind the parapets. We were not alone. Someone…
something was out there in the dark. '*Get out of here girly; you have
no idea what is waiting for you.*' But curiosity overcame me, burning
like glowing coals in the night as I looked down at The Manual. I
could swear it was grinning in the gloom, eager to get some exercise
again.

"Come on; I want to see what it is. Just a quick look." Grabbing
a forgotten plank, I scaled down the steps; the flashlight, turned off,
was gripped firmly in my other hand. Night had fallen, and specters
danced around every corner, fuelling my paranoia. The wet ground
crunched underfoot as I picked my way carefully forward, eyes
peeled for any sign of a monster lurking in the dark. All remained
calm, belying my sense that things were about to become batshit
insane. Another light appeared as if from nowhere. "How is that
possible? There's nothing but flat earth for miles around. Unless…"
I scampered over a mound of dirt and crept closer to the light.
Eyebrows furrowing, I stopped and took a knee. I could just make
out the faintest of sounds.

"There! Do you hear it?" The Manual grunted as I pushed it
down to the ground. "It's below us," I whispered in trepidation.
Putting my finger to my mouth, we scooted forward through the
darkness, continually stopping and checking. It was almost too
faint to detect, but soon the chipping of metal on stone grew
louder.

"Down." I hissed. A dim orange glow appeared before us. It was a lantern, but it was too dark to see what was holding it. My suspicions were confirmed, though; there was a hole beneath us, and something was going in and out of it.

'*This is your common sense speaking. Turn around and get help; it's the sensible thing to do.*' But how could I get help? Nobody would ever believe me; I was stuck with my finger up my ass. I had no choice but to investigate the mystery below. "Stay quiet and watch my back." The Manual nodded vigorously and flexed its pages in an act of bravado. We scampered across the ground to the hole's entrance and waited in the dark.

"As soon as the next one is clear, we go inside, and if we run into trouble…" I didn't have to finish the sentence; the Manual picked up what I was putting down. An image of a blood-stained sword and people running in terror formed on its cover. We didn't have to wait long. The sounds of footsteps soon appeared and grew louder. Ducking down, we didn't have time to see what it was disappearing into the dark.

Easing down into the hole, I immediately felt a warm glow around me. I didn't need the flashlight; a faint light bathed the cavern walls in an orange hue. The sounds of hammering began to grow louder with each passing step, echoing around the walls.

"What the hell…" I barely had time to think as a figure came wandering around the corner, a knapsack slung over its shoulder. Ducking down a side shaft, I watched in disbelief as the pointy red hat disappeared around the corner. I heard swearing and cursing as the figure lugged the bag topside.

It was a gnome.

"You're fucking with me, right?" I asked the book. It merely shrugged sheepishly in reply. '*And now the garden ornaments have come alive. Fun times.*' Shaking my head, I waited till the pint-sized creature was gone before moving on. This was not just a cavern; there was an operation of some sort going on. We worked our way forward as more gnomes appeared, some pushing carts loaded with rocks, others carrying burlap bags over their shoulders to the surface.

"Got to get a better look, stay close." I saw a rocky ledge not too far from me, leading to the main cavern. The intense orange light was radiating from inside. I had to be careful and not give the game away. Taking a deep breath, we ran for it, diving into a dark corner as two gnomes marched past. They stopped and looked around, billy clubs in their hands. It felt like an eternity. Clutching the Manual tightly, I waited with bated breath. We could have taken the little shits, but there was no telling how many of them were inside. After a few moments, the gnomes moved on, satisfied that all was well. I nodded to my companion; we crouched low and headed up the ledge.

Moments later, we were entering the main cavern. I peered out from behind a rock, and what I saw next took my breath away.

A gigantic red crystal, easily a few stories tall, stood in the center of the cave. A hundred gnomes were hammering away at it with pickaxes, dragging the stones into the dark. The hairs on my neck stood on end as I looked on. The stone had a power about it, stronger than anything I had ever experienced in my life. It radiated energy outwards, filling the dark corners of the cave. We had stumbled on a massive mining operation. There was no going back.

CHAPTER 8

On the other side of the wall, just outside a town in Middle America

I couldn't stop staring at the pulsating orange crystal, its power locking my eyes to it and refusing to let go. I could feel it filling the cracks and nooks of my soul with warming energy, overwhelming me. As if in a trance, I stood up behind the ledge, tilting my head sideways, trying to understand its otherworldly presence. The Manual tugged on my leg, trying to get me to snap out of it. Ignoring the book, I walked back down the ledge to the main entrance. I was oblivious to the danger around me. I had to see the crystal up close…touch it…embrace it.

Eyes wide, a picture of calm, I walked into the main cavern. My face was bathed in the encompassing orange light. A sudden silence fell around me as the gnomes' jaws dropped, and they stared back in shock. It didn't take them long to regain their composure. They came at me with their pickaxes, but I was oblivious to their presence; my eyes glazed over in the presence of the crystal. Seconds away from disemboweling me, the knee-high terrors froze in their tracks. The Manual had appeared behind me, a picture of a hand calmly cleaning its nails appearing on its cover. An uneasy silence settled over the squad of miners as they nervously looked at each other, one even erupting into tears. This wasn't the first time they had run into the possessed book.

The Manual blew them a kiss; then vicious fangs appeared as it leaped at the helpless mob. Utter chaos broke out in the cavern as the gnomes scattered in all directions. Any thoughts of resistance were long forgotten. The Manual snapped at the heels of a fat and tasty looking gnome. Panicked miners climbed over each other haphazardly, trying to escape the vicious creation. Packs went cartwheeling into the air and red hats littered the ground as the Manual barrelled into them, hoping to snag an errant leg or arm in the process. A young gnome tried his luck and swung his pickaxe wildly around, but he did not last long. The Manual knocked him down and applied a perfect Camel Clutch to the hapless pest.

The carnage continued around me, but I was still caught in my trance. I moved forward like a zombie, hand outstretched and mouth agape. The crystal was looming large over me. The sounds of the fighting did not reach me. I heard nothing but the low humming of the strange artifact mere inches away from me. It was speaking to me, calling me. It seemed distant, detached, as if adrift from my body. Finally giving in, I reached out and touched the crystal. Instantly, the power grabbed me, pulling my essence away—leaving behind an empty husk and sightless eyes. I was thrown across the cosmos, my screams dissipating into infinite space. Galaxies rushed past me in the blink of an eye, entire universes appearing and collapsing in seconds. Curling up in a ball and crossing my arms, I drifted through the impossible darkness, the glow of the burning red sun illuminating my face.

I was alone.

It was the same feeling I'd had when mom died, when I was sitting hunched up in a little bundle on the cold hospital floor. The same feeling of emptiness when I realized she was gone and that I would never see her again. The same tears running down my face. Wet glints echoed the starlight around me. Spinning around in the lunar glow, I heard the distant call again. It was human and it was willing me closer.

Succumbing to its call, I bowed my head and let the energy take me where it wanted. Dark space faded away to soft gray light, swathes of blue and white swirling around me. I was falling to earth again, closing my eyes and smelling the bittersweet smell of fresh dirt. When I opened my eyes, I was kneeling in a field of bright yellow corn. A hand stretched towards me, but I could not see who it was. The face was obscured by the intense morning sun.

"Hey, Pumpkin."

"Dad?" My father's voice washed over me as his rough hands pulled me up. It had to be a dream, but there he was, his broad smile chasing all my darkness away again.

"I…I don't understand." It was so much to take in. I looked at him with confusion etched into my face.

"Listen, sweetie, I know you have many questions, but you've got to let me talk now, okay? We don't have much time left." I nodded as he led me through the swaying, golden cornfields. "I always knew you would figure out a way past the wall and find the crystal down below. We raised a brilliant girl; there was never any doubt about it." I looked on in awe as my father swept his hand across the universe, showing me an infinite number of wars and battles fought over eons of time. Standing in awe, we watched the Israelites at the gates of Jericho; we heard their chanting as they faced the giants of the impossible city.

"What does it mean?" I asked, unsure of what I was witnessing. The sounds of battle filled the air.

"Look, Michaela," my father replied, pointing to a group of nearby men as they opened an ornate golden box and took out a shining crystal. The same one I had seen in the cave. "The Arc of the Covenant. Housing the most sacred texts of Judaism and the Aurora crystals. Its origins are known only to the gods themselves, but some say it has been around since the first dawn of humanity."

The scene changed again, and we were standing on a cliff overlooking a swirling and mighty ocean. The clashing of steel against steel echoed through the mountain walls as I looked upon a tiny group of soldiers holding the line against a vast army sweeping in from the ocean. At its rear, I saw the now-familiar glow of the crystal.

"Leonidas defying the Persians at Thermopylae. He and the brave few held on longer than anyone could have dared imagined. Fought till the crystal ran out of power and shattered." My father spoke as if in thought, almost as if he'd walked those blood-stained beaches with them.

"But what does it do?" I asked as the brave warriors made their last stand, falling one by one.

"Isn't it obvious, Michaela? The Aurora Crystals are concentrated power. It's where earth's lay lines come together in solid matter. Whoever possesses the crystals, even a tiny sliver of them, has power beyond mortal understanding. They can change the world as they see fit."

"But can people be trusted with so much responsibility?"

My father smiled proudly, pulling a cloak tight around him. "Clever girl...but to answer that: sometimes, no." The ancient cliffs faded away, and soon we were standing on an empty field, heavy clouds thundering overhead. I peeked past my father's shoulder and saw a soldier standing nearby. Gripping a rifle tight in his hands, he stared at the heavens as dark shapes appeared and bombs rained down death and destruction. "Battle of Britain, 1940. England is facing its darkest days. Somehow that son of a bitch got his hands on the Aurora Crystals, and he brought hell with it. The world changed in those turbulent days and not for the better."

"But he lost the war, how is that possible? You said the crystals gave immense power to whoever held them." The gray skies of England lit up with the sounds of dogfighting as Spitfires and Messerschmitts tore at each other.

"The crystals eventually ran out of power, but it was the strength of the human spirit that held them safe. You humans are stronger than we give you credit for." My father smiled softly to himself, tapping the Tommy on the shoulder. "But then the crystals I saw back home..." My words trailed away as the grim reality of the situation dawned on me.

"Are the largest collection ever found." My father finished my sentence. "Who even holds it, well, their power will be unimaginable, and not even the gods will be able to stop them. The destruction of planet earth will be complete and final."

"What kind of human being could crave such power?" I

asked, shaking my head in disbelief. Then I watched as the earth imploded in a sudden and violent ball of flame, leaving nothing but choking dust behind.

"He is not human, sweetie," my father replied. "He is the final resolution that you must all face one day." We were now floating above the nothingness that I once called home. "He is Death."

"You mean the black cloak and scythe? The grim reaper?" I raised an incredulous eyebrow in his direction.

"Not the Hollywood version you mortals know. No, he is concentrated but necessary evil. What he plans is beyond the normal. Death aims to seize the Aurora Crystals and bring an end to humankind and its ways." He shrugged sheepishly. "Family."

"But why? What can he hope to gain out of all of this?"

"Death believes there is no hope left for you mortals and wants to end it all. Eventually, the universe and the gods will shape another earth, and he can start again. He could never be trusted alone with you humans."

"Then I…"

"You prepare for the coming of the next Paladin. That is your duty and nothing more. Everything must be ready by the time he arrives. Ready the defenses, but you must not get involved beyond that. The engineer stays behind and never comes out of the shadows. Do you understand me, Michaela?"

I nodded. "But I am alone, how will I know what to do?"

"You've got a friend. I know it's weird, but you can trust it with your life." He smiled warmly and raised my chin again.

"The Manual?"

"He has kept many an engineer before you alive. You will find no more trustworthy a companion. Just remember to keep feeding him daily. And no junk food, okay? He gets bloated and cranky. That's how the city of Troy fell, but that's a story for another day. Together, I know you will be just fine." I nodded again, already feeling the weight of the world on my shoulders. I bit my lip. I didn't want to ask the question, but somehow it just slipped out. "You're not human, are you?"

"No, but I was always your daddy." He hugged me tightly. "I have to go, Pumpkin; our time is almost up."

"What? No!" I exclaimed in shock, gripping his hand tightly. "You can't go, not yet. Please stay?"

"Your mother is calling me, but I know you'll be just fine. Hold the line, and I'll see you soon. Love you." My father kissed me on the forehead, and I felt him slipping away from me. I held back the tears as long as I could, trying to show him I could be strong and that he could be proud of me. Eventually, he faded away into golden sunlight, and I was thrown back to reality. The pulsating crystal was before me, my hand still stretched towards it. Awakening from the haze, I looked around at the carnage around me. The Manual was sitting on top of a pile of gnomes, picking his teeth with a little red hat.

The reality hit me like a sickening blow to the stomach. I turned and started running, grabbing the Manual and stuffing him into my backpack. Through narrow corridors, I flew back to the surface. I fumbled for my bike and rode as fast as my legs could pedal through the deserted town, tears streaming down my face. I pedaled till there was nothing left in me. I kept whispering to myself, over and over, "No, please, God, no."

I didn't have time to park the bike; I left it there in the hospital gardens and ran up the steps. The corridors were quiet, the only sounds made by the night nurses shuffling on their rounds. The receptionist waved at me to stop, but I ignored her, no time to waste, had to make it. '*Come on…not again, please, no.*' One corner to go. I was almost there. I froze in my tracks as a nurse grabbed me tightly in her arms. She shook her head sadly as I wept inconsolably.

"*He's gone, baby.*"

CHAPTER 9

The human body has a strange way of protecting us, of sensing when harm is coming our way. It shuts down and blocks out everything around us. I felt nothing. A cold numbness settled over me as I stood watching an open grave. What did they expect me to do? Scream and wail on the ground like some lunatic as they frantically tried to console me? This wasn't the fucking Kardashians; it was real life, and every moment that ticked by hit me that little bit harder. The cold reality that my father was really gone and that he would not be sitting at his workbench when I got home. I hadn't even begun to process what happened when we last spoke—that fantastic story he told me before leaving. It was too much to take in. I was in a daze.

At first, I had sat next to his hospital bed, holding his limp hand in mine. I refused to let go, gripping it tightly. The nurses and orderlies gave me some space; maybe they remembered me from the last time when my mother passed on. Must have sat for hours next to him, saying nothing, my head resting on the edge of the bed. The Manual had fallen asleep on my lap, snoring softly. I swallowed my tears and hid my grief down deep. The same walls I had put up all those years ago were up again, and I wasn't about to let anyone over them. I was the girl alone, sitting quietly next to a shroud-covered body in a tiny little hospital somewhere in a town in Middle America.

The next few days passed by in a blur as funeral arrangements had to be made. The state sent over a social worker to assist me, a somewhat overweight woman who kept calling me the wrong name. She even tried contacting my father's next of kin. It was of little avail, as there were no family members I knew of. It was always just us, and Dad never mentioned any brothers or sisters. So in the end, it was just me, Naz, the caseworker, and a local priest at the funeral. I never said it, but I was genuinely grateful that my friend had shown up. It couldn't have been easy convincing her parents to allow her to attend a Christian burial. We didn't speak much, though, as she gave me space to grieve.

It didn't even rain that morning, but then again, this was never the movies. I watched with red puffy eyes as they lowered his black metal coffin into the ground, only vaguely hearing the priest's prayer next to me. I couldn't take my eyes off the grave; it had a morbid, magnetic pull that I simply couldn't shake. The priest's benediction finally died away, followed by a hymn that nobody sang to. Eventually, everyone left, the caseworker saying she'd be back in a few days, but I mostly ignored her. Only Naz remained behind. She held my hand tightly in hers as a slight breeze ruffled her hijab.

"I'll pop in later, okay, sweetie? My mother has made some Nasi Kandar for you, and I'll bring it over later."

I didn't answer her, merely nodding and gripping her hand a little tighter. It looked like she wanted to say something but thought better of it. Instead, she clasped my shoulder and walked away. I didn't have the heart to run after her. Had to be strong now, that's what Dad would have wanted from me.

Dad was buried right next to Mom. I looked at the inscription on her tombstone. Must have read it a thousand times, every Sunday afternoon when we'd come to put flowers on her grave, always daisies; she liked those the most. Leaning on my father's tombstone, my fingers tracing over the morning dew on the granite, I whispered, "I don't know what to do." Stupidly, I almost expected an answer, but nothing came. Forcing a smile, I kissed the tombstone and walked away. I didn't shed a single tear. Had to be strong. Had to make him proud of me.

After two days, the trickle of fakers and phony well-wishers had died away to nothing. As much as I hated it, I knew I had to get back into a routine, force myself to carry on. My legs felt like lead; each step was pure torture as I headed back to school. After everything I had witnessed in these last few days, it was almost comical coming back to this society of flat-nosed mouth breathers. Truth be told, I barely noticed the people around me. I walked past them in a total haze, my eyes pointed straight ahead.

'*Get to class, do the damn work, and get home.*' I kept repeating that mantra in my head. The Manual had been very quiet, not doing much but mope around the shop. I could see it was hurting by the way it picked at its food. It would usually curl up on my lap in the evenings, grumbling vague threats at an unknown adversary. Though I was still wary of bringing it to school, I liked the comfort and safety it brought riding in my backpack.

The place was the usual zoo, students milling through the

halls on their way to class. Others were wasting time in front of their lockers, talking shit, and generally being the bunch of talentless Philistines I knew and despised. I was almost at French class when I noticed the unpleasant presence of the Dolls in my way.

'Don't have time for this shit.' Flat out ignoring the dolled-up whores, I moved past them, accidentally bumping Bethany's shoulder. She smiled cruelly, twirling a half-smoked cigarette in her fingers.

"One less Jones in the world. Thank fuck for that." She snorted pig-like as I stopped dead in my tracks. I don't know what came over me at that moment, a total loss of consciousness; devils chanted wildly in my mind, beating the drums of war ceaselessly—my hand forming into a fist, knuckles white with anger.

Then I hit her.

I hit her harder than anything I knew I possessed. Fist crashing into the Doll's face, teeth shattering, blood spurting on the floor. My face was an emotionless mask as I whaled on the cheerleader. Punch after punch rained down on her till my knuckles ran red with blood. The other students' screams were a distant din, static lost in the miasma of my cold anger. A teacher's hands wrapped around my waist, pulling me away. Bethany, wearing a bloody mask, sprawled on the floor. I felt nothing, no pity or remorse, just cold anger bubbling underneath my own mask. I only emerged from my trancelike state when the teacher dragged me to the principal's office. I felt the Manual raging in my backpack and prayed that it wouldn't try to escape.

"You're dead, bitch! You hear me? You're dead!" The Doll

screamed in anger between flowing streams of blood. I saw Naz's face briefly in the throng of shocked students, a tear appearing in her eye as she lowered her head and looked away. Moments later, I was placed unceremoniously in a chair in Principal Saunders' office. A formidable woman. Rake thin, she was an ice-cold adversary to all who got on her wrong side. I sat quietly, barely taking in the Spartan surroundings of her office as she tapped her fingers in anger on the faded oak desk.

"What the hell, Jones?" Her perky pixie cut bobbed up and down in anger. "What the hell?" She kept repeating in disbelief. I said nothing, merely staring ahead of me. "I know Bethany is a Class A bitch, but this is not how I know you. A near spotless disciplinary record in all the years you've been here. And now two incidents in the space of two weeks." She reached for a brown file and rifled through it. "First, I get our star quarterback in pieces in my office, complaining that you assaulted him with a book or something like that. That's all I could understand of his nonsensical babbling. I couldn't get him to stop rocking on his chair, for God's sake. He's been in a state and won't even go near the football field or the library. What did you do, Jones?!" I said nothing, the merest smirk of delight forming on my face.

"This is not funny! And now, I'm expecting Bethany, her brain-dead son-of-a-bitch father and their lawyer here any moment. As if I have nothing better to do with my day, keeping this zoo in order, and now I have to work my ass off to stave off a potential lawsuit." She calmed down for a moment, sitting back in her chair. "Just tell me why you did it, Jones. I know you are hurting, with everything that has happened to you, but this is not the Michaela I know, the one with her heart set on college.

Just give me an answer, and I'll take it from there."

I looked at her intently, my eyes cold to the world, and stood up and started to walk out of the office.

"Fine! If that's how you want to play it, you're suspended from school for two weeks. Go cool off and pray you don't see the inside of a courtroom." She slammed her fist down on the table.

"Who gives a shit?" I answered, leaving the shocked principal behind. It felt surreal walking through the empty corridors, seeing the students pressing against the classroom glass, so eager to see the girl who lost her mind that morning. Ignoring them, I walked out of the school, slamming the door behind me. The Manual peeped out from the backpack and gave me a worried look. I silenced it with a stern glance, not really in the mood for conversation. It was a long and lonely ride back home, my thoughts scattered. The shop was quiet and dark; I fell into a comfy chair and promptly fell asleep. Didn't want to deal, didn't want to think about anything. Just sleep, cold, uncomfortable sleep.

It must have been after ten that night. I was lying on the bed and staring at the ceiling. I hadn't done much that afternoon—just slept for most of it before finishing off the leftover stew in the fridge, remnants from some funeral well-wishers. It was cold and tasteless, but it didn't matter to me. Sleep eluded me as I replayed the events for the umpteenth time in my head. I didn't want to, but it kept appearing like some sort of horror movie. I looked down at the Manual as it slept at the foot of my bed. I could see it was restless and unhappy at everything that took place.

Running my hand over its black cover, I quietly climbed out of bed and left the room, pulling a coat over my shoulders.

'*Got to get out of here.*' It felt like the walls were closing in; I needed some space to think. I left the shop unlocked and walked out into the night, not even bothering to take my bicycle. Must have walked for hours in the deserted town streets, snowflakes gently sifting down on the icy streets. Past closed shops and darkened houses I wandered, my bare feet blue from the winter cold. Somehow I found my way past the abandoned railway tracks and forgotten warehouse, back to the wall and everything that lay beyond it. The dark expanse was quiet, with only the briefest glimpse of lantern light moving in the distant forest. Even the gnomes were gone, the mine abandoned for the time being. My feet aching from the cold, I climbed the brick wall and stood motionless in the dark.

In that instant, the dam finally gave way, and I screamed till there was nothing left inside me. All my rage, pain, and frustration poured out like a gushing river, sweeping everything away before it. My ragged banshee screams went into the void. In my unbridled rage, I grabbed the bricks lying by my feet and threw them into the dark with all my might.

"Is this what you wanted? Is this what you wanted? Answer me, for God's sake." I screamed, rivulets of blood running down my hands. Brick after brick flew into the night as I stood alone, tears flowing freely down my face. I just wanted answers, was that too much to ask? My jacket flapped in the wind as I grabbed another broken brick—and then sensed there was something behind me. I spun around, ready to destroy whatever it was. Tears were running down The Manual's cover as it looked at me forlornly. I realized at that moment that it was hurting as much as I was. I wiped my tears, picked the book up and held it tightly in my arms.

"I'm sorry," I whispered as we both broke down and wept. I had lost my father and he had lost his friend. We were united in our grief, standing alone on the brick battlements. Through the tears, I looked back at the battlefield behind us, and in that instant, I knew what needed to be done. "Come. We have work to do."

A girl in her pink pajamas walking through the dark that night, a book resting calmly on her shoulder—it must have been a strange sight. However, this was no ordinary girl. No, she was a warrior thrown into the most impossible of situations. The odds were laughably, hopelessly against her, but on that cold winter's night, somewhere in Middle America, she made up her mind.

Someone had to make a stand against evil, had to stand resolute against the impending wave of darkness about to wash over her. One girl armed with nothing but her wits and a simple manual of the damned.

The engineer on the wall.

CHAPTER 10

Somewhere in a town in Middle America

I could barely feel the cold wind on my skin as I walked home that night, my mind racing with ideas and outlandish thoughts. Though terrified, I forced myself to stay calm and think rationally. There was much preparation that needed to be done, and I had no idea how long before the monsters would come looking. Those damned gnomes must have snitched to the higher-ups by now. I grinned ever so slightly as I pictured them trying to explain to their boss that a girl and her book got the better of them, a conversation unlikely to have a happy ending.

I pulled the Manual up tightly against my shoulder and felt it breathing in and out slowly, completely content as it snoozed. In those quiet moments, walking alone on the dirt track, I realized that this strange tome would have a more prominent role than I had thought. My father had had a reason to send the Manual across my path. It was more than a bodyguard. The feeling was palpable that much more would be revealed very shortly.

'*Okay, girly, you've had your epic moment of venting. Now, what do you plan on doing?* Pursing my lips and stepping around an errant stone, I mulled the obvious question. My charm and sparkling personality wouldn't get me far when a monster or two came knocking. I would need weapons and lots of them. *"Big, shiny fuck-off ones. That would make an orc go screaming home to his mother.'* I liked the idea for some terrifying reason, even though I had never handled a gun in my life.

'*Nothing like on the job training, I suppose.'* With words of war shuffling through my head, we passed through the wall and headed back to town. It was just after midnight, and the place was as quiet as the grave, with hardly a soul stirring. The Manual yawned loudly. "Let's get you home; it's way past your bedtime." The Manual simply snuggled tighter against my shoulder and flapped its pages contentedly. I was about two blocks from home when I caught a glimpse of red and blue shop lights down the street. An idea began to form in my head.

Smith's Outdoor Warehouse and Gun Shop had been around since I could remember. It catered to the odd lost hillbilly and to rich city folk who came down over the holiday weekends. Specifically, those who had to use the equivalent of Rambo's entire arsenal to hunt Bambi. It had everything I needed, and I doubted old man Smith would miss a few choice pieces here and there. Besides, it was for a good cause. I was saving the world and all that. I looked over my shoulder for any sign of the cops, sure that Joe and Earl, our useless police force, had settled in for the night with a box of doughnuts and some mild porn to while away the hours. No, I was safe to carry out my plans unhindered.

I was soon standing in front of the gun shop; the flickering red and blue lights danced across my face. Nobody was around for miles. I spied a loose brick lying nearby. Gently putting the Manual down, I walked over to the brick and weighed it in my hands. '*Perfect.*' I reached back to chuck it through the window. By the time Joe and Earl woke up, I would be miles away with my stash well in hand. Then I paused, mid-throw because the Manual was staring up at me with disapproval plastered on its cover.

"What? I need those weapons. Don't you dare try to stop me." I tried pushing the book out of the way, but it would not relent, even grabbing my legs. "Will you let go?" Without warning, the Manual leaped up, knocking the brick from my hand. Things quickly got out of hand, and we were soon rolling around on the pavement, fighting like barbarians.

"Stop it, damn you!" I shouted, really not caring who could hear me. Every time I tried scrambling for the brick, the Manual would wallop me with its cover, even biting me on the arm once. "That hurts! Get off me!" I shouted in anger, but the book would not relent. It eventually pinned me to the ground and sat on my back. "I give, I give." I finally gave in. The Manual climbed off me and I sat up, wiping my lips and hanging my head. "I don't know what else to do. How do I fight the monsters without weapons?"

The book paused for a moment. Then it reached out and gently turned my head around. At first, I didn't understand what he wanted me to see. The only building in sight was The Handy House DIY Shop across the street. It was one of those obscenely large chain stores that had everything and its mother inside it. When they built it a few years ago, it pushed a lot of local shops into closing up. I looked down at the Manual and saw a devilish glint on its cover.

"Oh, you have to be kidding me." I sat staring in wonder as the book skipped happily away across the street, only stopping to motion me to follow it. "I must be insane, completely and utterly batshit insane," I mumbled, dusting myself off and running after the book. Already wondering how the hell I was going to explain this to anyone who caught us, I looked up at the imposing building. It was almost grotesque in size, but that was a minor worry. The first problem we had to overcome was the large iron padlock on the front door.

"Now what, genius? Maybe I should go get the brick and try again," I said sarcastically. The Manual rolled eyes on his cover and flipped himself open. I leaned forward and studied the thin, spider-like writing.

"Practical lock picking for beginners."

"Well, aren't you just handy?" I muttered, reaching for the hairpin in my hair. It took a good couple of minutes, many swear words on my part and a few impatient coughs from The Manual, but eventually the lock popped open. "I hope you know what you are doing," I said. The book waltzed past me like butter wouldn't melt on its covers. Just as I was about to enter the building, I swore I saw movement in the nearby bushes. It was only there for a split second. I stared intently at it, but nothing moved and all remained quiet. '*Lack of sleep, Michaela, lack of sleep,*' I thought, stifling a yawn and heading inside. Who would be mad enough to be awake at this ungodly time of night?

'*Don't answer that.*'

The shop was more of a warehouse than anything else, a gigantic cavern full of all sorts of weird goodies and stuff. 'Stuff': that summed it up nicely. Aisle upon aisle of all sorts of building equipment and hardware, stacked to the rafters, just the thing for any handyman to end his weekend in the emergency room.

"Where are you?" I hissed. The terrifying thought of the Manual running around unsupervised loomed uncomfortably in me. I caught sight of it near the wallpaper stands, cooing affectionately and rubbing up against the garish decorations. "We do not have time for this. You can sort out your love life later. Come on." The Manual grumbled and moped off behind me. It didn't take me long to figure out why it had brought me here. This place was a treasure trove of destruction, everything a budding savior of the world needed. Running my hand over steel beams and wooden planks, something dawned on me.

"I was never supposed to use weapons like guns and rockets. That's a coward's way. No, an engineer uses her wits and knowledge to beat whatever comes at her." In the dimly lit warehouse, it suddenly started to make sense to me. This was how I was going to hold back the darkness, for however long that might be. The gears twirled madly in my head as I started thinking up elaborate traps and defenses— from homemade catapults to slingshots and spike traps. The amount of damage I could cause was infinite.

"We will need to set up a shopping list and work out exactly what we will need," I said to The Manual, who was happily shuffling behind, almost like a proud parent on their kid's first day at school. "Tools as well, but let's keep that separate." I was already wondering how the hell I was going to carry all this. My father had a pickup truck tucked away in the back lot of the shop, but the damn thing hadn't run since the Vietnam War. Just another issue to overcome.

'*One thing at a time, girly.*' My thoughts were suddenly interrupted by a beam of light coming down the far aisle. "Quickly, hide." I grabbed the Manual and dived behind a stack of wooden pallets. Stupid girl. I had forgotten about the rent-a-cop the shop employed, a fat slob of a man who couldn't catch a cold but could mess up matters in a hurry.

"Sit dead still, and no biting understand?" I whispered under my breath as the beam of light came closer. The Manual growled softly, and I had to hold him tightly to keep him from escaping. Painstakingly slow, the cheap dime store shoes shuffled closer over the polished gray floor. I could hear the slob chewing on a doughnut, a trail of crumbs falling to the floor behind him. Shuffle and chew, shuffle and chew. Ever closer he came; I pressed myself deeper behind the wooden pallets. Then he stopped. Wheezing slightly, he placed his flashlight inches away from my head. The son of a bitch only had to turn his head ever so slightly and all would be lost. A drop of sweat ran down my forehead and hung Judas-like for what felt like an eternity before falling in slow motion to the ground. I flinched as it landed with what sounded like an explosion. In my mind, I was ready to scramble for the exit. '*Out the door and gone before he knows what hit him.*' Gripping the Manual tightly, I placed one foot on the ground, my body itching to make a run for it. The guard coughed loudly and adjusted his belt.

"Damn ulcer is going to kill me," he snorted before fumbling with the flashlight and moving on. I only dared to relax the moment he disappeared around the corner. Nodding at the book, I motioned for him to follow me. I had seen all I wanted to, and it would be best to come back another night. '*Got to sort the transport out first,'* I thought to myself, sneaking through the darkened shop and out the front door with the Manual in tow. Fireworks were exploding in my mind at the possibilities that lay inside, waiting for me. It was just going to take some planning; with a bit of luck, I should be well on my way. There were guilty thoughts, too: what I would be doing was considered stealing, but I would make up for it later. The world was at stake. Like a phantom, I flew home through the quiet streets, excitement bubbling over inside me. There was so much to do and so little time; I would have to haul ass to get everything done.

A few minutes after I'd left the shop behind, Naz poked her head out from behind some nearby bushes. Unbeknownst to me, she had been observing my movements; she'd watched the scene with the Manual and me at the gun shop with widening eyes. She had even followed me into the DIY store.

"Inna lillahi wa inna ilayhi raji'un. What are you up to, Michaela Jones?" She shook her head in wonder, seeing the distant figures of the girl and book disappearing down the street. The little Muslim girl made up her mind. She was determined to get to the bottom of this mystery and find out exactly what her best friend was up to.

Try as she might, she could not shake the feeling that it all led back to the Southern Reaches and the darkness that lay waiting behind it.

CHAPTER 11

No rest for the wicked. I got back to the shop at one in the morning, but I couldn't sleep anyway. I lay tossing and turning all night long, my mind racing at what still needed to be done and what was waiting for me out there beyond the wall. I would sit on the edge of the bed, my fingers twitching in anticipation as plans slowly started to form in my mind. Time and again, I would lie back on the crumpled bed sheets, trying to find some peace in my raging soul, but I would fail every time. As the sun rose a few minutes before seven on that cold winter morning, I'd had enough.

'*Screw it, let's work.*' Yawning and stretching, I headed to the kitchen and put a pot of coffee on. I was going to need a few to get through the long and lonely hours facing me. Pouring a bowl of Captain Crunch, I stood and looked over the workshop's unabbreviated chaos, munching loudly as the gears turned in my head. '*I need space to work, and God knows what I'm going to do with all this junk.*' Another thought occurred to me: there was no way I could construct all my traps and weapons out here in the open. What if the neighbors saw something or, even worse, the cops dropped by? I would be screwed if that happened.

'*Then where else, genius? The only other place with space is the school, and that's not happening anytime soon.*' As I pondered my latest dilemma, the Manual walked in, rubbing its cover tiredly and removing a hairnet. It got into the same cross-legged, rubbing-the-chin pose I was in. The book looked up at me and then back at the vast pile of junk. Pulling my leg, the Manual beckoned for me to follow it.

"What is it? Can't you see I'm busy thinking?" Annoyed at the interruption, I ignored the book, but it would not relent, and it eventually started to push me away from the kitchen.

"What are you doing? Let go." The Manual pushed me until we reached the locked door to the basement.

"It's just the boiler room down there. Nothing to see," I said. The book rolled its eyes and hurried over to a nearby cupboard. Reaching underneath, it stretched its cover and clicked a previously unseen button. Looking on in amazement, I could hear gears spinning deep below us. The door silently slipped open. It seemed my father still had more cards up his sleeve. Grinning and shaking my head, I carefully walked inside and down the dimly lit, winding steps. The Manual trailed behind me, twittering in excitement. I couldn't imagine what was waiting for me down there; with my father, anything was possible. Finally, the staircase ended, and I came face to face with a white painted door. It had strange symbols painted on it, something right out of a fantasy novel. Maybe Viking runes, but I could not be sure. Taking a deep breath, I pushed through. A sudden blinding light lit up the room, and I stood staring in awe.

It was a workshop. A vast subterranean basement with row upon row of gleaming metal tables and tools lined up against the walls. I couldn't believe my eyes; it was here right under my feet all these years. Walking past the immaculately packed toolboxes, I noticed that nothing had been touched or used. And then it struck me. Father was preparing this place for the arrival of the next engineer.

'*Waiting for you, girly.*' Blinking a tear away, I walked around the room and saw an elevator in the corner and a garage door on the far side. He had wired this entire place in secret below the shop, and everything fit in perfectly. Nobody in a million years would have expected all this to be down here. It was the perfect hiding place. '*And all the parts I need are upstairs…unbelievable.*' I looked down at the Manual in mock anger, and it sheepishly turned its cover away, blushing beet red.

"He had his ways, I guess, and it's not your fault," I said, ruffling the book's covers playfully. "But we're going to need transport to carry all this." The book nodded and pointed at the garage door. It didn't take me long to find the handle to crank it open. It led to another covered garage, and as expected, dad's old junker of a truck was standing there. Whether I could even get it going was an open question, and I shuddered at the state of it. Only rust and spit and various colorful swearwords kept it together.

"Well, add this to our list; start with getting it running and go from there." The Manual nodded, then paused as it looked up at me. I stood frozen on the spot. "I have no idea how to fix it and…" God, I felt so stupid for saying it: "I don't know how to drive. But I guess I'll have to figure it out as I go. Come on; we have lots of work to do." The Manual nodded at me, and we got down to it. The daughter of an engineer took over as we started dragging parts to the dilapidated truck. I was working methodically and systemically, as any sound engineer should.

"Are you even lifting?" I shouted at the book as we lugged a car exhaust system down to the workshop. The Manual threw me a middle finger but carried on relentlessly. It still boggled my mind how much assorted junk father had upstairs, but it was all part of the plan, I guess. Progress was bitterly slow as we toiled away under the truck. I had no idea what I was doing half the time, but somehow my hands just knew the way. I could visualize the problem in front of me and see the solution as well. And when I got stuck, the Manual was there for me, an almost unlimited source of information. I started to understand why my father had sent him to me, but more importantly, in those lonely hours in the garage, he became my friend. We argued, fought, philosophized, and bantered like only those who knew each other a lifetime could.

"Those lug nuts? Perhaps we should just push the truck there; it will be quicker than you suggest."

"I saw you rolling your cover at me."

"You do know this thing is supposed to go forward as well as backward, right?"

"Of course Star Wars is better than Star Trek. Oh, I am trading you in for a Mills and Boon."

We worked through the morning and late into the afternoon, diligently going after each problem that cropped up its head. Just before four that afternoon, I felt confident enough to have a go. Covered in oil and grease, I stepped back and shouted over the raised hood to the Manual. "Start her up. What do you mean, you don't have any hands? Make a plan, I say." The truck sputtered and coughed like a demented asthmatic, smoke pouring from its exhaust. "Come on now, turn over, you bastard. Give her more gas." Just as I thought we had made a breakthrough, the truck's engine died away and silence filled the room again.

"I told you it's the solenoid; it has to be. No, it being made by Ford doesn't automatically make it a piece of crap." I jumped back under the hood and started fiddling around as the Manual slowly hit its cover on the steering wheel. He was just as tired as I was, but we had to keep going. We had barely even looked at the traps and weapons yet, and there was still so much to do. I was so engrossed in the engine that I didn't hear the knocking and loud voice behind me. After a few minutes, I stopped, blinked a few times, and then looked over to the book.

"Was that you? I told you to take it easy on the Sriracha on that sandwich." The knocking became louder. I spun around and ran to the outside garage door. Peering through the dirt-encrusted top window, I saw a white pantsuit and the rather large figure of a woman standing outside. Instantly, it dawned on me who it was. "Social worker! Hide and don't you dare show your face," I hissed, scrambling down and trying to make myself presentable. It was a lost cause. With a resigned sigh, I opened the outer garage door (having made sure the inner one leading to the workshop was firmly shut). An oil and grease covered teenager in overalls, white teeth sticking out from a blackened face, greeted the shocked caseworker.

"Miss Jones, I…I knocked, but you didn't answer." She stammered, wrinkling her porcine nose at the smell and chaos before her.

"No problem. I was just working on the old truck here." I

realized how incredibly stupid and awkward it sounded. "Come on in." I waved the social worker in with a dirty rag. Dumbass here had forgotten that she said she would look in on me in a few weeks at the funeral. The timing could not have been worse.

"It is good that you have a…um…hobby, Miss Jones, but I am here to discuss your case with you." She tried to keep her aloof demeanor intact, but she could barely hide her disgust.

"Right, of course. Want a sandwich?" I offered her a half-eaten bologna sandwich, which she politely turned down.

"My apologies that it took so long to get to you, but that's the government for you." She laughed a laugh usually reserved for rich people at country clubs. "It's very unusual, but we couldn't locate any of your relatives or any people with a history or connection to you. Most strange. Now, seeing that you are still a few years away from being an adult, we have decided to place you into foster care."

The Manual appeared behind the caseworker on the tool case, wrench in hand, ready to bean her. Subtly, I shook my head, warning the demented book off. He looked at me sternly and then motioned to the steel tool again. I whispered "No" through clenched teeth as the social worker rummaged in her briefcase. I was just about to throw something at the book when she looked up again and caught me in the process. Her eyebrows furrowed for a second, then she coughed and read through my file.

"Ah yes, I see there was an incident at the school. Got into a fight with a fellow learner, case outcome still pending. Suspended for two weeks…oh, this is not good, Miss Jones, and it simply speeds the process up. I know you are hurting after your father's passing, but this is no way to act. The state simply cannot allow you to live alone much longer."

"You can't do this. Please, you don't understand," I pleaded with the rotund woman. I was already dreading what would happen in the Southern Reaches without me there: no engineer getting the defenses ready and nobody to wait for the next Paladin to show up. The darkness would simply take over everything in a heartbeat.

"I'm sorry, Miss Jones, the state believes you'd be a danger to yourself if left unsupervised. You have a week to get all your things ready before we come to fetch you. A foster parent down in…oh, where was it again? Ah yes, Florida, is just what you need." She stated this matter-of-factly, reaching for a bright red shade of lipstick in her bag.

"You don't know what you're doing…" I said through clenched teeth, already feeling the world collapsing around me.

"We're the state, dear; we know exactly what we are doing. And you are going to love Florida; I hear its lovely down there— much better than this…place." She looked around haughtily, noticing the strange black book on the shelf. Curiously, she reached out to take it down but thought better of it when she looked around at the mess in the garage. "I'll uh…show myself out. See you in a week, Miss Jones." I looked on in horror as the portly woman wobbled her way out, disappearing around the corner. I gazed over at the Manual, still suspended on the tool case. The breaking news had hit him hard as well. His cover slumped forward in despair. We both knew this was a disaster on an epic scale. One week before they drag my ass off to goddamn Florida! One week before it all goes to kaka and the world ends in a spectacular shit show of monsters and horrors.

"Well old buddy, I guess there is only one thing to do." The Manual looked up at me; an eerie stillness had fallen over him.

"Brew us another pot of coffee, love. We have work to do."

CHAPTER 12

Somewhere in a little town in Middle America

It was mortal tiredness, the type that sinks right down into your muscles and bones. I kept pushing myself through those lonely hours, long past the breaking point. The thought of what was going to happen kept driving me forward. I couldn't quit, no matter how tired I was. Another pot of coffee, more energy drinks, and back to work. I barely slept those last few days; the odd nap under the truck was the only luxury I allowed myself, with restlessness haunting my dreams. It was a small mercy that the Manual and I got the truck working. It took some BFI (Brute Force and Ignorance) to get the son of a bitch going, but eventually it spluttered into life, much to our overwhelming relief.

With one problem ticked off our list, we could finally focus on getting the weapons and traps up and running. I couldn't afford to go overboard now, had to keep it simple and then expand our operation later on. Luckily, my father had left us many schematics behind. The Manual was another fantastic resource that I relied on heavily as the hours became days, and the sun rose and set.

"Nothing too fancy here. I've got to keep it simple and brutal. We will focus on projectiles later on when we are more settled in. At this moment, I'm thinking spring traps. We have enough metal around here to keep us going for a while," I explained to the Manual, who perked its pages in rapt interest. "The springs around here are a bit too rusty to trust. My main problem is getting power to the traps. Not mad about the idea of manually running out to activate them. We need a small, powerful generator." I was reaching for my jacket when the book stopped me in my tracks and looked up at me with determination etched on its cover.

"What? Go on your own? No, not a chance," I protested loudly. "It's simply too dangerous. And what if someone sees you out there?" The Manual flashed a set of razor-sharp teeth, looking sure of itself. I shook my head and tried to push past it, but the book was having none of it, standing its ground resolutely. It tapped its cover, warrior-like, growling in bravado.

"Oh, for God's sake, I'm not getting this stupid idea out of your thick spine, am I?" Pinching the bridge of my nose in frustration, and already seeing the numerous scenarios where this could all go spectacularly kaka in a hurry, I looked down at the little black book and sighed. "Fine, but you get what I need and get your ass back here as soon as fucking possible understand?" The book punched the air a few times, moving around like a prizefighter. "No biting, no maiming, no making people orphans. You get me six car springs and one portable generator, and then you hightail it right back here." I explained it all in painstaking detail, making sure the book was clear on every point. "And no biting the security guard. There are some of

Dad's sleeping pills in the medicine cupboard upstairs. Slip one or two in the guard's coffee, not the whole container, and wait for him to pass out. It's pretty strong stuff, so it should knock him out quickly. Do we understand ourselves, my dearest Manual? You will behave yourself, and you will not cause the fall of the Roman Empire again, is that clear?"

The Manual clicked its pages and saluted smartly before turning and heading for the stairs. Visions of bloodshed and carnage were dancing before my eyes. The very thought of leaving the Manual unattended was horrifying. It gave me a bit of time to get myself settled in with the traps, but I could not shake the feeling that I had inadvertently started World War Three.

An hour or so later, we zoom in on the seemingly docile surroundings of the hardware store. Not a soul is stirring in the early morning hours with only the odd streetlight flickering in the distance. Upon careful inspection, we notice the outside lock has been chewed off, a sure sign of the Manual's lack of patience and picking skills. The store was quiet as a grave, a basketball game on the TV in the guard's office the only sign of life. The book managed to carefully wriggle his way into the office and up the file cabinet, watching the guard like a hawk. At first, he contemplated throwing the sleeping pills into his coffee from a distance, but then thought better of it—a chance too risky to take. Spying a bit of rope nearby, the Manual tied it around himself and made a little grappling hook from a forgotten pen he found. Deftly, he threw the pen at the ceiling fan, wincing as it clattered to the ground. The guard grunted in his sleep but thankfully did not wake up. Pulling in the hook, the Manual braced itself and tried again. The pen twirled around the fan and locked tight. Humming the theme song to *Mission Impossible* under his breath, the book acrobatically launched into the air, suspending inches above the sleeping guard's face—so close, he could smell the peanut butter and jelly sandwich the obese guard had had for lunch on his breath. The book carefully unscrewed the lid of the container, pearls of sweat forming on its cover. He almost had it when one tiny white sleeping pill tumbled out, as if in slow motion, plonking on the guard's wrinkled forehead. Recoiling, the book quickly reeled itself upwards and then waited with bated breath.

The guard stirred, blinking his tired eyes a few times. Smacking his beet-red lips, he stared at the TV screen and muttered: "Damn Carmelo, can't shoot from outside the paint to save his life." He settled back into the comfy chair, head swaying tiredly before his eyes fell shut again. Not even daring to breathe, the Manual waited an agonizing two minutes, until the guard was asleep again. Finally risking it, he lowered himself slowly downward, level with the wheezing face. Wrinkling his cover in disgust, he poured three sleeping pills into the lukewarm cup of coffee below him. Satisfied his mission was complete, the book reeled himself up again and acrobatically swung across the room, landing with a flourish. Striking an Olympic pose, the Manual slammed the door ever so slightly, waking the guard. The fat slob got up and looked around in bewilderment, shining his light down the shop's dark corridors but seeing nothing. All was peaceful as he reached for the coffee mug.

Thirty-odd minutes later, the dull thudding of his head on

the desk indicated that he was out cold. The Manual was busy in the wallpaper section again, cooing like a French lover to a rather smooth roll of living room paper. Declaring his undying love to the roll and promising to be back soon, the book set off on his gathering mission. He snagged a nearby trolley and scooted across the polished floors, capturing the odd bits and pieces his mistress needed back at base. The generator proved to be a bit more of a hassle. Taking various planks of wood along, and using many unprintable swear words, the Manual finally managed to lever the heavy box into the shopping cart. Paddling gondola style, he zipped past the quiet shelves, snagging a can of gas in passing. The book rode out the damaged door and into the night, atop the shopping trolley like a victorious Viking leaving the scene of a great battle. I would later hear of the local cop's utter bafflement at this strange crime. It remains unsolved to this day.

Finally, after a few near misses, including a *Jackass*-style ride down a steep hill, the Manual returned to the garage, flicking the shopping trolley around with a showman's flourish. I had made great strides in the few hours he was gone, having gotten the essential framework down beautifully. In theory, it should work, but I needed the other parts to be sure.

"Should I even ask?" I stated, lifting an eyebrow at the book. It only shook its covers and looked around innocently. Deciding ignorance was my best course, I took the parts and started fitting them into the trap. A couple of hours of hard labor later, and the prototype was ready. An old crash test dummy from the workshop would perfectly suit my purposes; I attached it to a rope and suspended it from the balcony. I handed the rope to the Manual, put on safety glasses, and stepped back.

"Right, Test 1, here we go. On my mark, let go of the dummy and take cover." The dummy swung forward and connected with the steel plate of the trap, which smashed the doll hard into the ground, leaving a ruined and disturbing image behind. Tapping my fingers against each other, I looked down at the book.

"This can work, but I want some variation in the traps. We'll keep this one as is but lower the tension on the springs on the other one. It should send any nasty flying backward and discourage them from trying again anytime soon. Let's get something to eat and finish up in the morning. I can barely see straight, and we need some rest." The book nodded as we headed for some hot soup and a nap upstairs. We never made it to the food, passing out on the couch as the tomato soup bubbled away unattended. Even through the haze of tiredness that had overwhelmed me, I could feel the energy pumping through my veins. I had started in a genuinely amazing way, but this was only the first step in something so much bigger than me. A few traps were slowly taking shape below me; they were the first shots in the looming war. It excited and terrified me to the core, but I had to see it through to the end. I had no choice in the matter.

I tried to keep some semblance of normality the next day, even though the excitement felt like torture inside. I went to get some supplies: milk, bread, and butter, just enough to tide us over for a bit. The rest of the day we spent tinkering in the workshop, trying to get the spring traps working as best as possible. I knew they would not hold back a large army for long, but perhaps they could buy us some time while we set up other traps. I tried to push the thought of the social worker to the back of my mind, but it wasn't easy. They would be there to pick me up in three short days. Still so much to do and so little time. But I simply could not afford to waste any time thinking about the matter; it was out of my control anyway.

Just after five in the afternoon, we had finished our first set of traps; we started loading them into the truck. It was an almighty struggle to get everything in, and we had to use ropes and pulleys to winch the heavier parts into the truck's flatbed. Three hours later, an exhausted girl and her book stepped back, satisfied that we had everything we needed. I didn't want to make it too obvious, but I was dreading this moment—I'd never driven a vehicle before.

'*Got to find your inner gangster, girly.*' I gave myself a woefully inadequate pep talk as I walked to the truck, resting my hand on the door handle. The Manual scooted in and started filling out an insurance form. Trying my level best to ignore the little shit, I pressed the garage button and turned the key with more than a little trepidation.

"Really? An oxygen mask and a brown paper bag? You are not helping matters and don't think I didn't see you cross yourself before you climbed in." I stared straight ahead and inched the car forward. It protested loudly and stalled, not moving an inch. The Manual tapped the handbrake, trying to be as infuriatingly helpful as possible.

"Not a word, book, or I donate you to the local kindergarten." I tried again, and the truck lurched forward, bouncing and hopping along. It was a truly pathetic sight to see. I crawled out of the driveway and into the street,. I wasn't exactly testing the limits of grip at the moment, pushing along at twenty miles an hour. The Manual's will finally gave out; he ducked under the seat and started whimpering. Desperately, I tried to remember the YouTube videos I'd watched the previous night, tried to remember something, anything, about what those smug assholes said.

'*Slow and steady, girly, take your time and watch for the cops.*' I knew the local cops were as useless as a washing machine at the Playboy Mansion, but with my luck, those idiots would pick tonight to be out on patrol. '*No officer, the trap of death in the back is for my grandma, she's feeling a bit under the weather, and I thought it would cheer her up.*' I kept looking around, frequently gnashing the gears as we crept through the quiet little town. Luckily for me, everything except the gas station closed at six, and nobody liked being out in the streets with the winter chill settling in. After a less than glorious trip that included many stalls and missed signals, we finally made it to the train tracks at the Southern Reaches. I was satisfied that nobody had followed us. No lights and no screeching of brakes or police sirens—all was well.

'*Don't get overconfident. Stick to the plan,*' I kept telling myself as we inched over the abandoned railway tracks and headed to the wall. It was always so much darker out here away from the town's lights—and it was quiet, very quiet. I could not hear a bird chirping or a bug rustling in the undergrowth. The place was bereft of life. Eventually, we reached our destination, and I pulled up with a graceless jerk of the truck.

"Oh, brave warrior, we're here, you can come on out now," I said sarcastically as the Manual peeked out from under the seat, a silver harmonica playing on its cover.

I calmed my soul for a moment as we stood in silence, looking out over the darkened battlefield. We would never be expected to last long out here; it should be over in a day—an hour perhaps? However, we had to make a stand here in front of this empty field, just to buy some time before the arrival of the Paladin. Insanity, thy name is Michaela Jones. I motioned to the Manual, and we slowly started unpacking the truck. A long and bitterly cold night was awaiting us, but we had to endure. Survive and endure.

Let's work.

CHAPTER 13

We worked like the devil himself was behind us that night; maybe he was in a way. The first order of business was to get all the material off the truck and get the spotlights set up. The little generator hummed away in the night as we started setting up in the pale yellow gloom of the lights.

"We'll have to funnel them in, can't defend a large area. Our luck is in the lay of the land." I pointed it out to the Manual. "It's sloping naturally towards us, so what I'm thinking is we put bear traps and spikes to that side and make the land almost impossible to cross. It shouldn't be too difficult with what we... ahem...*borrowed* from the hunting and hardware store. We'll need a shit-ton of them, though, may even need to think of making some of them ourselves," I said, mentally mapping out the battlefield before me. "Plus, it won't take power to run them, which works in our favor. And then over there..." I walked a few paces, seeing the dark outline of the dam in the distance. "We flood the area, maybe use some gunpowder or dynamite to put a hole in that son of a bitch." The Manual looked up worriedly at me. "What? Oh, I'll be careful, and nobody is going to miss a bit of explosives." It was sheer madness overtaking me. I took a pencil from behind my ear and twirled it in my fingers. I could already picture the scene before my eyes.

"Perhaps bring that sucker down on their heads as they march past…no, that's a stupid idea, we need to be here to operate the traps." Flicking my fingernails a few times absentmindedly, I looked down at the book again. I could see the worried look on his cover. I bent down and hugged him tightly. "It is going to be all right, but I need you, okay? I cannot do this on my own. You with me, sweetie?" The Manual nodded, steeling himself for the mammoth task ahead.

"Good, okay, let's cover the center run first, and then we can sort out the flanks later on. I just hope they don't catch us with our pants down. We just have to hope Death is overconfident and taking his time" I already had visions of being overrun while we were still working. Then again, all this could have been for nothing, the demons and monsters laughing at us as they trampled the traps on their way to the wall.

'You can't think like that girly. You just can't.' I knew my inner voice was right. I glanced up to the dark forest in the distance, wondering what horrors lay waiting for us inside it. The Manual nudged me on the leg, bringing me back to reality. We sauntered back to the truck and started lugging the heavy wooden boards across the uneven ground. It was hard, merciless work, and soon sweat poured down my brow as I fought through the mud with each weary step. Truth be told, I would have given up a long time ago if it hadn't been for my faithful companion. The Manual carried me in those lonely, dark hours as we struggled to get the spring traps up. Every time I felt like quitting, he urged me to carry on, willing me forward, even though my legs felt like jelly.

"No, no, space the traps out a bit. In a V-pattern; we'll cover more ground that way. Get me the electrical cables from the back of the truck, will you? And we'll have to cover them up; the usual raini is still a few months away, but I don't want to take any chances." We had to prepare for every eventuality, cover all the bases. I toiled away in the mud, fighting to get a stubborn motor to turn over. The damn thing had likely been lying in my father's workshop for years and had rusted like a bastard. The Manual appeared over my shoulder and helpfully held out a sixteen-pound hammer.

"BFI?" I asked, grinning. It took a few shots, but soon the motor was purring away like a spoiled kitten. "Great, let's take this puppy for a run." We walked back and climbed the brick wall. The Manual fit a set of safety glasses to its cover.

"Generator is running, motor is good to go, cables connected. Here we go." I picked up the control box, shut my eyes, and pressed the red button. My faith was beautifully rewarded as the trap sprung forward with a loud *whump*, shattering the churchlike silence around us. Our luck was holding for the time being. I reset the trap, reaching down and high-fiving the Manual.

"That's a start, a good start. Okay, we'll grab some bags and cover the traps for the evening and then…" I froze in mid-sentence, the controller box still suspended in my hand. For just the briefest of moments, I swore I saw something move near the tree line. It was a flicker of light, gone in an instant. Must have been my overtired mind imagining things, seeing ghosts where there was nothing. Taking two steps, I paused again and scanned the dark vista, my eyes straining in the gloom.

'*Had to be imagining it, there's nothing out there.*' Something made me stop and look a third time. Then I saw it, a glint of metal in the pale moonlight, a slight movement betraying its presence.

Oh fuck.

It couldn't be anything else; it had to be! Oh God, there were monsters by the tree line, and they were heading this way. They must have come to see what was going on after the incident at the mine. Damn reconnaissance party had rocked up earlier than I had expected. Fuck, fuck, fuck!

"Do we run or do we…?" I looked out over the set traps hiding in the dark. A vicious smile formed on my face—the Manual grabbed its crotch and licked its razor-sharp teeth. "Okay, got to play this carefully. I'm going to pull the truck up and hit the horn. With luck, they'll come straight at us and not on our flanks. Stay here and keep an eye on them." I ran back to the truck and quickly got into position. "How many out there?" I shouted, already counting down the seconds. The Manual leaned over the brick wall and flashed the number three on its back to me. Damn, more than I expected. Couldn't back down now, had to go for it.

'*Not your brightest of ideas, girly.*' I ignored the voice of reason and punched the hooter. The sound reverberated across the battlefield. It was like dropping a wet fart in church, and I knew all hell was about to break loose. A loud grunt of disgust sounded in the distance. Whatever it was, it was not happy at all. Running back up the steps, I took my place next to the book and scanned the dark horizon.

"Can you see what it is yet?" I asked anxiously. The Manual shook its pages, straining to see above the parapet. "Come on…come on, show yourself, fucker," I whispered under my breath, waiting for whatever hell was coming across our path. I didn't have to wait long for my answer.

Orcs.

A three-creature squad was rapidly making its way towards us. Perhaps it wasn't the brightest idea to get their attention, but I simply couldn't risk them flanking us. Their piglike grunts of indignation came closer with each passing moment and their shields rattled as they clanked their swords against them. It was enough to drive any mortal to madness—but then again, they'd never had to deal with me. The orcs were over-confident, barely pausing as they trampled over the muddy ground, not expecting any resistance. I could just make out their hulking physiques in the gloom. Big bastards. I knew that hand-to-hand confrontation would end badly for me.

"Do not move an inch; let them just get a little bit closer." I peeked over the crumbling brick parapet, the control box shaking in my hand. So close. I could hear the metal rings clinking on their chainmail, could smell the stink of rotten fish and cheap wine.

"Almost there…wait for it…wait for it…" I hissed, slowly exhaling. Then I pressed down hard on the control button. It was the sweetest sound possible: the spring traps sprang to life. The first one crunched the nearest orc into the ground with a sickening clap and smashing of bones. It barely had time to grunt before the heavy wooden plank turned it into red mush. Screams of disbelief echoed around the battlefield from the remaining two orcs. They soon regained their warrior composure and charged forward, eager to disembowel their unknown adversary.

"Count with me! Five...four...three...two...one!" I shouted above the war cries, hitting the second and third buttons. Trap two worked beautifully, sending the stunned orc careening backward through the air. The last I saw of it was its ass hurtling through the trees at a tremendous pace.

And then our luck ran out.

The third spring trap was just a split second too quick, grazing the last orc's shoulder. The beast howled in pain, scrambling to its feet and roaring at the brick wall. "Oh, we're fucked. Let's get out of here." I grabbed the Manual on the run and hurried down the brick steps, the truck keys fumbling in my hands. I'd woefully underestimated the speed of the orc. It was on me in seconds, jumping on the truck's roof and slashing at me with wicked-sharp claws. I didn't have time to think! I had to react. I left the truck behind and started running, weaving in and out between the brick walls. The brutish monster charged after me, plowing through the red brick battlements. An unholy scream was lighting up the darkness as it hunted its prey.

'Don't stop...don't stop.' I kept weaving back and forth, hoping to confuse the monster. Had to throw him off our trail, just needed a few second's space to get back to the truck. I doubted the lug could keep up with a speeding vehicle. I tried my luck one too many times, though, and ran straight into the muscular demon. With a roar, it swung its crude metal sword at me, smashing it into the battlements and sending shards of red brick flying in all directions. I scrambled off the ground and ran up the steps, the Manual thrashing in my hands.

"No! He'll tear you to pieces." I stumbled backward over a loose plank, hitting the ground hard and seeing the book tumble from my hands. The orc knew it had me trapped. It licked its bloody lips at the thought of an easy meal and brandished its crude metal sword in the air.

'*Game time, girly...*' I dived forward past the desperate clutches of the orc, its claws flashing inches above my head. An electrical cable lay on the ground, spluttering bright orange sparks where it had been ripped loose. Damn Orc must have trampled on it earlier. Without thinking, I jammed it into the orc's chest, and a massive electric bang ripped through the air as the monster crashed backward, smoking vigorously as its body came to rest. The impossibly bright light was fading away into nothingness.

"Wow..." was all I could manage, sitting back stunned, eyes still adjusting from the sudden light show. "You okay?" I asked the Manual as it shook the dust off its cover. It whistled at the sight of the fallen orc. "Let's get out of here. No telling if the rest of the Chucklewood forest critters are coming back for more." We'd barely made it three steps when the orc slowly stirred behind us. It was burnt a lovely crispy black, but the fucker was still standing. It was now a straight race to the truck between us and the monster. For obvious reasons, it was pissed beyond belief. It picked up its sword, its eyes raging red as it walked towards us. Glancing over my shoulder at the waiting truck, I knew there was no chance in hell of us reaching it before the monster turned us into cat kibble. The orc laughed softly, running a lime green tongue over its lips, already savoring the human taste. Then it stopped and rolled its eyes backward in its skull—the sound of wood connecting with bone lingering in the air.

"*Namaste*, motherfucker!" A veiled figure appeared in the dark behind the now comatose orc, dropping a wrestling-style cross chop over the fallen monster. My eyes nearly popped out of my skull. My situation had gotten a hell of a lot more interesting in a hell of a short time.

"*Salaam Alaikum*, Michaela Jones." Naz smiled at me, a two-by-four plank of wood in hand.

'*Oh shit.*'

CHAPTER 14

Somewhere in a little town in Middle America, on the other side of the wall

"What in the holy fuck are you doing, Naz?" I exclaimed in anguish, looking up and down at the girl and the unconscious orc at her feet. She simply twirled the two-by-four in her hands, aiming another shot at the monster.

"'Thank you for saving my ass, Naz.' 'Oh, it's a pleasure, don't worry about it.' 'That orc was about to turn me into cat food. I'm so glad you're here,'" She said sarcastically, studying me intently in the dim yellow glow of the spotlights.

"No, no, no," I kept repeating. "You have no idea what you've gotten yourself into here." I took her by the shoulders, shaking my head all the while.

"Always said I'd be there to watch your back, sweetie." I could hear the hurt in her voice as she turned away from me. I reached out and pulled her back gently.

"Naz…oh, kiddo, what have you done?" I hugged my friend tightly, the worry lines running deep on my forehead. "But, yes, thanks for saving my ass back there."

"It's what any good Horseman would have done. Now, young lady, I think you need to explain what this delightful bag of ugly is that we are so calmly standing on."

I knelt and took the orc's pulse. It was still living but was knocked out cold and in no danger of waking up soon. Sighing wearily, I sat down on the brick battlements and ran my hands through my sweaty hair. "How much weird can you handle in one day?" I asked, knowing things were about to take a turn for the strange.

"Hello? Mister jolly green giant catching forty here not enough?" Naz replied, eyeing me suspiciously.

"Not exactly." I nodded at the Manual as he poked his cover out from behind a pile of bricks. "It's okay; she's a friend." The book crawled forward, unsure what to make of this new person. Naz's eyes were growing wider by the second, not daring to believe what they were seeing.

"It's ... it's…"

"Yes."

"But, it's…"

"Very much so."

"Will it bite?"

"Only if it's hungry or cranky." The two stared at each other for what felt like ages until Naz bent down and reached for something in her pocket. The book was recoiling until he realized she had candy in her hand. Ever so slowly, he came forward and gently took it out of her hand.

"See? She won't hurt you." The Manual slinked behind my leg, chewing methodically on the toffee and the thought of this strange new person.

"Okay, now while I am trying to process all…this…you had better start explaining your ass, woman," Naz said, folding her arms defiantly.

"You were never supposed to be here, and I need you to forget everything you saw here tonight, please."

"Fuck, no. I find out my best friend is out here alone, doing God knows what with these ugly creatures and a talking book, and I'm supposed to just turn around and leave? Pull the other one, Michaela."

"Please, Naz. I'm fighting a war here, and I cannot allow anyone else to get hurt." My frustrations boiled over, but I instantly regretted my anger. She didn't deserve it.

"Hurt? You did happen to notice that I'm Muslim, right? I have been called every name under the sun, and my family persecuted like you would not believe. I was told to go back to Arabia on my magic carpet countless times, even though I was born in America, but do I get treated like it? I think you know the answer to this, so start talking." A slight smile formed on her face. "I'm a big girl, and if I can survive a couple of hours being stuffed in a jock's locker, nothing will hurt me. I'm all ears." I groaned loudly, not believing what was going on, but realizing I was not getting rid of her that easily. I truly hated dragging her into this mess, but I guessed it was too late and that I might as well spill the beans.

"There are things lurking in the dark—demons and monsters that will take your heart. I'm the only one standing between them and the end of everything we've ever loved. I know it sounds like the script of a bad Hollywood movie, but it's true. I so wished it wasn't, but it is. This is a gateway to our planet, the only one, as far as I can tell, and the darkness is coming right through here.

"We have to tell someone!" exclaimed Naz, standing up and pacing around anxiously.

"Would you believe me if I told you?" I laughed bitterly. "No, they would lock me up in the funny farm if I did. I'm alone in this battle." The Manual coughed and looked up at me. Smiling, I picked it up and placed it on my lap. "'Scuse me; *we're* alone in this battle."

"So it's little Miss Badass versus whatever nasty things come crawling out of the dark. And where does the book come in?"

"He's my guide. The only engineering I know is what I saw growing up with my dad. He helps me with the technical aspects and construction. I'd be lost without him," I replied, pulling the book closer to me.

"Why don't you just shoot the things and be done with it?" Naz asked curiously, placing her feet on the comatose orc.

"No weapons. Don't ask me why, but something tells me it's not the way to go." The Manual vibrated angrily in my arms. "And besides, boo-boo here would not like it. He gets nasty when he gets upset."

"I noticed it at school the other day," Naz replied, looking out over the dark battlefield.

"When? And speaking of which, I think it's time you start explaining yourself." I threw the ball back in her court. Naz blushed beet red, shuffling her feet back and forth.

"That afternoon when I saw this little paperback from hell chasing Jake Mathis across the schoolyard. I first thought I must have fasted too much and was seeing things, but I just couldn't put it out of my mind."

"So, you started following me."

"Yes," she replied sheepishly. "It's not hard slipping out of the house, so I trailed you for a few nights. All very quiet till your little excursion to the hardware store, I saw you leave, and then I knew you were up to something."

I sat pensively, playing a slow rhythm on the bridge of my nose. "Naz…if anyone finds out what I'm up to…there's no one else that can do this."

"Well, all I know is you have a kickass little buddy over here. I happened to be watching the hardware store the night it went on a shopping trip. It was epic, by the way." The Manual perked up and tapped its cover in appreciation.

"But it could all be for nothing," I sighed and flicked a pebble against the orc's head.

"Do I have to pull everything out of you, Michaela Jones?" Naz exclaimed in exasperation, standing up and kneeling before me. I think she knew her friend was hurting inside, that I was waiting to explode.

"So little time left to get everything ready…never going to be ready before they come for me," I muttered distantly, shying my eyes away from her.

"Dammit, who? Tell me for God's sake!"

"They're going to take me away, Naz." My eyes shot full of tears, as the reality of having to leave everyone I ever loved behind dawned on me. "I've got less than a week before I get sent into foster care." The words hung horribly in the air before settling down on us.

"I won't let them; you hear me, my friend? I'll raise hell itself to stop that." Her voice was calm as the night around us and steady as a rock. "You showed me kindness when everyone else shunned me, and I will repay that favor if Allah so wills it." Naz hugged me tightly, and I bit my lip hard to keep from crying. Even the damned Manual hugged me around the legs.

"Now, you are going to explain everything to me, slowly and carefully till my ass is one hundred and ten percent clear on the situation. And then we are going to work our way through this mess you've landed us nose-first in."

"Us?" I asked, looking my friend deep in the eyes.

"Well duh, you expect me to shut up about all this? My silence has a price, and it's straightforward—bring me on board and let me help take care of the nasties. A sort of partnership of the damned, if you will."

"What? Oh, hell no. I am not dragging you into this. What if you get hurt and what happens when…" I began to protest, but was cut off immediately by her level voice.

"And there is no way you and fifty shades over here can do everything by yourself," she said. "Simply put, you need me, bitch." I could have punched her smiling face at that moment, but there was no way of convincing the little Muslim girl otherwise.

"And nobody is going to notice you've gone missing? That thought ever occurred to you?" I protested.

"Dude, partner, buddy of mine, I have been running my madrassa like a boss for years now. The maulana is terrified of me. I got this. We'll work on this when we get time in the afternoons and at night. Your suspension from school will be ending soon, and then we carry on like normal. Nobody will find out. What do you say?" She held out her fist in expectation.

"I can't fucking believe I'm doing this," I muttered in disbelief, staring at her before fist-bumping her.

"Yeah! Apocalypse buddies. This is going to be epicness." Naz smiled broadly and looked down at the orc at our feet. "So…what are we doing with gorgeous here? Can't just leave him, right?"

A sly smile formed on my tired face as I eyed the control box nearby. "Want to take the trap for a test drive?"

Thirty-odd minutes later, we had managed to drag the unconscious orc down the steps and place him on the wooden spring trap. The beast was just starting to come to; it looked around groggily at its surroundings. Only too late did it realize the world of pain it was about to enter. Just as it was about to scramble off the board and tear us a new one, Naz pushed the button with relish. The orc's green eyes went wide with terror as we waved goodbye.

"Life's hard for a pimp. Nothing personal, sweetie." Naz shrugged as the trap launched the screaming orc into the night sky. We three watched with wonder as he disappeared back over the tree line, and I felt sorry for the poor bastard. Maybe for like a second.

"Alas, poor Yorick. I knew him, Horatio," I stated, cold as ice, tying my loose hair up again.

"You getting cultured on me here, darling?"

"A girl's got to have some qualities. Okay, I think we need to get back home and catch some Zs. Seeing that I can't talk you out of this, you might as well see the rest of the operation tomorrow afternoon."

"Can't wait to see it all," Naz replied, gripping my shoulder tightly as we slowly walked back to the truck, the Manual resting in my arms. Even though I was terrified for her safety, a part deep inside me was glad I had someone else to watch my back. All I knew was that the next few days were going to be very interesting indeed.

It was make or break time.

Meanwhile, somewhere down south, Death was sitting on his throne, raising an eyebrow a barely perceptible inch upwards. He was staring at a pathetic looking set of bloodied and bruised orcs before him. Not believing their sob story, he dismissed them with a flick of his fingers. A massive fireball turned the hapless orcs into charcoal. Death sat back and drummed his fingers angrily on his arms. Though barely a nuisance at this moment in time, this slight setback was irking him, and he was not happy about it.

Not happy at all.

CHAPTER 15

Somewhere in a town in Middle America

It was one of those mornings. Just before eleven, I think. It felt like someone had tap-danced on my head as I slowly opened my bloodshot eyes. I lay back in the bed, gently pushing the Manual to the side as I contemplated everything that happened last night. For a brief moment, I believed that it was a bad dream and that nothing had changed—just me and the little black book facing off against the Darkness. No Naz, no complications, everything simple and easy.

'*And then she woke up, the coffee was cold, and her cushion was missing.*' The acid-like thought trampled through my mind as I grimaced, yawned, and painfully got up from the bed. Scratching my ass through the blue pajama bottoms, I headed to the kitchen. I needed coffee. Something black and sweet as all hell, it was my only salvation at this ungodly hour. As I waited for the kettle to whistle, the Manual motioned into view. It somehow looked in worse shape than me as it hopped onto a chair nearby me. I watched with detached attention as it reached for a bottle of headache pills and swallowed it whole.

"What a night, huh?" I sat back in deep thought for a moment, reaching for the kettle. The Manual said very little, resting its cover on the counter table. Even though I was mortally tired, a surge of excitement was running through my veins. We had managed to take down a group of fearsome warriors by ourselves, without guns and bullets, just our wits and some engineering knowhow. I still couldn't believe it. It just didn't seem real, yet it was.

In those quiet few moments, the coffee mug temporally forgotten, I started slowly thinking ahead. The die has been cast, and there was no going back now. We had started something, and there was no choice but to finish it. In my sleep-deprived mind, I already started envisioning different and more elaborate traps. Those spring traps would only last so long, and God only knows what other monsters were coming down the pipeline. I would have to start thinking about using fire and electricity as well. However, that was for later, my priority was a warm shower and then clean up the workshop downstairs—anything to get my mind of the insanity of last night.

It was a weary and broken Michaela who dragged her carcass into the workshop a good hour later, the shower doing precious little to ease my tired muscles. With my head still pounding in agony, I took in the mess I had left behind. Piles of timber and screws lay scattered across the tiled floor. Silently cursing myself for working so sloppily, I got down to work—the Manual pitching in when it wandered down a bit later. The monotony of the labor gave me a chance to clear my head, and I could see ideas for traps forming in my mind. I would sort out the construction later, but the concepts were coming together— though at a frustratingly slow pace.

"No, sort those screwdrivers by size. Do not sass me, or I'll turn you into a romance novel." Our banter carried on through the hours as the workshop slowly regained some semblance of sanity. Lunch was a subdued affair, a peanut butter, jelly, and banana sandwich for me and a chunk of frozen turkey leg for the book. I sat paging through the Manual, seeing elaborate schematics and drawing for traps against the monsters. It was mind-boggling, the absolute shitstorm contained within its pages; I knew I would be utilizing a lot of them before this war was over. My father's notes were excellent, all of them in his thin, spider-like writing. They helped me tremendously when the schematics looked too complicated. I tried hard, but I was missing him today and would have given anything for him to be back here again. Sighing deeply, I finished up my lunch and got back to work.

It was barely half an hour later when I heard the doorbell ring. My father had installed a second bell downstairs to make life easier. Wiping my hands clean on a grimy rag, I looked down at the Manual. "Now, who can that be?" The book just shrugged and trotted after me upstairs. I was in no mood for company. Probably another salesman—just had to get rid of the pest, and quickly, as there was still much work to be done.

"No, I do not wish to change my long-distance carrier, and no, I don't have a soul to save." I flung open the door. Instead of an overzealous salesman, a small figure stood looking up at me, smiling broadly.

"*Salaam alaikum*, Michaela Jones," Naz stated, folding her arms. I had hoped beyond hope that last night's incident would have maybe, just maybe, scared her off. Then again, this was not a woman who took 'no' for an answer. She was dressed in a vintage Shawn Michaels wrestling shirt; she made for quite a sight standing at front of my door.

"Naz…you know this is not a good idea." I protested in vain as she leaned past me and saw the Manual behind my legs.

"Is that you, Mills and Boon? How's my favorite book from the dark side doing? Come give Mama some love." The Manual bounded past me and jumped into Naz's arms.

"Naz, I think you should go home…what are you doing?" I protested. They both looked up at me with puppy dog eyes.

"That won't work on me; this is a foolish idea." My words fell on deaf ears, as they got cuter by the moment. With a scream of resignation, I threw my hands in the air and marched back into the shop. The Manual fist-bumped Naz and hummed as she carried it inside. I stood with my head against the elevator, eyes closed, already knowing this was going to bite me on the ass.

"Are you sure this is what you want?" I asked her, not looking back. Naz placed her hand gently on my shoulder.

"You watched my back once; now I'm returning the favor." That's all she needed to say.

"Shouldn't you be in madrassa now?" I asked as we rode the elevator down.

"Bitch, please. My maulana was still sitting in the corner, rocking back and forth on his heels when I left him. I got this, woman."

I simply shook my head, knowing I was dealing with a force of nature and that the word 'no' was not in her vocabulary. The elevator shuddered to a gentle halt, and the doors slid open. Naz's eyes went wide as she walked in awe through the subterranean workshop.

"This is where the magic happens, I guess," she said. A part of me felt sheepish that I had kept it a secret from her, but I'd had no other choice in the matter.

"Dude…"

"I know, I know," I replied, fiddling with a wrench on the worktable.

"Dude!"

"Trust me; I had the same reaction." I tried to keep calm, but Naz's enthusiasm was infectious. She walked past the rows of shiny tables and tools.

"This is fucking amazing! My best friend has a bat cave. Holy shit." Naz started looking through the pile of schematics on a nearby table. "And this is where you start putting the plans together, right?" Her eyes were shining in wonder as she explored the workshop.

"Yeah, and some of the material is over there. I, um, borrow the rest from the hardware store."

"Very cool indeed, but there is only one problem."

"And what, pray tell, is that?" I asked suspiciously.

"You got the basic idea down, but good god, woman, your ass needs to go Wile E. Coyote on this motherfucker." She waved her arms around in exasperation.

"What do you mean?"

"We're facing the forces of darkness itself, right?" She didn't give me time to respond. "Got monsters from every nightmare, every creature coming for us, trying to bone us into the next Pornhub advert, right? Well, then we got to get medieval sister. Our homeboy the Manual must have some damn fine goodies in there, so let's fucking use them."

"It's all yours. Go mad." I smiled genuinely and watched as Naz flipped open the Manual and quickly paged through him.

"See? Right here. Plans for a homemade trebuchet. The construction doesn't look that bad, and we can easily find ammunition for it. We light their asses on fire, I say."

"I did see some gunpowder at the hardware store. Shouldn't be that hard to break into the back rooms." I thought for a moment before continuing. "Heavy stone ammunition will be too difficult to make and transport, but if we can pour tar or resin out over the battlefield, then we can set fire to it from a distance."

"Now you are thinking like an engineer. Show me what else you got cooking over here." We spent the next few hours blissfully discussing weapons and strategy in the workshop. For some bizarre reason, we just clicked, and the ideas flowed—everything from spikes to bear traps, and even something that looked disturbingly like a gigantic mousetrap. Our ideas just got more demented as the hours ticked by, but we kept at it. There could be no mercy for whatever demon was coming at us. Because if we failed…no, I couldn't even entertain that thought. Had to push through.

"Have we got any of those springs left over? I saw a nice recipe in the Manual for phosphorus grenades, and I think we can combine them nicely," I hollered over to Naz as she and the Manual were knee-deep in the parts bin.

"We might have just enough for one or two. We can fit it to a pressure plate. Should be epic," Naz replied as we slowly started putting the crude traps together. We were almost finished when the doorbell rang. We looked at each other worriedly.

"You expecting visitors, Michaela Jones?" Naz asked, rubbing her hands clean with a grimy rag.

"Not that I know of. You better hope it's not your parents looking for you."

"Oh, I'd be royally fucked if it was." She hurried upstairs with me. Something was off; it was way too late for customers or salespeople to come knocking. Making sure the secret entrance was closed and hidden away, I hurried to the door.

"Who's there?"

"Social Services. We've come to collect you, Miss Jones." My blood instantly froze at the ill-fated words. The bastard was early; I expected him in a few days at most. I could hear the Manual growling behind my legs.

"No, we don't hurt civilians. Just give me time to think,' I said to him. 'Coming! Just looking for the key," I shouted to the closed door. The truth was that I had no idea what I was going to do. Cornered and out of options, I looked back forlornly at Naz; her face dropped in despair. Our whole plan had come crashing down upon us, and the very fate of the earth itself was about to be wrecked by this overzealous bureaucrat. With a heavy heart, I unlocked the door and watched as the portly man walked in.

"I do hope you are packed and ready to go, Miss Jones. Yes, I am aware I am early, but we are trying to improve our efficiency." He looked around haughtily at the messy room, his eyebrows twitching in disgust. He spotted Naz standing in the corner and looked down with a sneer at her.

"And I trust your, um, immigrant friend's papers are all in order? We do not want ICE involved now, do we?"

"You son of a bitch!" Naz went for the social worker, but I managed to restrain her. "It's okay, sweetie; I got this…I got this," I whispered in her ear as she calmed down a bit.

"Just let me get my things, and I'll go with you," I said to the shocked social worker. He kept his distance, and a sturdy table, between him and the still seething Naz. The adventure was over before it could even begin. I was going to get shipped to goddamn Florida, and there would be nobody to man the wall.

'*The end is here.*' I thought miserably, head hanging low as I headed to my room. I'd barely made it a few steps when I heard a loud and unmistakable "ka-thunk" of steel on bone. I wheeled around in horror.

Naz.

She had beaned the social worker with a monkey wrench and was standing over his unconscious body. The poor bastard had hit the floor like a sack of potatoes.

"What the fuck are you doing, Naz?!" I exclaimed, running over to check on the poor man.

"Relax the mammaries, dear; he's still breathing. I didn't hit him that hard, and I can't help it if pussy boy here can't take a shot."

"Oh, that is brilliant, just brilliant! You just assaulted a government official. What can you possibly hope to gain from this? Apart from spending years behind bars?" I was beside myself with rage, already seeing myself in a lovely orange jumpsuit getting felt up by the local lesbian/prison tackle machine.

The little Muslim girl smiled wickedly and glanced back at the hidden elevator. "I'm thinking we're going to save your ass, woman. Now, help me get this sack of lard in the truck downstairs. I have a plan to solve all our problems."

Let's work.

CHAPTER 16

Somewhere in Middle America

"We need to talk about this demented obsession of yours of hitting people on the head," I grunted between clenched teeth as we dragged the unconscious social worker down to the workshop. He weighed a ton, and I cringed every time I looked down at his yellow-stained pits.

"What? Concussions build character; everyone knows that. Now help me get this fucker into the truck. Lift with your hips, woman, come on now." I just shook my head, scarcely believing I was willing to go along with Naz's insane plan. Then again, the thought of crossing her didn't sit too well with me, either. After a mighty struggle, we eventually got him into the back of the truck. "Beautiful. Now you go get the parts for the trap, and I'll get the chemicals from the back." Naz pulled a tarp over the social worker, smacking him on the backside in passing. I looked down worriedly at the Manual; we shared a moment somewhere between wonder and utter horror. We were simply going balls-to-the-wall, dragging behind the wicked machinations of her yet-to-be-revealed plans.

A half-hour or so later, we had everything we needed loaded into the truck. Still taking it slow with the whole driving thing, I carefully pulled out of the garage and into the crisp evening air. Naz was sitting in the back, periodically kicking the social worker to see if he was stirring. "Don't even say it," I hissed at the Manual. The little black book simply folded its pages and snuggled into the truck's seat, a morbid curiosity forming inside its mind. Though equally freaked out as I was, it wanted to see what Naz had up her sleeve.

"I cannot believe I let you talk me into this. I need to have my head examined," I said morosely, pulling the blanket tighter over me. We had carefully set out the traps a hundred yards away from us and then constructed a basic wooden yardarm. The body of the hapless social worker was swinging upside down from a rope attached to his leg.

"Random acts of violence can solve any problem. It was either Gandhi or Betty White that said that; I can never remember," Naz replied, cool as a cucumber and sipping on a mug of hot coffee. It must have been a curious sight: two girls sitting on lawn chairs in front of a dark battlefield, waiting for something to stir in the distant gloom. Our patience was soon rewarded, as we heard the distant clinking and clanking of bone and steel rambling towards us from the forest. A group of ten skeletons emerged from the tree line, the orange glow of fiery torches lighting up the faceless horrors.

"Mind waking him up?" I asked, stirring my coffee. Naz picked up a stone and, taking careful aim, careened it off the social worker's skull. He woke with a splutter, eyes wide in shock, arms flailing around wildly, his screams echoing over the field.

"Let me go! Let me go!" He wailed loudly, as we watched. The Manual looked up from Naz's lap, slightly annoyed at the sudden interruption, then snuggled back into the blanket.

"Why do I always get the screamers?" she said with a deadpan look on her face. The social worker clawed at the air and then saw the advancing line of skeletons. In a voice that could only be described as Kanye West seeing Kim Kardashian without her makeup, he started yelling his lungs out even more.

"Oh, God! Get them away from me! Help!"

"We'd love to, but you want to send me away to Florida. Mama no like banana hammocks and tiger print G-strings," I stated with a wicked smile forming across my face.

"It's the law; you cannot change that!" He protested, seeing the skeletons marching across the field, getting ever closer.

"Well, that's a shame. I wonder what they are going to do with him?" I said, turning to Naz.

"Bone him, I imagine," Naz replied, running her hands over the Manual's cover lovingly.

"Oh god, did you come up with that all by yourself?"

"I didn't have much time to work on my material." She shrugged and looked back at the ball of flop sweat hanging from the rope nearby. "Yo, homeboy, you ready to deal?"

"Damn you; I'll make sure you are deported for this!" His voice was raising a notable octave or two every passing second.

"Can't we just let him, you know…?" Naz pulled a finger over her throat, eyeing me hopefully.

"No, we have to do the right thing." I slowly got up, walked over to the social worker, grabbed him by the nose, and looked into his eyes. "Well, what's it going to be? Push a couple of papers around and help me out here or…" I motioned to the skeletons, now in full charge mode. "They looked pissed; I wouldn't want to be around them."

"You're out of your fucking mind! This is madness!" the ball of lard wailed even louder.

"Okay, no worries. Naz, if we hurry, we can still catch tonight's wrestling."

"Sweet. Pentagon's got a new package piledriver I've been dying to try out. Might have to enlist one of my brothers again, though," she replied, starting to fold up the lawn chair. The skeletons were less than two hundred yards away and closing fast. I could see the fire shimmering off their off-white bones as they jabbered and groaned in the night.

I'd barely made it a few steps away when I heard his panicked voice calling after me. "I'll do it! For God's sake, I'll do it!"

I paused and casually looked back at the dangling man. "Do what, dear?"

"I'll sign the paperwork. You won't have to go to Florida. Just get me down from here!"

Looking past the man at the onrushing horde of skeletons, I decided to torture him for a few more agonizing seconds. "Naz, sweetie, what do you think? Should be we let him go?"

She calmly cleaned her nails and thought deeply about it.

"If we have to. It would be messy otherwise."

I smiled broadly as the first skeleton stepped on the homemade phosphor landmine, a massive flash of pure white light exploding in the distance. Like a set of cascading dominoes, the rest of the traps were set off, sending a deluge of bones raining down from the sky. It was quite the fireworks show, and though I didn't show it, I felt relief inside. For a second I'd doubted our crazy contraptions were going to work, but they came through beautifully. Soon the intense white light of the phosphor died away, leaving a scattered field of broken bones lying around. It was over in seconds. I turned to the social worker, reaching for a knife in my pocket.

"Make sure I'm left alone, now, you hear me? If I see any government people near me... Now run, buddy, and don't you dare look back." I cut the rope, and he flopped to the ground. Scrambling to his feet and dusting himself off, he looked at me with wide, terrified eyes.

"You're insane, completely insane," he stammered, gulping for air.

I glanced over at Naz and the Manual. "I guess we are. Now get." The social worker started running, disappearing into the night with blind panic. I wasn't worried that he would tell people what was happening out here. Nobody would believe him anyway. I watched him fade from view as Naz joined me. There was a distant look about her, unusual for the normally buoyant girl.

"You know we are playing with fire, right? We can only keep poking the bear for so long before it all comes crashing down."

"I know, sweetie, but we got no choice left. It's just us now," I replied in a hushed voice. We stood watching over the still-smoldering battlefield, knowing that things were going to get a lot worse from here on out.

"Let's get going; I think there's still some Chinese takeout in the fridge. And I want to see if we can do something about the generator. We're going to need a lot more power if we want to keep this show going." I was thinking about the mysterious crystal underneath our feet. If we could somehow hook up to it, it could provide us with all the energy we'd need. But that was for another day.

"You're the brains of the operation. They keep on coming, and we'll keep on knocking them down. I'll just look dope and fresh over here while doing it," Naz said. I laughed and punched her on the shoulder. Laughing, she chased me back to the truck.

We spent the rest of the evening back at the shop eating takeout, watching wrestling, and coming up with even more insane ideas for traps. I never told her, but I truly valued these precious times with my best friend. It got my mind off the terrible task waiting out there for me in the dark. She kept me going when I felt my spirits started to fade. I knew we had dodged a bullet with the social worker, at least for the time being. Just before ten, Naz headed back home, and I was alone again. The shop suddenly felt cold and empty as I fell asleep on the comfy chair with the Manual snuggling tightly in my arms. Another day survived, another day to be grateful for, as my eyes fell shut.

Somewhere in the darkness.

Death was pacing up and down in the vast and empty dining hall. All the elite demons he commanded had wisely chosen to make themselves scarce. It was not beneficial to your health to stick around when Death was in one of his moods. He had gotten word that another of his legions had met their fate near the wall, and he was less than pleased. A goblet of blood-red wine crashed against the dark stone walls as he flicked his fingers in agitation. There was nobody to defend the wall, with the last Paladin having died years ago, yet something was out there screwing up his well-laid plans, and it was pissing him off to no end. Storming past a terrified goblin cowering in the corner, Death headed downstairs, a black cloak trailing behind him. He went to his sanctuary, deep in the heart of his fortress, where he could think. None of his minions was allowed to come down here. Pushing open a heavy oak door, he exhaled slowly and looked up. A gigantic scarlet heart was beating against the far wall, blackened veins crisscrossing its fleshy texture. Death crossed the room, ran a hand over the abnormal heart, and then slowly lowered his head against it. Drawing dark energy from it, he clenched his fists in anger. Fire raged in his soulless eyes; he knew what he had to do.

Bring hell itself down on those who dared stand in his way.

Unleash the demon.

CHAPTER 17

Somewhere in Middle America

A few days had passed since the social worker incident, days of constant work for Naz and me. We spent every possible moment building and refining our traps. We tinkered and argued good-naturedly over what could potentially work and which of our ideas were suspect at best. I started to notice that something was driving Naz, an invisible yet tangible force pushing her to work harder and longer into the night. I wanted to talk to her about it but held back time and again, glancing anxiously down at the Manual. We both knew what was at stake, but Naz kept pushing herself, only taking breaks when we had virtually pulled her away from the work. I thought it best to talk to her later on; I had to get the first line of traps up and make sure our defense line was secure.

A bond was forged between us without anyone ever saying anything. Between the sparks from the welded steel and the hammering of nails, between cuts and bruises and pure exhaustion, we found each other. Naz and I had gone beyond being two schoolgirls way in over their heads and playing heroes to becoming an alliance of women, forged in desperation and extended beyond our understanding. With our faithful companion helping as best as a book could, we carried on unabated, willing each other forward. Maybe there was an element of fear that surrounded us. We had seen but the merest glimpse of the shadow and we knew worse was to come.

Simply put: It was 'fuck it and carry on' time. And besides, two badass bitches defending planet earth had a beautiful ring to it. We were in it to the bitter end.

It had been suspiciously quiet since we last saw any monsters, and it was stirring an unease inside me. We should have been up to our tits in all sorts of assorted nasties, but there was nothing. Not that I was complaining, as it gave us a chance to put the finishing touches on a line of glue traps attached to a set of swinging hammers. If I read it correctly in the Manual, these traps should keep any monster busy just long enough to turn it into marinara sauce. Did I feel any sympathy for said nasties that were stupid enough to walk into our traps? Fuck no. It was them or us, and I preferred us. Our job was simple—stall the monsters long enough for the Paladin to show up and kick some heavy-duty booty, as Naz so ineloquently put it.

One problem facing us was the lack of power. My little generator simply could not handle the requirements of our rapidly growing field of traps; it soon started to smoke violently. We could have, ahem, 'bought' more, but it wasn't feasible in the long run. No, the operation was needing something with a bit more kick.

The crystal.

Very reluctantly, we headed down to the cavern one late

Thursday afternoon. I could smell the lingering stench of gnome in the narrow confines of the subterranean hole; it had sunk into the cavern walls themselves. The Manual paused over a fallen red hat, smacking its pages and probably reminiscing over a snack that lingered in the memory. Shaking my head, I led them both deeper underground. It wasn't long before we were standing in front of the massive, glowing red crystal. We looked on in silent awe, feeling the hum of the unearthly stone shifting through our bodies. For once, Naz was lost for words, looking at me with her jaw dropping open ever so slightly.

"*Inna lilahi.*"

"So yeah…" I said after a few moments of pregnant silence, finally breaking the ice.

"Dude…"

"I know."

"Dude…"

"I know."

Then Naz looked over suspiciously at me, her eyebrow rising just perceptibly.

"If I grow a pair of testicles overnight, bitch we are going to have words. Long and complicated words," she said, grinding her teeth ever so slightly. Nodding, I reached for a small pickaxe the Manual thoughtfully handed to me. I mean, what could go wrong? I was just hacking off a piece of crystal that held ancient power that nobody understood and that had the potential to change the fate of planet Earth. Nope, nothing at all. Naz and the book shuffled back to safety. Gulping noticeably, I gripped the handle of the pickaxe a little tighter and closed my eyes. I swung with all my might; cold steel met radiating stone, and it felt like the whole world was shaking around us.

It was alive.

I could feel my soul twisting and weaving, vivid strands of it reaching out and connecting with the crystal. Like hands suspended in time, they felt the crystal; it was almost childlike. It was afraid, terribly afraid. The pickaxe slid from my grip and clattered dully on the ground. Streams of white light flowed past me, I stepped forward. The crystal's essence recoiled, pulling back into itself.

'*I'm not going to hurt you.*'

The crystal hesitated, unsure of the new presence in its consciousness. This one is different. There is no hatred in her heart, but she's been hurt before. Black tendrils were mixing with red and white light—kindred spirits connecting in the empty space. Ever so slowly, it relented and allowed me inside its inner sanctum. I could see images of wars long forgotten rushing past me, of bloodshed and agony. And all the while, the crystal looked passively on, tears running down its surface. It was tired, incomprehensibly and irrevocably tired.

'I'm *sorry...*' I hated myself now, knowing I needed to ask just a bit more of it. I didn't have a choice, had to do it. The crystal wrapped its essence around me, blanket-like, comforting, and safe. I think maybe it understood the dilemma facing me, but it didn't make it any easier. I was using a living entity to keep a bunch of selfish and stupid people alive. What a life. I lowered my head in shame, unable to look up.

'*Michaela Jones.*' The crystal's voice was all-encompassing, filling the corners with life and energy, but it was also soothing and comforting. Its essence formed something like fingers that raised my chin. I looked up with tears running down my cheeks. *'I see you, Michaela Jones. You are worthy.'*

'Tell me what to do,' I whispered, staring deep into the scarlet infinity. Fireflies of crimson energy streaked about aimlessly from point to point.

'Faith. It is all you two have now. You must believe in each other. Let go of the hatred and believe, Michaela Jones.' I exhaled slowly and watched wisps of cold air drift away from me.

'We're so small. How can they expect us to do this?' The demons of self-doubt kept tugging at me, dragging me down.

'Sometimes, that's all the world needs—two women just unwilling to take "no" for an answer.' A slight smile formed on my lips as I heard her words. I nodded, understanding. *'But you will have to walk in the shadows and face the horrors of the shade yourself. Nobody is coming to help you; you will have to save yourself.'*

'Show me the shadow,' I replied, the words bereft of life, chilling to hear. The crystal darkened and shuddered at the mention of the great evil. It wanted to pull back, but I held on and stood my ground. *'Please. I have to know.'* Even though my whole body was shuddering at the thought, I had to know who my enemy was. I needed to see its face. The crystal relented and reached out, laying a single finger on my forehead.

Pain. As if a million stars vaporized before my eyes. I could feel myself screaming in horrific silence, my mouth contorted in agony. The shadows were driving wicked daggers into my body, pulling the seams loose, unraveling, tearing me apart. Hatred, pure hatred coursing through my veins like rivers of black ink, gushing forth into an empty void. The stygian horror was forcing me down to my knees, willing me to bend down. My eyes turning gray-white, I looked up.

I saw him.

Death.

The final gambit of all our pathetic efforts on this planet was standing across from me, black cloak fluttering in the wind. His face was bereft of color, skeletal, as he stared at me, arms crossed in mounting anger. He couldn't believe this human, this worm was standing in his way. Death grabbed me by the chin, lifting me off my feet. Suspended in midair, I felt him gaze into my soul and then froze. An irrepressible spark kept flicking inside me; the unconquerable willpower that has driven me my whole life remained steadfast. I looked Death straight in the eyes, unwilling to avert my gaze. For a split second, this threw the reaper, and he blinked. This was not possible; the humans always cowered in his presence, pissing their pants at the mere mention of his name, yet this girl refused to back down.

'*Engineer—you have no hope. Embrace the pain and give up,*' Death hissed, maggots crawling from his empty eyes.

'*You think you…scare me?*' I said in a hushed tone, fighting back the pain with everything inside me, holding on by my fingertips. '*I saw my mother pass before my eyes, watched as cancer ate her alive. I was there, day by goddamn day, as she withered before me. You took her away. I held her hand and felt my whole world collapse as her time ran out. I have felt more pain than you could ever even imagine.*' Anger flowed from me as I ripped Death a new one. '*But once was not enough, no—you tried to break me a second time. Leaving me alone. I've had to grow up without my parents, so don't fucking talk to me about pain.*' I could feel his iron grip loosen on my collar as the ground started shaking underneath us.

'*But you are just a woman…*' the skeleton spluttered. Death was used to dealing with warriors dripping with male bravado, proud and exalted human beings whom he relished breaking. However, this girl…she was different. She honestly did not give a damn, and that disturbed him more than anything he had felt in eons.

'*That's all I need to be, motherfucker.*'

Death let go of me and stepped back. The ground caved in, splitting us apart. Two polar opposites were staring at each over the chasm—the girl versus the shadow. The reaper hissed at me in anger, his skeletal hand clenched as he pointed a bony finger at me. '*As you wish, engineer.*' Death faded back into smoke and disappeared. At that moment, I finally let go and gave into the torturous pain. Tears streamed down my face as I convulsed in agony, my body shuddering. I grabbed my head and screamed. I felt someone grab me, holding on tightly. I was back in the cavern, a hunched-up ball on the ground as Naz and the Manual hugged me.

"I saw him…I saw him," I muttered, staring into nothingness. I felt like I was freezing, shuddering at the unspeakable horror I had seen. Cold sweat bathed my face as I fought hopelessly against the images still running in my mind.

"I got you, girly," Naz whispered protectively, holding my head against her chest. "I got you." The crystal glowed brightly then slowly died away into nothingness. It had served its purpose and was ready to embrace its final act.

'*You are worthy, Michaela Jones. Use me wisely.*' I said nothing, merely shielding my eyes as I burrowed into my best friend's arms. We had found our source of power, but at a terrible cost. The crystal had died to give us a sliver of hope.

Just a little.

It was the day after the events in the cavern, and our machines and traps were humming along merrily. The crystal had provided us with tremendous power, more than we had ever dared hope for. With one of our problems solved, we turned our attention to the next issue on our list. The dam on the far left of the battlefield proved to be a stumbling block in our preparations. It had to come down in order to channel the incoming monsters into our path, but getting the bastard down was another matter altogether. It was not like we could get explosives at the local Kwik E Mart now, could we? I came up with a solution as we were sitting on the wall, taking a break and eating hamburgers. We were going to use the power of the crystal again. What's the worst that could happen?

"You got issues, white girl," Naz said pensively as we looked up at the dam later that day. I had managed to rig up a few shards of the crystal at the base of the dam with det-cord running away from it.

"Unless you got a better idea?" I handed the detonator box to Naz. She looked down at the switch and then back at us.

"Oh, of course, the Muslim knows all about bombs. Let me get that for you," she said sarcastically.

The Manual and I gave her a blank stare. "Well, at least your sense of humor is still intact," I said.

Naz paused over the switch then sniffed the air. "Did you just fart and let Fluffy off the leash? Good God, woman, I told you those extra onions were going to bite you in the ass—pun intended."

"What are you talking about…?" Then I smelled it as well. A sulfuric stench somewhere between rotten eggs and burning flesh. The wind started to pick up, whipping our hair about, and then I saw it coming towards us across the field: a gigantic monster bathed in raging flames, screeching at the air as it flapped its leathery wings wildly. It turned slowly in the gray air above us, spiraling before diving down on us. Cinders dripping from its ragged fangs, the monster streaked through the air, eager to devour its hapless victims—an easy meal for the lord of the skies.

The Fire Demon cometh.

CHAPTER 18

"Well? What are you waiting for you overhyped budgie?" Naz shouted at the incoming fire demon, grabbing her crotch in defiance. Swathes of hot wind lashed over us. Hearing the crackling of burnt grass in the distance, I grabbed my friend by the collar and pulled her back.

"That's quite enough of that. Move your ass, woman!" Naz dropped the detonator and we started running for our lives. Jesus! We never thought such a thing even existed. We must have pissed Death off more than we realized. There was no time to deliberate as the behemoth crashed through the clouds, sending down a stream of hellfire. I glanced over my shoulder as we ran, pulling Naz to the side with all my strength and then tumbling over the grass.

"Hold on!" I yelled. The monster streaked past us, its eyes glowing demon red. It was like standing in the turbulence caused by a passenger aircraft; the wind threw us around like rag dolls. As I fell, I clutched my shoulder, shaking in pain. The fire had singed me, barely, but it still hurt like a bastard.

"Oh, hell. Hold on, I got this." Naz pulled my jacket off, all the while looking for the demon circling above us. Luckily it was so massive that it couldn't turn quickly and had to take the long way around. Naz ripped a piece off her hijab and wrapped it tightly around my arm.

"Just keep pressure on it, okay? We'll get you help." We both knew she was lying through her teeth, but it didn't matter. Eyes wide with terror, she saw the demon coming for a second time. Our time and luck were rapidly running out. The fire monster flapped its wings even harder, agitated that its prey was not yet turned to ashes.

"Listen to me, damn it! Listen, will ya? We got to stick and move; it's our only chance; use that fucker's size against him." Naz paused for a moment, smacking her lips. "We're going to run straight at him."

"We're going to do what?" I exclaimed, open-jawed, thinking she must have lost her mind even further.

"Bitch, if there was ever a time to trust me, it's now." Naz tried to fake a brave smile, but I could see in her eyes she was afraid. I nodded, going along with whatever craziness she was about to drop on me.

"Okay, but you know 'bitch' is not really a term of endearment, right?"

"I know." She grinned wickedly, summing up all her courage as the demon made its final turn high above us, its shadow blocking out the dim yellow sun. "We got to time this just right, or our asses are toast." Like stunned deer in headlights, we stood our ground, alone on the open battlefield.

"Naz…" I hissed under my breath, barely audible above the horrific roar of the fire demon.

"Wait for it…"

"Naz…"

"Wait for it…"

"Nazmirrah!"

"Now!" She grabbed my hand and ran straight at the winged monster. Instantly it was thrown, sending the stream of hellfire far above our heads. It scorched the earth mere meters behind us. Like a roaring freight train, the demon swept past us. We fell to the ground and held on for dear life. Almost as if in a trance, Naz lifted her head to stare in awe at the incredible goliath mere meters above our head. She marveled at the shimmering orange scales and its gigantic muscles twitching in flight. Naz was oblivious to anything around her, not seeing the incoming danger until it was almost too late.

"Down!" I grabbed her with my good arm and pulled down. A razor-sharp claw flashed mere inches past her covered head. It was a miracle it didn't rip her to pieces. We lay stunned on the ground, gasping as the fire demon hurtled past us. My mouth felt like sandpaper. I watched in morbid fascination as the creature flapped off into the distance. Then it struck me; something was missing.

"Naz…where is the book?" I asked in the sudden silence.

"What book?" She turned to me and asked.

"The Manual, goddammit." My question was answered mere moments later when the little black book came charging like Boudicca past us.

"Oh, my…" That was all I managed to get out as we watched the Manual chase after the demon.

"Can I borrow him for Ramadan? He's going to be a hit at the dinner table," Naz said, standing up and dusting herself

THE GIRL'S GUIDE TO THE APOCALYPSE

absentmindedly off. The fire demon never saw the incoming book behind him, not until it was way too late. The Manual opened its magnificent jaws and launched itself through the air, clamping down on the monster's trailing hind leg. The demon screamed in agony and thrashed about wildly. Darting back and forth through the air, he tried everything to shake the pest stuck to his leg, but it was to no avail. As previous monsters could attest, once the Manual has sunk its fangs into you, it won't let go for anything on this earth.

"He's bought us some time…got to think…got to think," I mumbled to myself, forcing my brain to come up with a plan. I knew it would not be long before the Manual's brave attempts would come to nothing. The odds were severely against us, and it would only be a matter of time before the demon would refocus and come for us again. Through the throbbing pain of my shoulder, I looked around and then saw the dam in the distance.

"One shot…got to go for the Hail Mary…"

"Naz, darling, how are you at playing bait?" I asked, seeing the dark specter above us, twisting and turning in anger.

She looked at me like someone who just crawled off your sainted mother. "Uh, no?" She replied incredulously, already making up her mind that the white girl was definitely off her meds.

"We gotta use our numbers advantage here; it's our only chance. Trust me, okay? I got you."

"Trust me, okay? I got you," Naz mimicked me sarcastically before howling out in frustration. "Allah help me; I must be insane. What…what do you want from me?"

"Keep that son of a bitch busy, just buy me some time to finish rigging the crystal," I yelled, before turning and running back to the dam—while I kept one eye on the rapidly descending demon above.

"What are you planning...oh, you utter bitch." She waved her fist in anger, not believing she was going along with this utter madness.

"And make it seem believable; get him off my ass," I shouted, ignoring the middle finger aimed in my direction.

"She must be having emotional issues, it's the only explanation, but instead of seeing a shrink, white girl is out here fighting dragons or demons or what the fuck ever." Naz carried on her brilliant if bitter monologue. "But did we mention that in this group therapy session, it's my ass that's on the line? No, let's just leave that convenient fact out." She aimed a kick at a nearby dirt clod and watched with cold anger as it bounced away. "So Nazmirrah, darling, what did you do today on this lovely sunny afternoon? I turned down a few marriage proposals, watched some wrestling, and just chilled my ass out. And no fighting some over-caffeinated demon spawn from hell? No? Good for you."

A hundred yards away, the Manual's grip had finally loosened; it let go as the fire demon streaked low over the ground. The book landed with a heavy thud and was obscured by dust. Breathing heavily, it stared as the demon flew further away from it.

"So what the fuck am I supposed to do now? Flash it? Do fire demons even like boobs?" Naz stood there, wrinkling her mouth to the side. Then her face went blank and her feet slowly started strutting back and forth.

She had found her stage.

"WOOOOOOOOOOO!" Naz whooped and hollered, channeling "Nature Boy" Ric Flair, even dropping an elbow into the dirt. "Do you hear me you overrated piece of monkey spunk? I am calling you out—if you even got the peaches to face me." She kept prancing back and forth like an insane person. The fire demon turned its head in mid-flight and stared in a mixture of wonder and utter horror at the strange sight below him.

"Are you deaf? Get the cum out of your ears and face me, you Cartoon Network reject." Naz was playing with fire and she knew it. "Then again, I'd also hang out backstage like a baby-back bitch if you had to come near all this. I'd make you tap so fast to the Figure Four, you'd wish you were back home, sucking on your housekeeper's tits again. WOOOOOOOOOO!" That got the desired effect. The Fire Demon howled in anger and turned to swoop down on her.

Adrenaline still pumping through her, Naz spread her arms wide and gratefully soaked up the applause of an imaginary audience. Then she turned and started running. I couldn't believe it, but her insane plan had worked: the demon was distracted just long enough for me to get to the detonator. The control box had busted wide open in the fall, and wires were all over the place.

'Damn, damn, damn…' I gritted my teeth, struggling to get everything back into one piece while keeping an eye on the monster. The fire demon was thundering after Naz, scorching the earth in his wake. At first, I thought she was running around randomly; then I realized she was leading him straight into the waiting traps.

"Damn it, what are you doing, Naz?" I had to fight the urge to run to her. '*Work the problem; it's the only way out.*' My hands fumbled clumsily with the wires. I gritted my teeth, wiped the sweat from my brow and tried to fix the detonator. Naz, meanwhile, was running for her life, plumes of dust dancing around her feet. Her lungs burning, she tried hopelessly to put more yards between her and the onrushing behemoth. Not looking where she was running, though, she tripped over a stone and hit her head hard on the edge of a rock. Her head spun in agony as she clawed at the empty air around her. With blood running down her forehead, she forced herself to her feet. Just a little bit more to go, so close now. Hearing the fire raging and thrashing in the beast of the belly, Naz dug deep into the cold ground and stumbled forward, seeing the control lever in the distance.

'*Move, bitch, move.*' Running blindly, she blocked out the demon's enraged screams and clambered up the brick steps to the wall. With hands made brown by the dust, Naz grasped the lever and slowly stood up. The demon flapped its gigantic leathery wings and charged at her, not thinking of the consequence.

Naz sprang her trap.

Two poles flew up from the ground; electrical cables shimmered in the sunlight. The fire demon crashed face-first into the coils of humming electricity, a hideous yellow spark lighting up the surroundings. Shielding her eyes, Naz turned away, only hearing the monster screaming in abject pain and fighting wildly to free himself from the trap.

"Shocking, Mister Bond." Her words were scarcely spoken when the demon started pulling itself up again. The shock had only incapacitated it for the briefest of moments.

"Oh, come on!" Naz shouted in frustration. I was almost finished with the detonator, just needed to put the last few pieces together. Out of the corner of my eye, I saw Naz running towards me, followed closely by the rapidly recovering demon.

'*Work the problem, Michaela, work the problem!*' Finally, the last stubborn screw was tightened and I was ready to go. I started waving madly, jumping up and down, screaming my lungs out. "On the far side, Naz! Bring him around on the far side!" She wasn't going to make it; I'd have to go and help her.

'*Stand your ground, play your role. She can take care of herself.*' Gesturing like an insane woman, I kept shouting, willing her to listen to my plan. '*Come on, Naz, come on. Just listen, please.*' Then by some miracle, she changed course, narrowly escaping a stream of hellfire. '*Got to time this perfectly, come on...*' The dam wall was mere yards away from her. The behemoth corrected his course, lining up his target perfectly. A cloud of vapor was forming in its terrible mouth as I took a deep breath and pushed down on the detonator button. The crystals exploded in impossibly bright light, tearing the heart out of the dam. The great walls cracked and gave way instantly, sending a deluge of roaring water cascading below. The demon shrieked in horror, its arms flailing wildly as it was engulfed by millions of gallons of white water. Naz kept running, her arms outstretched as the water crashed wildly behind her. My hand was gripping hers tightly, pulling her away from the chaos erupting behind her.

"Do not let go...don't let go..." the tired and bruised little body kept repeating, clutching at me. I closed my eyes and refused to let go of my friend, the screams of the fire demon washing away in the torrent of raging water. We stood there for what felt like hours, sisters in arms alone in the chaos of the surroundings. The water finally relented, its energy spent. All that was left was the now still body of the demon, its fire extinguished; only a blackened husk remained. Wading through the mud and pools of standing water, we carefully approached the monster. I could hear its labored wheezing as it struggled for air, slowly suffocating.

"Naz...it's still alive," I said solemnly, reaching for a jagged piece of metal. One strike to the head and it would be all over. One less demon to worry about, simple as that. My hand was ready to deliver the *coup de grâce* when Naz stopped me.

"Stop." Her voice was bereft of her usual bravado.

"What are you doing, Naz? We gotta finish this thing before it gets up again." I exclaimed, trying to free myself from her grip.

"It's already gone, and this is not what we are here for." She slowly let go of my arm and turned her attention to the fallen Fire Demon. "We do not fight with anger or hate; didn't you tell me that over and over? We fight to defend what is precious to us, not to butcher a defenseless animal. Otherwise, we are as lost as they are." Naz bowed her head and walked over to the demon, placing her hand on its forehead. "O Allah, ease upon him his matters, and make light for him whatever comes hereafter, and honor him with your meeting and make that which he has gone to better than that which he came out from." I nodded, seeing a pearl of wisdom in my friend that belied her years.

We stood by the dying Fire Demon. The Manual arrived a short while later, its pages slightly burnt. It climbed into my arms and snuggled deeply into my chest. An hour later, the demon finally died. Strange as it may seem, I could see the calmness that had come over it as it realized that its passing was near. As it sighed its last breath, I closed its eyes and bade it a peaceful journey into the afterlife. It must have been a surreal sight: two battered and bruised women standing side by side near the fallen leviathan, all three finally at peace.

As the sun threw its last few rays down on the earth, we sat on the wall and stared out into the distant vista. Both of us were deep in thought, trying to make sense of it all. The only sounds were that of the distant rustling of trees far ahead of us and the gentle snoring of the Manual in my arms. Slowly Naz turned to me; we were both in a world of pain, every movement causing us to flinch slightly.

"So, school starts for you tomorrow," she said, a slight smile forming as she wiped a thin blood trail from her mouth. I laughed softly, my hand pressing down on my sore ribs.

"How are you going to explain that shiner and the rest of the injuries to your parents?" I asked, reaching for a nearby thermos of coffee.

"I'll leave that bit of entertainment for later, tell them I got into a fight at madrassa. They are used to it by now." She paused as I held the thermos out to her for a drink of the now ice-cold coffee. "Are you ready to go back?"

I sighed and ran my finger over a loose tooth. "Things will never be the same again, not after everything we've gone through. A normal life?" I laughed and coughed loudly. "Mathematics is going to be a breeze after all of this."

Naz nodded as the dying rays of sunlight danced on her tired face. "I have an idea, but you're going to need to trust me."

"What is it?" I asked suspiciously, raising an eyebrow in her direction.

"At this moment, you are Sting, pre-1996; the kids love you, but you ain't scaring shit, honey." The old, familiar spark was dancing in her one open eye.

"So what are you suggesting?" I asked, already knowing I was going to regret it.

Naz smiled wickedly between bloodied teeth, turning towards me. "We got to go to the dark side."

I sighed good-naturedly, knowing there was no denying this force of nature. The only way was to give in and go along with whatever insanity she had cooked up next in her mind. Nodding, we bumped fists and slowly got up and stumbled from the battlefield to home, sisters in arms.

Later that evening, back at the shop.

"Is your hijab on too tight? You must be insane." I exclaimed in horror as Naz revealed her nefarious plans.

"Michaela, darling, you must trust Naz. Naz got your booty covered. Now sit still and let me work." I groaned as she applied the hair coloring. I was being dragged into her deranged little world, and there was nothing I could do but hang on for dear life.

"We'll talk accessories afterward; now I got your wardrobe covered. You have a serious lack of ass-less chaps here, but I can work with that."

"Naz…"

"Leather, love, as black as my mother's cooking, yes. Just a bit…a lot of makeup, and we will be ready to go. You are going to be just lovely, my little Halloween decoration."

"I swear if I have to get out of this chair…"

"And hurt your beloved partner in crime? Ya right, darling." She stepped back, eyeing her work in progress. "This is going to work very nicely, indeed."

The next morning back at school

"I feel like a complete tit," I moaned as we approached the steps of the school.

"Embrace the badass side of the force, darling," Naz replied, taking off my jacket. Sighing deeply, I pushed open the door and heard the gasps of students inside. They stared in horror as the leather-clad hellion with pitch-black hair walked past them, eyes hidden by dark makeup. The once bright and bubbly midwestern American girl was a long-forgotten memory. I was a bitch on wheels, and somewhere deep inside me, I loved it. Naz walked beside me, challenging anyone to say anything to us. I saw Jake Mathis standing by the lockers, talking shit to his little inbred jock buddies. I paused, staring a hole through his back.

"I said, what the fuck do you want, nerd…" He swallowed his words mid-sentence, seeing the reborn hellion before his eyes. "Jesus…"

"No, more from the south. How's my little plaything been?" I grabbed him by the crotch, lifting him slightly. "Still short of a first down, I see, Jackie, such a pity." His eyes widened as he saw my backpack slowly unzip, and the Manual peek out from behind my shoulder, its burnt pages ruffling in anticipation. I pulled him close, eyeball to eyeball. "It's a new world order, bitch. Pray you don't catch my eye. Now, fuck off." The terrified Jock broke loose and fled down the hallway, screaming. I stood alone, smiling wickedly at the students staring at me in terror.

This was going to be fun.

CHAPTER 19

Somewhere in Middle America

I've had weirder days at school, but not many. It took me a while to grow into this good-girl-gone-bad creation of Naz's, but slowly I started to embrace it. I didn't want to say it out loud, but it was fun being on the devil's side for once. It was lunchtime; my 'makeup artist' and I sat side by side, just watching the residents of the jungle passing by. Taking the long way around us. It was fun seeing the terror in the asshats who had always made my life a misery, watching them whisper behind their hands as they scurried for cover. I looked at Naz and smiled through my bright red lipstick, slowly twirling a straw between my fingers. I was having fun in a demented way.

However, a strange thing happened as I moved silently and menacingly through the halls, staring down anyone who got near me. I started seeing the school's fringe members—the outcasts and freaks for whom every day was an almighty struggle just to survive. I caught one of the Dolls harassing a chess geek near the gym, pulling on her pigtails and laughing as her chess set clattered on the polished floor.

She never saw me coming.

I appeared like a wraith behind her, cleaning my polished black nails and grinding my teeth slowly. The Doll turned around, eyes growing wide as she saw the demon before her. Long story short, I dry humped her down the corridor till she fled in terror. While I wanted to put an unholy fear into the school populace, I didn't want to be a bully. It was never my style, nor would it be. Carefully, I helped the girl pick up the fallen pieces, not saying much, just giving her a wink as she collected her belongings. The girl nodded at me, clutching the chessboard to her chest.

"Thank you..." she whispered before quietly turning and walking down the empty corridors.

Then came the interesting classes. Picture it: Darkness herself right in the middle of the class and the rest of the students subtly pulling away on the tables along the walls. I had to stop myself from pulling out my textbooks as usual. No, that would not do, so I adopted a strategy of listening to every word the teacher said while pretending to be half asleep and then writing it down in private, later. All the teachers screamed at me as I put my feet on the desk and even once lit up a cigarette. All except Hammersmith and Perry. For some reason, they tolerated and even gave me some leeway. I couldn't figure it out; but I only pushed the boundaries just far enough to get under their skin. With the rest, I was full-on bitch-on-wheels, and it wasn't soon before I was in the principal's office again. I got a couple of demerits and a good shouting at, especially after I set fire to one of her plants. I then simply put on a dumbass smile and watched as the vitriol and screaming washed over me.

But it didn't matter; I played the role to perfection and embraced it with everything I had in me. I had to keep the others at a distance and could not afford to let them get close to me. The only thing that mattered was holding the line and getting ready for the incoming storm. The rest was just coffee-house and bullshit.

Later that afternoon, I was relaxing on the bleachers, watching the Jocks playing football: a rubber band and a set of needles provided endless pleasure. I sat grinning like the Cheshire Cat as deflated football after deflated football floated to the ground. Naz saw me and climbed up the steps, sitting down next to me.

"Dude..." that was all she could come up with. Her eye was still swollen shut. In fact, she looked like she had been through hell, but she still smiled contentedly.

"Had a good day?" I asked, throwing a can at one of the cheerleaders.

"Like you would not believe. No comment of Camel-fucker or Sand-jockey all day long. You, my dear, have put the fear of the devil himself into them. How's the new persona fitting you?" she asked, opening up a bag of chips and munching absentmindedly.

"It's different, but I like it so far. Takes some getting used to, though."

"All in good time, dear. We can't afford nosy people getting too close to us, especially not now," Naz replied, feeding the last of the chips to the Manual. It casually opened its mouth in my backpack and swallowed the packet whole.

"It's true," I said pensively, staring out over the lush green football field. "What did your parents say about..." I motioned at her blackeye and slightly swollen face.

"Grounded, of course. They plan on having a long and very serious conversation with my maulana," she replied matter-of-factly.

"Will that be a problem?" I didn't want to say anything to Naz, but I was worried about the so-called Paladin not showing up yet. I had no idea how long two women (and a book) could hold the line before being overwhelmed by the monsters. Not wanting to scare up any ghosts, I shelved the thought for later. We would cross that bridge when we came to it.

"Bitch, please. I got this covered so much it's scary. I have been sneaking out since I was ten and as for my maulana…" She winked and tapped her nose conspiratorially. It was better not to ask.

"Good to know. I've been thinking: we need to lay off the hardware store for just a bit. We've been hitting it too hard lately. They'll get suspicious before long."

"Then what do you suggest, *Herr Capitan*?" Naz asked, playing with the Manual's pages in my backpack.

"The janitor's office," I replied with a wicked glimmer in my eyes. "They have all sorts of goodies there ready to be donated to the cause."

"And Harry, the janitor will never notice it's gone. Too busy watching Eastern European midget porn on his phone. Terrible selection of websites, by the way."

"Wait, what?" I asked, raising an eyebrow in her direction.

"Nothing. Nothing at all. But what do you need there? We got enough stuff to keep us busy for a bit," Naz quickly changed the subject.

"We can always do with more steel struts and bolts, but I had my eye on two barrels of glue he keeps in his office."

"Glue? Dare I ask what for?"

"Patience, dear, patience," I replied, shining a hand mirror at the Dolls trying to form a cheerleader pyramid below us and watching it crash to the ground. "I have some less than delicate plans I want to use it for. We hit it tonight?"

"Crazy girl," Naz laughed softly, still sore from our encounter with the Fire Demon.

"But you love me," I said, fist-bumping her without looking.

"Do I have a choice?" We cackled like hyenas on the bleachers, not caring who saw us. It made me feel better, and all my worries were pushed to the side for a bit. With my friend by my side, I always felt we had a chance, even if it was only a small one.

6:30 p.m.

I went through my usual evening checklist back at the shop, making sure we had enough equipment for the build. I worked meticulously, checking each item off on the clipboard helpfully carried by the Manual.

'Got enough spikes and bolts for at least five more traps...will have to check the structural integrity on the wire traps; not sure if it can withstand a sustained onslaught...maybe replace the wooden struts with metal.' I tapped the pen on the clipboard and leaned over to look at the contents of the truck. *'Once we get the cans of glue tonight, we should be set for what I think is heading towards us...might have to test*

the idea out first.' Only then did I pause and look up at the clock. It was already after six, and Naz was late. Her evening prayers were done by now; it was unusual for her to be late. I glanced at the Manual, but the book just shrugged.

"Maybe her parents locked her in her room," I remarked to no one in particular, turning and checking my inventory further. I barely made it two steps before stopping and tapping my feet. Something was wrong; I could feel it in my bones. Nothing on earth could stop Naz from doing something, and if she'd been detained, she would have been on the phone ASAP.

'You are making a mountain out of a molehill here, Michaela, and it's most likely nothing.' I tried to convince myself but failed miserably at it. My father always said to trust your gut and go with what you believe, and I fully believed something was way rotten in the state of Denmark. I grabbed my coat and lifted the Manual into the basket of my bicycle. I just had to calm my worried nerves, nothing more. I pushed the bicycle out into the cold evening air. It was best to leave the truck in the garage. Naz's house was on the other side of town, and I didn't want to risk going past the police station. This was screwing up our schedule, but the safety of my friend came before all else.

The bicycle flew across the sleet-covered streets, crunching frozen leaves as I pedaled ever faster. The Manual kept lookout from the front basket, scanning the horizon for any possible dangers. Thank God the streets were deserted. The little light of the bike bounced up and down as I tore through the streets, barely paying attention to stop signs and running every red light. *'No time to waste. Move, Michaela, move.'* Cold fear was slowly growing in me, and try as I might, I couldn't convince myself I was irrational and stupid. Maybe I was paranoid and worrying for nothing but could not shake this horrible feeling inside me.

I made excellent time, soon arriving at Naz's house. Stowing the bike behind a tree, I headed to the front door and was about to knock when I paused, my hand suspended in midair.

'*Yes, this is a brilliant idea, you clod. Show up at someone's front door dressed as the missing member of KISS; that will end well. Use your brain, you stupid girl.*' Taking a step back, I quickly headed around to the back of the house. I'd visited Naz once or twice over the years. Her room was on the ground floor. I just had to work quietly. I wasn't in the mood to get shot by a Malaysian gun owner with a twitchy trigger finger.

'Naz...you there?" I tapped on the window, leaning and peeking inside. All was quiet, with only a bedside lamp shining. 'Naz...oh, I swear...' Gritting my teeth, I lifted the sliding window and slid into the eerily quiet room. '*I can see it now, Michaela Jones, savior of the earth arrested for breaking and entering. Me love you time.*' Catlike, I walked over to the bed and shook the prone figure lying under the sheets.

"Naz, goddammit..." I pulled the sheet off and stood in quiet shock.

A doll stared lifelessly at the Manual and me.

She had snuck out, but where could she be? '*Think, dammit, think.*' She can't be back at the workshop; it's a small town, and I'd have seen her along the way. The school, perhaps? Maybe, but doubtful; she would need help getting in and carrying the items out. The hardware store? No, she wouldn't risk it, not after I warned her off. Naz was fearless but not stupid. That leaves only one place...

A chill ran down my spine as I looked out into the cold winter's night.

The battlefield.

'What are you doing, Naz?' I thought in panic, grabbing the Manual and running to the open window. She was alone out there with God knows what, waiting in the dark. Heaven help me that I'm not too late.

'What the hell are you doing?'

CHAPTER 20

Somewhere in Middle America

I sat alone on the metal bleacher steps, watching Michaela walking away. It was late afternoon, and the winter sun was shining brightly, but there was still a chill in the air. The football team was running sprints up and down the field like mindless lemmings. There was nothing else to do, seeing that someone had put a needle through the football. It was never my sport; I preferred half-dressed monsters body slamming the hell out of each other. The sport of kings.

My mind wandered away from wrestling (and whether I had set the TIVO for the evening's festivities) and towards everything I had experienced these last few weeks. It was just pure insanity. Any normal person would have run for the hills a long, long time ago.

'Then again, when have you ever been normal?' I shrugged in acknowledgment, tightening my hijab slightly. The truth was, I would have followed Michaela to hell and back. She was the only one in this miserable dump of a school who had my back and stood up for me. Bitterly, I thought of all the abuse I and my family had received. How many hours thrown into a cramped locker or having to help my father clean rotten eggs off his car? I

could feel the hatred boiling up in me, hearing their racist chanting as they pulled my headscarf off, or sitting in a forgotten part of the school crying my eyes out. Allah frowned upon violence, but I could feel myself losing this fight every damn day.

And then a white girl showed up.

I had never felt this alive in my life, and I had a purpose now. I was helping my friend construct the defenses, preparing for the inevitable storm. I wasn't just some sidekick, I was her friend, and she treated me like an equal. I couldn't ask for more. However, there was this nagging feeling I simply could not shake as I crumpled an empty chips packet in my hands. We were getting ready for whatever devilry would soon be coming our way, but what if there was something else we could do?

The thought kept milling through my head as I headed out of the school, past the band geeks waiting for a lift home. I needed to time this perfectly, though, madrassa should be finishing any time now. My attendance, or lack of it, was never really a problem. I mean, the maulana even sent me a thank you gift for not showing up one year. Chase a man around with a stick once and you get branded as 'difficult.' Typical. An idea slowly started to form in my head as I walked past cookie-cutter middle-American houses, noticing the bare and leafless trees along the way. It was at times like these that I missed home. It was not always comfortable living in Malaysia, the heat, the terrorist groups, the heat, but it was home. This place was so gray and lifeless, well, till a certain madam decided to stare down the very face of evil and all his demons. Sighing and cleaning my nails while I waited at a streetlight, I thought of the battlefield and the dark forest that lay beyond it.

'*What if you can stop the horror before it even reaches the traps?*' Deep in thought, I wandered across the street, replaying the sentence over and over in my head. A jackass in a pickup truck honked at me, and I gave him the evil eye, visibly taking pleasure as he tensed up. That's right, bitch, piss off the Muslim, why don't you?

Try as I might, I couldn't shake the idea. I absentmindedly went through evening prayers and mostly ignored my parents at evening meal. It was the usual nonsense and questions of when I was going to get married, and had I decided on Harvard or Stanford for my doctoral career. Telling them I wanted to become a professional wrestler was always good for an evening's entertainment, but I wasn't in the mood. I had other things on my mind. I excused myself early from the dinner table and locked myself in my room. It was my sanctuary from my idiotic brothers and their nonstop discussion on all matters related to soccer. Putting on Hogan vs Warrior for the millionth time, I sat back on my bed, and with all thoughts of studying long gone, I stared out my window.

'*You can destroy the darkness; hit them before they even realize it.*' I had gone toe to toe with the monsters and lived to tell the tale. What if I could do it again? Turn their whole world upside down in one go and then look like a certified badass afterward? The more I thought about it, the more I liked it. Michaela might be a bit upset at me, but nothing I couldn't charm myself out of. I looked up at the Ultimate Warrior Gorilla Press slamming the mustached fool, and pulled a face, growling fiercely.

'*There is much to do, girly. Get your ass focused.*' I turned up the TV, ensuring my parents would not come within a mile of my room. '*Same procedure as usual.*' I grabbed a life-size doll from my closet and carefully tucked it under the bed covers. Okay, the insurance policy is taken care of. I've used it a million times before when I've snuck out for an evening of fun and games. Quickly dressing in a black shirt and pants, I pulled a leather jacket on and reached conspiratorially for a secret drawer at the back of my dresser.

Tapping a nightstick on the palm of my hand, I allowed myself a moment of quiet reflection on the times I'd used her to keep my belligerent brothers in line or to chase off a potential suitor. Good times. To quote Dr. Suess: '*Oh, the places you'll go.*'

Fully armed and dressed to kill, I sent up a quick Dua and headed for the window. Common sense should have taken over here, and I should have trusted Michaela and her plans, but the thought of her getting hurt was just too much for me to bear. No, I had to do this. I commandeered one of my brother's bikes and set off for the wall. The wind was bitterly cold, but I barely felt it; my heart was racing at a million miles per hour, and it took everything I had to calm myself down. Rhythmically, the bicycle's tire ground and twirled in the night. The empty streets were freezing and deserted; not even the police were out tonight. Too busy hunched up in the station, watching basketball.

'*Keep it together, girly, just keep it together.*' I raced past the houses and darkened factories. Soon the railway lines loomed before me. I stopped for just a second, rubbing my cold hands together—a freezing stream of vapor escaping into the night. I had never been alone on the other side of the wall before; I'd always had Michaela and the Manual to watch my back. It felt different. I tightened my jacket and pushed off with the bike again.

"*Dammit, Naz, get your mind straight,*' I admonished myself, pedaling ever faster. It wasn't long before I had passed through the wall, and the battlefield was before me. It was quiet, almost tense, as if it were waiting for something to happen. There had always been the banter and good-natured ribbing of my friends to put my mind at ease, but now? Nothing but darkness folding and undulating like black velvet cloth into the distance. I should have listened to my inner voice, turned around, and went home. This was a bad idea and I knew it, but maybe it was pride spurring me on, or perhaps I wanted to prove something to Michaela. Naz the brave sidekick, the great backup, the Marty Jannetty to her Shawn Michaels. It was my time to shine, and dammit, nothing was going to stop me!

Stowing the bike by the battlements, I took a deep breath and started walking, carefully picking my way through the field of traps. I would look like a real jackass if Michaela found me tomorrow morning strung upside down on one of the rope traps. For just a moment, I allowed myself to marvel at the incredible range we had constructed together—everything from basic steel bear traps (jacked up of course) to slingshots and electrical wire traps. There were spike pits on the far side and net traps for flying nasties to the rear. Our old faithful spring traps were standing ready, and then there were the tar pits, fire sprayers, mace tension traps, and blades primed and ready. It was amazing how we had managed to scrape everything together, robbing the hardware store blind under their eyes, working marvels in an incredibly short space of time. For just a moment, a piece from Hunter S. Thompson passed through my head (I did pay attention in English class now and again).

"*I never knew where I was going, but I ripped the tits off everything that got in my way. By the time they figured me out, it was too late."*

The people out there in the real world, their heads would explode if they saw the level of fuckery we were up to here. Flashing a brilliant smile, I ran my hands over a spring trap, feeling the crystal's presence. Quiet energy ran through the battlefield, enveloping the traps, powering their dark purpose. I knuckled down and headed for the forest. It suddenly seemed so much bigger than it had from the battlements. The jagged black trees loomed over me. I exhaled and peered into the darkness.

'You had better find your inner gangster and quickly, girly. Have you got iron ovaries, or are we just pissing about here?' My inner pep talk sounded better on paper. It didn't help much to stop the icy fear clamping my heart. I had to show Michaela that I was worthy and could hang with her. Sucking it up and quieting down the chorus of common sense raging in my head, I left the battlefield behind. My little pocket penlight was the only thing lighting up the gloom. I was ill-prepared, and I knew it. Leaves crackled under my feet as I slowly moved through the stygian forest. Wraith-like ghosts danced between the ancient tree trunks, long-forgotten voices jibbering and jabbering into the night. The pathetic little penlight was doing nothing to light my way. Spinning around, I looked wide-eyed into the unknown. The whole forest was alive, teeming with dark energy, crackling, fizzling with unholy terror. I wanted to turn around, flee to safety, but it was too late. Interlocking tree limbs blocked any escape. My penlight crackled and died in my hands as I heard footsteps and the clattering of bones around me. Fiery orange torches cast jagged shadows around me.

Skeletons.

I had run headfirst into an entire legion of the faceless monsters. Stupid, stupid girl. They were closing in on me, brandishing dark bone swords, sharp enough to slice the very soul from you. I had no choice but to stand my ground, clenching my fists in anger. But I was scared, horribly scared. They took their time closing in on their prey, knowing there was no place for me to run. Sightless eyes were staring into pure nothingness; I could feel the blood lust bubbling up inside their soulless bodies. I tried making a break for it, but a skeleton grabbed me by the head and flung me to the ground. A thin stream of blood trickled down my lip as I got painfully to my feet.

Surrounded and outnumbered, I looked around at the circle of death around me. "Well? I haven't got all fucking night!" The last thing I remember was the pack crashing into me. The world swirled around me and went pitch black.

I slowly came to, blinking my eyes and looking around. My head was splitting like someone had taken a guitar to it. No idea where I was…inside a room somewhere. Could hear screaming in the distance, hideous cackling floating down the stone corridors. I couldn't move. My arms were secured to a wall with iron shackles. I frantically tried to free myself, thrashing wildly but to no avail. The wooden door creaked open, and my eyes went wide in terror. A shadow was standing before me, its eyes burning deep red, an iron gauntlet on its hand.

'Oh, fuck.'

CHAPTER 21

Somewhere in Middle America

I climbed through the window, the blaring sounds of the TV still ringing in my ears. Cold fear about what had happened to my friend was growing inside me. I quickly placed the Manual in the basket of my bicycle and took off. How could Naz have done such a stupid thing? I knew she was impulsive and hot-headed, but this was just universally stupid. It was dangerous enough to be out on the battlefield in the daytime, but at night? That was suicide.

'Take it easy and think this thing through, Michaela. Maybe she's somewhere else that you didn't think of.' I knew it was bullshit. In a town of only a few hundred people, there weren't many places to go. Pedaling like the devil himself was behind me, I thrashed the bike around the corners, showing scant regard for my safety. I could rest when that nutcase was back safely by my side.

The Manual sat in the bike's metal wicker basket, leaning forward, scanning the streets all the while. In a short space of time, Naz and the book had struck up a famous friendship; they would often sit together in the workshop at night while I worked on new traps. She even managed to show him a few wrestling moves—not that the Manual needed any help in that department. Sometimes she would fall asleep with the book by her side. The Manual would be crushed without his partner in crime. "We're bringing her back buddy, we're bringing her back." The wind raced through my hair as the little book looked back and nodded determinedly. Heaven help the poor bastards if they so much as touched one hair on her head. Whatever was left after the Manual got done with them would have to deal with me.

My lungs were burning violently when we reached the train tracks a short while later. Steadying the bike on one leg, I quickly caught my breath and looked around. Just as I expected, a trail led off into the darkness. Nobody ever came out here, and we always made sure to wipe away our traces. It had to be her. Pushing off with grim determination, we headed into the darkness, leaving the town's fading yellow lights behind. We had made the trip to the wall and back so often, but this felt different and just wrong. My little buddy had kept me going, talking my head off about anything and everything. Now it was so quiet out here by the wall. The only sounds were the crunching of the bike's tires on the dirt road and the restless fluttering of the Manual's pages in the wind.

"Dammit," I whispered to myself, pulling up next to the battlements. Naz's bike was parked against the crumbling brick wall, but there was no sign of her. "Naz! Where are you?" I shouted as the Manual looked forlornly at the bike. We were ahead of schedule, and there was no reason to come out here, especially alone. And we always worked together on the traps; it made the heavy lifting that much easier. No reason for her to be out here unless...

I looked down at the book, closing my eyes in disbelief.

'*No...no.*' I glanced up at the forest in the distance as the cruel and cold reality set in. My best friend had walked straight into the jaws of the night itself. What madness had possessed her? It was suicide going in there. I knew I had no choice but to go in after her; I would never forgive myself if something happened to Naz. Shaking my head in frustration and tying my hair in a ponytail, I motioned for the book to follow me. It didn't hesitate for a second, puffing its pages out and following me into the dark. It didn't take us long to find her tracks in the mud, and as I suspected, they led straight to the forest. She'd dawdled around a bit near some of the traps, where I caught her scent in the air. She insisted on overdosing on John Cena cologne. She couldn't be too far ahead of us. "An hour at most; come on." An earlier brisk rainstorm had turned the battlefield into a mud bath, but we plowed ahead. It was hard going, but the thought of my friend lying out there in the cold, even possibly...

'*No! Don't think like that,*' I admonished myself angrily. I picked up the Manual and carried him over this last part of the field. We paused before the daunting looking forest, peering into the infinite darkness. There was a silence about the place that seemed to suck the life out of everything around it, as if Death itself had passed his skeletal hand over the land. All we could hear was my shallow breath and the cracking of twigs.

"Let's go." I mustered all the bravery I could summon in my tiny body and marched on. Heaven knew what would have happened if we ran into a monster out here, but I was so pumped up on adrenaline that I could have run nose-first through a brick wall.

It was difficult trying to get through the forest, and soon Naz's tracks started to fade. It was impossibly dark, as if light itself had died in this horrific place.

"Hold on; I want to try something." I fished in my pocket for a lighter. I didn't smoke, but it was part of Naz's insane makeover plan. Then I reached out for a tree branch. A shudder swept through the forest as I broke it off, almost as if this place could feel pain. Blocking out the mournful howling, I tore a piece of material from my jacket and wrapped it around the branch. With a quick flick of the lighter, our faces were soon bathed in a dim orange hue. I was fully aware that we were standing out like a pair of porkchop panties at a vegan festival, but I decided the risk was worth it. I had to see where we were going.

"Keep going," I whispered in a hushed tone to The Manual. The book simply nodded; I could see it was furious. Deeper into the pitch-black forest we went, weaving our way into the dark tendrils. Naz's footsteps had long faded between the scattered leaves, but I took an educated guess and kept going in her general direction, praying she hadn't changed course along the way. The forest was humming with the sounds of insects; blue fireflies buzzed erratically around. The tension was growing with each passing moment, and I expected to get jumped by some jacked-up nightmare waiting in the dark. The torch sputtered. I could see it was dying, but our luck held out: I saw a beaten footpath opening up before us. Had to be extra careful now, there were bound to be monsters along the way.

"Wait," I hissed at the Manual, holding the book back. The engineer in me took over, the one who planned and waited for the right opportunity. The book was restless by my feet, but I calmed him down with a gentle hand on his cover. My patience was soon rewarded as we heard dull footsteps coming down the path. I quickly doused the flame in the ground and waited. Three skeletons were marching down the track, bones clattering as the soulless demons strode past us. I saw something in one's hand in the half-light, but it went by too fast for me to properly make out what it was. I had to take a calculated risk here. I leaned down to the Manual and gave him a gentle push forward. It was all the encouragement he needed. Bounding out from the undergrowth, the rabid book seized upon the startled skeletons and took them to town—a cacophony of bones flying in all directions. Screams were silenced in an instant as the gnashing of teeth mixed ever so delicately with the woodland sounds. I turned my head away from the carnage; the Manual finished the job in record time.

"Feeling better now?" I asked as all became quiet again. The Manual was sitting on a pile of bones, picking its teeth with its last hapless victim. Picking my way through the bones, I quickly found a piece of black material. It had Naz's scent on it. As I studied the pile of bones, I saw a nightstick lying underneath it. I pulled it out, realized what her insane plan was; she'd just gone charging in, trying to cause chaos.

'*Damn it, Naz.*' She had run straight into their waiting arms, but they hadn't killed her. No, I would have seen a blood trail somewhere, surely. She must still be alive. It was the faintest of hope, but it was all I could cling to. If I gave up on her now…no, keep your head up, Michaela. "Let's go." I'd barely made it a step further when I felt something approaching. A wave of energy burst through the forest, sending spiders and woodland denizens fleeing in panic. Crows flew into the air, flapping their wings in terror. The wave washed over me like a tsunami, forcing me to my knees in pain. Gasping for air, I clawed at sheer nothingness. I could feel screams ripping through my soul, tearing sinews asunder and cutting flesh to the raw bone. A red mist descended, boiling and scraping open nerves to the very core. Somewhere in the maelstrom of agony, I could feel the Manual, hammering but failing to get in. I was alone in an ocean of torment, and I was drowning by the second. My fingernails were digging deep into cold mud, and my jaw was ajar in a silent scream; I looked up with scarlet tears running from my blinded eyes.

Naz.

I saw her vaporous essence before me, screaming out in distress and radiating pain. A shadow was torturing her, tearing her mind to shreds. My friend was brave, braver than I could ever be, but I felt her resistance fading as the demon dug his claws deeper into her subconscious, probing for something just out of my reach.

'*Just hold on.*' I tried to connect with her across the void, but her essence was faint and fading fast. The shadow pounded relentlessly on her walls, tearing and thrashing away with all his dark power, breaking her resistance with jagged claws. And then, just for an instant, I saw something in his mind.

A heart.

Massive and corrupt, it beat rhythmically, deep below the earth, pumping stygian blood. I felt the sheer wickedness that permeated the abomination. With every hit Naz took, it thudded quicker and quicker, taking perverse delight in her pain. The heart was willing her to give up and allow the shadow over her defenses. But there was something else standing in the gloom, watching from a distance. It was curious about the little girl holding on for dear life, scratching and clawing with every bit of faith she possessed. Why would the demon take such an interest in a normal girl? I searched for answers as the hooded figure turned around and pulled his hood off.

Death.

Fires raged in the cold, empty eye sockets of the skeleton as he commanded the shadow to continue lashing Naz, driving the poor girl to untold levels of agony. Why would he do this? Why? I sensed Naz starting to slip. She was close, terribly close to losing this fight and letting the demon inside. Death's sadistic laughter rang in my ears as I clawed at the dew-laden ground, willing myself forward. The crimson mist faded, the forest opened up to reveal a fortress bathed in lunar glow; jagged spikes from the unholy presence reached mockingly to the heavens.

'Get up, Michaela. For once in your goddamned life, you are not doing something just for yourself. Get up now.' The lioness inside me spoke up, demanding that I raise my spent body again. I refocused and looked up at the spires of the distant fortress. Naz was in there, and I was going to bring her back, come heaven or hell itself. The Manual nudged my leg, propping me up with great effort. I looked down at the brave little book and whispered a thank you. I knew my ordeal wasn't finished, but somehow having him by my side helped more than I could say. Painfully, I started walking again, each step a labor unto itself, but I had to keep going. Couldn't stop…don't stop. Keep going.

Three solitary figures stood in the distance and looked at my plight.

"We should do something. She cannot do it alone." The shape of Miss Hammersmith slowly morphed into the form of the Horseman Famine. Her rotund belly protruded as she licked her greasy lips and wiped a tear from her eyes. She had seen untold eons of suffering, of hungry masses slowly dying in the streets of Paris and the refugee camps of Somalia. She knew what it was like to see a person erode to nothingness and watch on passively as her brother took them away. She wished she could break the rules, just this once, and help the brave girl before her eyes.

"We can't. Michaela has to do this by herself. We cannot break the thread," Mister Perry answered, laying a hand covered with plague sores on Famine's shoulder. The crippled old figure leaned tiredly on his cane as insects crawled through his ashen gray beard. He didn't believe his own words and wanted nothing more than to run towards the girl and clear the way for her. But Pestilence knew the plan had to play out as it was prophesied.

"I'm sorry, Pumpkin, I'm so sorry," War whispered, a red tear running down his cheek as the other two Horsemen bowed their heads in sorrow. They dared not intervene; there was simply too much at stake. The very fate of the planet depended on their standing back now and watching the events unfold.

Only she could save the world now, nobody else. Billions of people on earth, and it all came down to one girl and her friend somewhere in Middle America. The three Horsemen knew how utterly insane it was as they faded back into the mist, leaving the tiny little figure and her trusty book in the dark forest.

The question was, could she save herself?

'*Just hold on, Naz, just hold on.*'

CHAPTER 22

Somewhere on the other side the wall

Steeling myself, I started walking again, heading in the direction of the fortress. I could still hear Naz's hollow screams echoing through me, but I had to block them out and focus on the next step. *'Work the problem, overcome it, and move on.'* My inner engineer took over my rational side, even as I was frantic to save my friend. *'It's not going to help to charge in like a fool. Think about what you're doing here.'* The sounds of grunting and the sharpening of steel drifted towards us on the night wind. We were closing in, and the threat of danger grew with each passing step. My only hope was that the guards would be overconfident and not paying attention as they should. I mean, who would be stupid enough to break into the fortress?

'Don't answer that.' I decided to move off the path a bit. I didn't want to run into any patrols along the way. Moving like a shadow from tree to tree, I constantly checked that the Manual was still behind me. I had little to fear there; nothing on earth was going to move the book from my side. Our caution was soon rewarded when I spotted a group of torches coming down the road.

I grabbed the Manual and dived for cover. Hunkering down at the base of an ancient and gnarly oak tree, we waited in growing apprehension. Screeching voices chattered through the night. Leaning ever so slightly from behind the tree, I spied five wiry creatures heading towards us. Their skin was a rotten, blackened green; their sinewy bodies ached with unreleased tension as they lightly feathered arrows in their crooked bows. I'd read about them in the Manual. The dark elves were the elite snipers of Death's army; they were capable of shooting the eye out of a sparrow at a hundred yards. It would be suicide to try to charge them. I just had to sit still and wait for them to pass by. The Manual squirmed ever so slightly in my arms, eager to have another go at monsters. I tightened my grip and shook my head ever so slightly, praying he would understand.

'*Come on…*' I urged the creatures silently on. I didn't have time to waste. The dark elves were almost past me when a woodland lizard scurried down the tree trunk. In a flash, three arrows streaked through the air, impaling the lizard. The creatures cackled and brayed as one of them walked closer to retrieve their arrows.

Right where I was hiding.

The scaly, crooked-back demon scampered over the dew-laden ground. With an audible plop, it pulled the arrows from the lizard and then swallowed it whole, licking his lips with a long, thin tongue. The dark elf turned to head back and then stopped, sniffing the air. It had caught the faintest scent of overpriced cologne in the wind. I looked down in horror and realized I still had the strip of cloth from Naz. The elf cocked its head and reached for another arrow, pausing as it looked around with beady eyes. Grinding broken and yellow teeth, it peered into the darkness, unsure what this strange new smell was. Pulling the Manual tighter to my chest, I closed my eyes and held on for dear life. If he spotted us, we would be dead in an instant, shot before we could make it twenty yards. Crooked fingers inched their way around the tree trunk, so close the monster could have reached out and touched us. It stank of stale pig blood, and I fought to keep from gagging.

The dark elf wheezed. A drop of black spit ran down his chin and dropped wetly to the ground before my feet. He was almost on top of us when the others called angrily out to him. Grunting in frustration, the creature scampered back to the other monsters. I didn't dare exhale till they were down the road and around the bend. That was too damn close for comfort. Sighing deeply, I looked down at the book as it wiped the sweat from its cover. *"Regular patrols; they must be getting ready to move. Let's get going, but keep your eyes open,"* I said, clambering from behind the tree. Sticking to the undergrowth close to the road, we made our way carefully forward, continually checking for any other nasty surprises. We heard the mournful howling of a wolf and saw a bright orange fireball streaking into the night. More horrors were waiting for us out in the night, that was for damn sure.

It took us a good hour to make the last few hundred yards, but finally, the fortress loomed before us as we peeked out from the undergrowth. Grotesque and imposingly dark, my eyes narrowed as I studied the stone castle intently. It was built like a brick shithouse, with solid stone walls; there was no way to scale them. Even if we could, patrols of guards moving back and forth on the battlements would have been on us before we could breathe. Besides, I had no weapons with me, only a little pocket tool. Not much use there.

"Maybe try to sneak in with the supply carts?" I said distantly to myself, seeing a line of carts being pushed up the path towards the massive iron gates by a group of orcs, their aching muscles lit up by orange torchlight. The Manual nudged my leg and motioned to something. The guards at the gate were carefully checking every cart. No, that way was out.

'Okay, we cannot go through or over the walls, but perhaps underneath them? See if there is a service hatch or drainpipe somewhere. It's a messy option, but we don't have much choice in the matter.' The fortress was built on an old rocky outcropping. They needed some way of getting water in. I would have bet there was a whole mess of caverns down there, and with a bit of luck we could work ourselves up into the main building. I tapped my foot a few times, running things through my head. "But if security is as good as I think it is, they will have secured that." A little gem of an idea came to me as I watched a witch circling lazily above us.

"How are your dancing skills?" I asked the Manual. It gave me an incredulous look, not liking already where this was going. "Get me a witch down here; I'll be right back." I scampered off into the woods, leaving the book behind. The Manual shook its covers in disbelief; it had been roped into another lunatic plan, and there was no option but to go with it. It stepped out of the undergrowth and looked up at the misty skies, sighing deeply. Slowly it started doing a little jig, shaking its spine back and forth. But the lone witch simply carried on her way. Exasperated, the book looked down at the ground and started doing a Michael

Jackson moonwalk, strutting his stuff like a badass.

'*Just need to find what I'm looking for...*' Moving quickly in the moonlit forest, I spotted the perfect branch. It would make an ideal slingshot. The blade in my pocket was working brilliantly. '*Don't have a rubber band...there, those vines will do nicely.*' There must have been a bit of hillbilly somewhere in my family line with a penchant for destruction, I thought to myself. Five minutes later, I had an admittedly crude slingshot. I grabbed a rock on the run back. My timing was perfect. The witch had spotted the Manual below and swooped down on him, screeching through the night.

'*One shot...make it count.*' Steadying myself, I let fly with the slingshot. The rock, arching perfectly, hit the stunned witch mid-flight with a dull thud to the skull. She never had time to react, falling like a sack of potatoes to the ground. "I always wanted to try that," I said, dragging the unconscious body into the woods. The Manual kicked the witch in passing. When we were safely out of sight, and we had made sure nobody had seen us, I quickly flipped the witch over and took off her backpack.

"I knew I smelled something earlier," I explained to the book, as I riffled through the witch's backpack. "Ah-ha, I knew it! Sulfur. And if I'm lucky...yes, more chemicals and potions." The Manual raised a page in derision at me, unsure where this was going. "Whatever is in here, I bet it will be good enough to get us through any gate or barricade." I ruffled his covers, smiling. "You did good, buddy, but the hard part is still waiting for us. We've got to get over the moat, and I'll understand if you want to stay behind." I knew the little book was fearless, but I also knew that water and fire could damage him beyond repair. He looked at me pensively and then glanced up to the fortress and the orange lights glowing in its towers. Though he had been a companion to countless engineers over the ages, he had never found friends like Naz and me. Summoning all the courage he could muster, he nodded quietly in my direction.

"Thank you," I whispered, hugging him tightly. "Now, help me tie up the witch, and we can get going." With the hag safely gagged and tucked away under a bush, we made up for lost time and started searching for a way into the fortress. It was hard going, moving through the underbrush and continually checking for patrols along the way. I did see a small fishing boat moored on a makeshift dock, but I decided against it. Someone might see it was missing and become suspicious. No, I couldn't leave a trail behind.

'A castle that size must have an aqueduct somewhere.' I tapped my fingers on the trunk of a tree, deep in thought. The Manual sighed unhappily, chilled to the bone from the cold. "Shh...do you hear that? There it is again." I listened intently for the slightest sounds drifting across the mist-covered waters. It was different from the clatter coming from inside the fortress, more rhythmic...constant. It sounded like a wooden wheel. That had to be it. "They must have hidden the entrance behind some rocks; we will have to go see," I said, lifting the Manual to my shoulders. "Hold on tight and don't let go, whatever you do." I pulled off my leather jacket, wrapped the witch's bag safely inside it, and tied it to my shoulders. Easing down to the water's edge, I looked around carefully for anything that could give the game away. The water was cold as hell, and I knew I was taking a big risk here—I would be a sitting duck for any archer on the wall—but I had to go for it.

We slowly waded our way across the watery expanse. Rivulets of water ran down my face and my long black hair trailed behind me. The Manual clung to my shoulders with everything he had, terrified of falling in. We were lucky in one way: the mist obscured us from the soldiers on the battlements above. My muscles aching from the unusual exercise, I drudged forward, seeing the far bank coming ever closer. With my skin turning blue from the cold, I crawled out on the other side, water streaming down my body. I was soaked to the bone and struggling to catch my breath. The thought that I had made a mistake was too terrible to contemplate.

"I'm okay… I'm okay," I wheezed. The Manual rubbed my shoulders as I sat shivering from the cold. I knew I had to carry on, but the swim had taken more out of me than I'd expected; I needed a moment to recover. A few minutes later, I picked myself up again and nodded at the book. "Come on, Naz is waiting for us inside." It didn't take long for me to see how they'd tried to hide the aqueduct from the outside—with large rocks and trees planted before it. Crude but effective.

"Keep your eyes open," I said. "We don't know what's inside." We clambered over the rocks and headed into the dark expanse of the cave. The squeaking of the wooden wheel was now as clear as could be. I hated going into the dark like that, but we had no choice. I could hear the gushing of water nearby. Soon we found ourselves trampling over a flowing stream. I just had to hope there was an access tunnel to the surface. The Manual pulled on my soaked pant leg and nodded to something in the distance. We had hit our first obstacle: a massive iron gate was blocking our progress. The book snapped its jaws confidently and was about to start in on the metal annoyance when I caught it mid-stride and pulled it back.

"Wait…I want to see something first." I ran my hand down the heavy steel bars, probing with my fingers in the dark. "Tripwire. I bet you it's rigged to the guardhouse above. If we break the gate, they will be on us very quickly." I stepped back and reached for the pack on my back. "You got any information on chemical engineering in there?" I asked the Manual. It paused for a second, then eagerly flipped its pages open. It took a bit of mixing and matching, but using ingredients and equipment from the witch's backpack, and continually checking the ratios in the book, I soon had a vial of bubbling, neon-green liquid in hand.

"Might want to step back on this one, chief," I said to the Manual. It dived behind a rock and gave me the thumbs-up signal. With great trepidation, I poured the liquid over the iron bars and hurried to join him. The wicked brew spluttered and splattered, smoking as it came into contact with the iron bars. The smell was enough to make a person from New Jersey back away in horror. I held my nose and tried not to barf a cat. The concoction worked better than I could have hoped, chewing the metal bars away but leaving the tripwire intact.

"See? Easy as that," I said, winking at the book, which simply rolled its eyes and sauntered after me. We made it through the first obstacle without hassle and without alerting the guards, but something was niggling at the back of my mind. '*Where are the other booby traps and other security measures?*' It didn't make sense to fortify everything in the castle and leave this gap open for any intruder to waltz in. Were they that careless? I kept my reservations to myself, not wanting to worry the Manual any more than necessary. We kept following the stream till we reached a massive subterranean cave with a large wooden water wheel.

"Up there, look! There's our exit to the castle. Just got to find some stairs, and we are smiling." For just a second, I became overconfident and relaxed my guard. As I took another step and looked down at the Manual, we both felt something stirring behind us. Something gigantic had been awoken in the dark. Rocks started tumbling and the ground began to shake. This was their safety measure, the backup plan I had been dreading.

A yellow, bloodshot eye the size of a house opened and stared down at us.

Cave troll.

CHAPTER 23

Somewhere on the other side the wall

"Move!" I shouted, as the huge creature stirred and the cavern rumbled around us. I should have seen something like this coming, should have known a simple rusted gate wouldn't be the only thing waiting for us down here. *'There's no time to feel sorry for yourself, woman. Move your ass.'* I grabbed the stunned Manual on the run, scooping him up in my arms and heading back the way we'd come in. I would have to find another way into the castle. Our escape attempt was cut brutally short as the cave troll thundered his fist into the ground, sending a shock wave crashing through the cave. An avalanche began raining down before us, instantly blocking our exit. Waving away the dust, I turned around, my eyes widening at the sight of the behemoth behind us. It was pissed, really pissed, that someone had dared wake it from its slumber. Colossal brown hands were clenching and unclenching in anger. Deciding it had had enough of us, the beast charged. Seconds felt like hours, but I forced my frozen feet to move and skirted around the edges of the cave, moving as fast as possible. Our only saving grace was that the gigantic monster could only turn very slowly.

'Well, that helped,' I thought sarcastically as the beast crashed into the cave wall, sending debris flying through the air. *'Christ, he's going to bring the whole fucking place down on our heads.'* The troll roared in anger, holding his head in agony and stumbling around. *'Come on, you bitch, think! Got to be a way to get out of this mess.'* Pulling my sweat-caked hair out of my eyes, I desperately tried to think of a plan. There was no way we could take on the troll face to face; he'd squeeze us like a zit. Shit….shit…shit…I saw the monster getting his bearings back and lining us up for another charge. There had to be a weak point on the monster, some Achilles heel that I could use to kill it.

'Dammit, Michaela, stop thinking like a warrior. You're an engineer, so plan like one.' I bounded past the giant waterwheel. Water rained down on us. The troll was already on the run, picking up speed at a frightening pace. It hit the ground again, its muscles flexing as his fist came down. Ducking and rolling, I managed to avoid the fist by inches. The shockwave hurtled us forward between its tree-trunk legs. The troll howled in frustration as I weaved around him like a running back heading for the end zone. The Manual looked up at me from my arms, knowing that we couldn't keep up this foolish game for much longer.

'Think like an engineer.' Trying to slow my thoughts down realized that the troll was chained to the cave wall. It was the way they could keep him here. *'Use his power against him.'*

"We're going to go Empire on his ass. You up for a bit running, little buddy?" the Manual stared at me aghast and nodded quickly, understanding my plan. Bouncing from arms, the little book stretched out, getting ready. He looked at me as the troll turned, its eyes blood red in anger. I timed the steps of the incoming troll, measuring his stride carefully. "Okay, on my count, move and watch where you're running." The troll picked up speed, assured that its victims would soon be nothing but a bloody spot on the ground. "Wait for it...Wait for it." The troll was getting closer, spit running down his chin and its hands clawing at the ground.

"Almost...wait for it...don't flap your pages at me, sweetheart...now!" We scattered, sending the flabbergasted Troll grabbing at empty air, the long chain trailing in his wake.

"Keep him moving and watch out for that chain!" I shouted on the run, keeping the monster to my left. The troll thrashed around, unsure of whom to go for. He had size and power on his side, but we had the speed advantage, and we made use of every bit of it. Too late, the monster realized what was going on. We twisted him from side to side, weaving the chain around his oaken legs.

"He's almost there, just a bit more." The Manual ducked under a swinging claw, sweeping around the back of the monster. I waved my arms like an insane person, distracting him even more. "Go around long; we're going to drop his ass." I was calling the shots like a badass, each decision thought out and timed perfectly. Approaching the problem analytically, I could see the beast's movements in my head even before he made them. As I came around him one last time, I suddenly veered off course and ran straight. The confused beast had little time to react as I harged underneath his legs. He grabbed at me, but the goliath's omentum threw him head over heels. Running at full speed, I scooped the stunned Manual up in my arms again and held it safe. The troll pirouetted through the air, almost as if in slow motion, a jumble of arms, legs, and tightly wrapped chains. I didn't dare look any further. I put my head down and ran like the devil was after me. Gravity eventually got the better of the troll, and he came down with thundering velocity, slamming chin-first into the unforgiving ground. Pulling the Manual close to my chest, I closed my eyes. Dirt and pebbles came cascading down upon us. It continued for a good ten seconds, until the monster finally came to rest, its chained body falling deadly still. Wiping the dust from my eyes and the book, I gathered myself and exhaled slowly. It still felt like the entire cave was vibrating with energy—or perhaps it was only us.

'*You're going to have to move quickly now; those chains won't keep him down forever.*' I don't know what made me do it, but I cautiously approached the fallen troll, looking for any signs of movement. I should have been looking for an escape route, but something told me to go to it. It seemed peaceful somehow, as if this was the first rest it had gotten in ages. I looked down at its calloused hands and then up to the slowly moving waterwheel behind it. Feeling a tug on my pants leg, I looked down at the Manual. It was holding a jagged piece of metal out to me. Grasping my hand around the rusted shiv, I fell silent, feeling its weight in my hands.

'*It would be so simple—one shot through the skull, and it would be all over.*' The helpless troll slowly opened its eyes. Then I saw something; it wasn't hatred, but fear that was hovering there. He was a prisoner, caught up in this horrible mess just like us. I looked down at the book and smiled softly.

"Mercy."

The Manual wanted to protest for a moment, but it nodded, understanding. I knew it was a terrible risk to take, but something inside me told me to free the trapped creature. Trying not to think about what could happen in the next few minutes, I scanned the surroundings and saw the grim, black padlock locking the chain in place. It was the size of a family car; no wonder the troll could never escape.

"How are your lock picking skills?" The Manual flipped through its pages and then gave me a thumbs up. Pulling up his imaginary sleeves, the book climbed down into the padlock, signalling me to pass him the metal shard. Five minutes, and many unpronounceable and archaic swear words later, the lock clicked open. I pulled a very greasy Manual out of the lock and tried to clean him up a bit. Now would come the moment of truth. *'Here lies Michaela Jones and random book—turned into cat kibble by an irate cave troll.'* It was a charming thought.

We stepped back from the monster, waiting for the inevitable fist to come down and splatter us. The troll moaned in pain, moving his sore shoulders around tiredly and trying to figure out exactly what was going on. Its first thought was to massacre the pests that sent him crashing to the ground, but then, slowly, he realized that his chain was loose. The gigantic fist stopped in mid-air, yards from our heads. Then the troll picked up the now slack chain and stared at it like a little kid. Trying to think of a time when it was not a prisoner down in the dark, the troll raised his fist and bowed his head. Tears started rolling down his rough-hewn brown cheeks, soaking me to the bone, but I didn't mind. The Manual tucked himself under my arm and looked up at the wailing creature before us, suddenly so vulnerable. The troll held out his palm, inviting us to climb up.

"Come on," I said to the book, gingerly climbing up the troll's thumb and sitting down on his outstretched palm. The book was hesitant, but it nevertheless trusted my judgment. The troll lifted us to his face, many stories into the sky, and looked at us intently, still trying to make sense of the strange black-haired girl and her faithful companion. I could see the leftover tears shimmering on his face. He thought about matters intently, as much as any troll could, and then smiled broadly.

"I am free?" he rumbled in a voice like distant thunder over the Kansas plains.

I nodded, returning the smile. "You are free."

The troll bowed his head humbly and exhaled happily, blowing my hair and the book's pages as if by a gust of wind. It was as if an immeasurable weight had been lifted from the creature's shoulders, and I could see the wave of relief washing over it. No more a prisoner having to work the wooden waterwheel for the castle, it was finally free to go live its life in peace again.

"Thank you," the creature stated simply, but with such meaning behind it. He then noticed me looking up at the gap leading to the castle at the top of the cavern. Instantly, he knew what we were doing down here in the dark and slowly started moving forward.

"Hold on!" I said to the book, letting out a yell of excitement as the troll carried us safely in his house-sized hands. The Manual was less than thrilled about being that far off the ground and had to swat away a swarm of bats fluttering past. Carefully, the creature lifted us to the narrow gap and waited as we climbed up his fingers to the waiting night air. I looked down for the last time. I could see he was at peace; I whispered a thank you to him. The troll smiled brilliantly and disappeared back into the darkness, but we could hear him ripping the cave apart to get free. Quickly, I scampered over the well wall with the Manual on my back and ran for a dark corner where the soldiers couldn't see us, and I could catch my breath again.

I didn't need to say it as I looked down at the book by my feet: we were in the heart of the castle, and there was no going back now. Come hell or high water, I was going to find my friend in this madness and bring her home.

Hold on, Naz, just hold on.

CHAPTER 24

Somewhere on the other side of the wall

I took a moment to calm myself down after the events with the cave troll. I had to think clearly, work out exactly where they were keeping my friend. I hated stumbling blindly into a situation, but every moment counted. I could feel that Naz was close, her pain radiating through the walls like a heartbeat.

'The tower perhaps? Find a staircase and work my way upwards from there. No, this ain't a fairytale. Come on, think, Michaela.' The Manual tugged on my leg and nodded downwards. Biting my lip, I thought about it and nodded. It would make sense for them to lock her up in the dungeon. The question was, how to get access?

"The main building—it's our best option, but we'll be running straight into danger there. You up for this little buddy?" I asked the book. The Manual put on his bravest face and gripped my hand tightly. Taking a deep breath, I dashed across the stony ground, the book in tow. Diving for the shadows, we made it just in time. Two dark elf archers appeared on the gantries above, faces lit up by flickering torches and moving slowly but surely, their eyes scanning the surroundings. Luckily, they were more focused on intruders coming in from outside than on what was happening inside the castle. I mean, who would be stupid enough to wander into this unholy mess?

'*Careless. That was too close,*' I berated myself. We could have easily been spotted if we'd been a second slower. I had to make calculated decisions from here on out. "Storage room, down the far wall. Get there quickly and douse the torches there. Keep an eye on those two clowns above us," I whispered under my breath, biding my time. "Okay, go!" We raced down the wall, constantly checking over our shoulders at the parapet. I grabbed the flickering torch and pushed it into the ground. The Manual had a more direct approach, swallowing the flame of his torch whole.

"So far, so good. Let's keep it going." I eyed our next move, seeing the faint trails of smoke escaping the book's mouth. We could cross the courtyard again, but the gap between us an safety was too large, and we would not make it in time before being spotted. It wouldn't work. Then I saw a door swing open, and an orc appear in the dim yellow light. The monster stumbled around, swaying a metal tankard from side to side.Most likely to get some fresh air. I pulled the book a bit closer to my chest. The main entrance had to be around the next corner, but we would have to take a terrible risk.

"Barracks. Do not make a sound." I waited patiently for the orc to head back inside, then I cast my eye up to the dark elves again. '*Small window of opportunity; move your ass, woman.*' Moving wraith-like, we set off on a sprint, always expecting an alarm to go off and all hell to be unleashed. The raucous sounds of drinking and laughing were growing as we approached the barracks. The orcs were in full voice, singing filthy songs between bouts of competitive belching. The Manual scrunched up his nose at the smell, trying to keep it together. It was like a million dying rats had farted in unison, and my eyes were soon watering at the unbearable stench.

We made it to the first window in record time, breathing heavily as we crouched low to the ground. There was no going back now. Crawling along the wall, we worked our way towards the door. With luck, we would cross the space before the drunken orcs could take notice. We had just made it to the second window when I grabbed the Manual and pulled it back. A hairy orc arm came swinging out, knocking the glass window to pieces and showering us with shards. Holding on to the book for dear life, I closed my eyes and waited for the inevitable. The orc howled in pain while the others roared with laughter, snorting and farting even louder. The party was turning violent as they guzzled pints of black beer. Just as I dared move again, another orc ran out the door, pulling his pants down and mooning the dark elves on the gantry. An arrow whizzed through the air, embedding itself deeply in the fleshy buttocks of the offending monster. That kicked things off: twenty orcs came racing out, charging at the archers above. The barracks quickly emptied, as the fight spilled across the courtyard. Shrugging at the book, I got up and quickly made my way across the entrance. The monsters were way too busy to notice us, and we were gone in an instant.

"Can't be far, almost there," I said, hoping that my hastily formed plans would work out. The third ring of the castle had to be close. We worked our way from shadow to shadow, slipping past the inner portcullis. Two goblin porters came running past, carrying supplies on a makeshift stretcher, their long green ears twitching and bobbing as they went. They soon disappeared from sight.

"There, that large double door," I said, pointing. "It has to be the main entrance." The way was clear, and all was quiet, and I was about to set off when another wave of red hot pain scorched through my skull, driving me to my knees. I could feel it; they were ripping the very soul from Naz, tearing at the bloody, frayed edges. She was holding on but was so close to breaking, her pain palpable inside me. Gasping for air, I fought through the waves of incoming pain, forcing my mind to focus. The book looked up worriedly at me, holding my arm as my body convulsed.

"I'm okay, just give me a moment," I lied. I had to keep moving before the pain overwhelmed me. Clutching my stomach and clenching my teeth, I stumbled out of the shadows and headed for the door, as if in a haze. I moved over rough cobblestones as fast as the pain would allow me, somehow making it to the far wall without being spotted.

Crouching beside heavy oaken doors, I rested my head on black stone walls, trying to keep it together. The pain was getting worse inside me with each moment, and my vision started to glaze over. Blurry images floated before my eyes. Then the earth started to shake ever so slightly; I looked worriedly at the book. Something heavy was coming our way.

I flattened myself against the wall, not daring to breathe, as the heavy castle door swung open. A legion of lizardmen marched past us, their green scales shimmering in the dim torchlight. They held razor-sharp halberds high and moved as if one. It must have been the palace guard, heading out to sort out the fight in the courtyard between the orcs and dark elves. Just when I thought they had passed, one last creature appeared in the glowing light of the entrance: a rock golem.

The dull gray monster folded its massive arms and watched the lizardmen march off into the distance. The damn thing was standing in our way, but perhaps there was just enough space for me to slip by. The Manual ever so carefully folded open its pages, making sure not to make any noise. It motioned down to me and then up at the brute only a few yards away.

'*Terrible eyesight but great hearing.*' I could work with that. I just had to keep the noise levels down, and we would be golden. Inching my way around the wall, I placed each footstep carefully, continually checking that the golem had not heard us. I was so close now that I could hear the stones rumbling in his body as he breathed in and out. One false move and he would easily crush us. It took everything in me to block out the pain of Naz's torture; I had to keep it together for just a little bit more. The golem shifted his feet slightly and stretched out his shoulders. Inches away, I could almost feel the rough stone texture of his skin on my face. If he moves back one more step…

'*Come on, asshole, don't you fucking move…stay right there…*' The golden rays of the torches inside were already playing over my face, and I wondered if I could make a break for it. Then again, no telling how quickly the Golem could move and what was waiting for us inside. No, just had to take it steady, one step at a time. Holding my breath, I rose behind the golem, eyes wide as I stared into the back of his rocky head. My nervous gulping sounded like gunshots in my head. I slowly backed away, pulling the Manual back with my feet. One sneeze, one cough, and we would be toast. The golem suddenly barked an order at a lizard man chasing a very drunk orc across the courtyard. His voice was like rocks tossed in a blender and put on high.

'*Stay still, goddamn you…almost there…*' I felt a metal vase against my back, but it was too late: the vase came tumbling to the floor as if in slow motion. I looked on for a moment in horror, then grabbed the book and ran. The golem swung around at the sudden disturbance and charged into the interior. I could hear him stomping around angrily. Luckily, I managed to duck into a darkened side room, where I held on for dear life and prayed he would not check the rooms. The stone monster moved up and down the corridor a few times, then stopped and grunted indignantly.

"Damn goblins, always messing around." A few minutes later, he moved off again, satisfied that all was well. I breathed a sigh of relief and looked down at the book in my arms.

"You okay?" I asked, realizing how close we'd come to blowing the whole thing. The book nodded and urged me to carry on. He knew I was hurting badly, but the longer we spent here the higher the chances were that we'd get caught. Summoning up more courage than a fifteen-year-old girl should ever have, I moved carefully out of the room, checking to make sure the golem had not decided to make a repeat appearance.

As we moved down the castle's grim corridors, we heard servants moving about and the distant clatter of pots and pans in the kitchen. The castle had settled down for the night, but there were still servants working. It only took one to give us away. It took a good half hour to check and recheck our steps as we tried to make sense of the byzantine layout of the castle interior, stopping constantly as lone servants moved along the corridors. My nerves were frayed to the breaking point when we finally reached what looked like the door leading down to the dungeons—its lock giving little resistance to my wiles. We worked our way down the cold and wet steps, feeling our way forward in the dark. The stairs wound their way deep into the earth until they ended at another metal door. I peeped through the bars and saw a disgusting blob-like creature squatting on a wooden chair at the far end of the corridor. It couldn't be helped; we had to take him out.

"Make it quick." I picked the lock and stepped back, whistling once. The pink creature grunted, upset that someone had disturbed his sleep, but it hobbled down the corridor and peered into the darkness of the stairwell. It would be the last thing it ever did. The Manual flashed its magnificent jaws and swallowed the monster whole. It never even had time to scream, a clear and defining chomp ending all discourse and discussion.

Wasting little time, we hurried down the corridor past sleeping prisoners to the far door. As I pushed through, a fresh wave of pain hit me like a sledgehammer to the gut. Dry heaving in agony, I dug my fingers into the crevices of the stone walls and pulled myself forward. We were in the heart of the dungeon now, within a heartbeat of my trapped friend. Crawling forward, I realized we were on a balcony overlooking the torture room below.

There she was. Naz was chained to the wall, her head slumped forward as some sort of shadow creature pumped dark magic into her. With clenched hands, he ripped and tugged at her soul. I knew she was close to breaking, and my first thought was to run down the stairs and beat the living shit out of the robed monster. *'And then what? Just hope it rolls over to have its tummy tickled? You have no idea how powerful that thing is, and it could pull you to pieces in an instant. Think like an engineer, Michaela.'* I forced myself to slow down and look around; brute force was not going to solve this—I had to think of a workaround. I spotted a metal gargoyle perched on a ledge just off to the side of us. It was right above the shadow creature. Perfect.

"I'm going to need your help. Come on," I whispered to the book. I inched my way forward, shuffling precariously closer to the horror on the ledge. *'Please don't be rusted...'* Gripping a wrench in my teeth, I clambered over the Gargoyle and then reached down acrobatically to undo a lug nut at the base of the statue. The damn thing would not give way initially, but soon I got it and the other three nuts loose.

"On my count, push with everything you've got." We braced ourselves, waiting for the shadow to take a few steps back. "Push, book, push!" I hissed and threw all my strength at the statue. Pearls of sweat ran down the Manual's cover as he gripped the legs of the statue and gave it his all. Creaking and cranking, the Gargoyle started to shift forward.

"Come on, you utter bastard!" I dug my shoulder even deeper into it and cursed it forward. Gravity finally took over as the statue toppled, end over end. The shadow looked up in stunned silence. In an instant, he was a black splat on the ground, his hands twitching under the grotesque metal block. It had made one hell of a noise—the whole castle had to be awake by now. I rushed down the stairs and lifted Naz's chin. She smiled at me through bloody teeth.

"Gargoyle to the face. Nice." She turned her head and spat out a gob of red saliva as we fought to get her chains loose.

"Can you stand?" I asked, lowering her gingerly down from the wall, her limp body resting on my shoulders.

"No, but I'll give you a lap dance if you get me out of here." Naz winced at the pain, holding her sides as we stumbled out of the dungeon. The Manual whistled and waved us over. He had found a quicker way outside. The little book was magnificent, a concerto of teeth snapping away in the dark, sending any monster brave or stupid enough in his way running for cover. We followed close behind, stumbling down the long corridor. Naz's body hung heavily on my shoulders; I had no choice but to dig deep and drag her from that hell hole. Already we could hear the shrieks and howls echoing through the castle corridors. The whole place was coming alive around us, and the monsters were hellbent on destroying the intruders who'd dared wander into their realm.

"How much further?" I shouted, elbowing a flying goblin in the face with a satisfying crunch. The Manual kept its head down and plowed ahead, bones and limbs flying in all directions as we followed in his wake. With our bodies screaming, our lungs racing, and our energy fading fast, we finally burst through into another courtyard, where a cold blast of air left me gasping. Stupidly, I had hoped the corridor would lead us outside the castle, but we were still stuck within it. There was no way I was dragging Naz out alive through this mess. The monsters would be on us before we even made it to the outside gate. Stay and fight? It was suicide. Then I heard the whinnying of horses. There had to be a stable nearby. "It's our only option. Come on

Naz!" I urged my rapidly fading friend on until we reached the stables. Never mind that I had never ridden a horse in my life— I would learn on the job. What could go wrong? After fumbling with the latch, I heaved the stable door open and peered inside to find the dark form of a resting horse, its head bowed. Just as I was about to step inside, the beast looked up with bright scarlet eyes and let out a snort of flames from its nostrils. I looked down at the Manual as it quickly flipped its pages open. Hell Horse.

Well fuck me, this made things interesting now, didn't it? However, I was shit out of luck and had to go for it. Steadily, I approached, never breaking eye contact with the demonic stallion. "Easy now. I'm not going to hurt you. Easy now," I coaxed the animal softly. Maybe it understood our plight, or maybe it was just tired of being abused by the castle's dark denizens. Somehow, in those dark stables, two damaged souls met and understood each other, even if the human was a strange sight. He could feel my soul was pure and true. The hell horse stamped a few times, whinnied loudly, and finally relented. Gratefully, I loaded Naz and the Manual onto it before climbing on myself. Knowing that this all could end spectacularly and painfully, I gripped the reigns tightly and pulled the equine nightmare around. Leaning down, I stroked his neck and whispered into his ear.

"Run, boy, run faster than you've ever run before."

Back to the battlefield.

War was coming.

CHAPTER 25

Somewhere on the other side of the wall

"On a fire breathing horse with my best friend. Good times," Naz mumbled.

"Just hold on," I said, glancing over my shoulder at her. I couldn't see any injuries, but I knew she was in a bad state. "I'll get us out of here; you keep 'em off us," I told the Manual. The little guy braced himself for what was coming. I tightened my grip on the reins, ignoring the fact that the last time my ass was on a horse was at the county fair when I was five. I could already see myself falling flat on my face and a hundred orcs laughing themselves to death.

I leaned down and whispered in the stallion's ear, "I trust you; take us home." The horse whinnied, wisps of white smoke escaping his nostrils. I felt the mighty beast beneath me and knew he could feel my fear. *'Just keep it together, Michaela; come on now.'* The stallion's hooves were clicking and clacking on the cobblestoned road; we were picking up speed as it started to stretch its long legs. Exhaling slowly, I urged him forward, hearing the clarion call of demonic screams erupting behind us.

The entire castle had come alive, its energy surging with calls for blood echoing from the towers.

"Go." I could feel his pulse accelerate, his heart pumping like a steam train under my open hand. We flew through the courtyards, hearing the zipping of arrows around us. Dark elves were rushing along the battlements, firing arrows and screeching in the night. "Keep your heads down!" Pulling Naz's arms tighter around my waist, making sure she was safe, I felt an arrow scream past my face, missing it by inches. We had to get out of there, and quickly. A lycan came leaping over a pile of straw bales, its fangs gnashing viciously. I managed to crack the wolf on the jaw, sending him slamming into a wall. We heard his howls of pain as he summoned his brethren to the hunt. Oh great, more shit to deal with, damn it. Monsters were pouring out of the darkness, their crude weapons ready to strike us down. The hell horse thundered forward, sending two goblins scattering as I fended off the intentions of an orc by kicking him squarely in the chest.

"I hope you know where you're going." I had to trust the great beast below me, using the reins only to guide it around the obstacles before us. I heard the beating of hooves behind us. A lizardman swung out of the dark, brandishing a sword, his long red tongue flicking from side to side. "Mind getting that sweetheart?" The Manual grabbed a wooden pole leaning against a wall and started prodding the chasing monster. Realizing it wasn't working, the book took aim at its head and nailed him square on, watching as the Lizard fell off his horse and got caught in the stirrup and veered off course.

"Nice one buddy, but more incoming, keep them off of us,

we have to be close to the exit." Another lizardman came up next to us, matching us step for step. The Manual looked at me cross-eyed and then leaped into the unknown, flashing its enormous jaws. I almost felt sorry for the scaly bastard as the book clamped down on his shoulder, sinking its jaws deep into green flesh. The lizard thrashed about, trying to get the literary pest off him, but to no avail; the book was locked on like a motherfucker! Hissing and screeching, the rider's attention was diverted just long enough not to see the wooden cart before him.

"Jump!" I shouted, snatching the book seconds before the lizard hit the cart, and went cartwheeling into the night. The Manual tried to catch his breath as I ran my hand over his pages. "I got you, little buddy, almost there." Then I looked back worriedly at Naz. "You okay, sweetie?" It was a dumb thing to ask, but she gave me the thumbs up. "This is better than live porn," she laughed, before starting to cough violently. She needed help and damn quickly. I urged the horse to go even faster; we flew around a corner and saw a group of lesser trolls barricading an entrance by throwing a pile of debris across it.

"No way through. We got to find another way out." I pulled the horse around and charged back the way we'd come, looking for an escape route. The monsters were coming out of the woodwork en masse and closing us down with each passing second. A pack of skeletons had set up a line of defense by the main entrance, hunkering down with spears pointed straight at us. I could see the dark forest just beyond them. Had no choice, had to go for it.

"Hold on kiddies, we're going to try an old navy tactic here and go straight through them." The Manual looked up wide-eyed at me and shook his head in disbelief. "That's my girl," Naz whispered behind me, holding on with all she had left as I turned the stallion around, looking intently at the waiting mob ahead of us. Clicking my tongue, I started him on a steady trot before picking up speed, faster and faster. Sightless eyes were staring black; the skeletons were steeling themselves for the suicidal run. Bony hands gripped swords tight. It was all or nothing. The wind rushed through my black hair; my eyes narrowed as we closed in on the barricade. Closer and closer we rode, the horse's hooves beating violently on the stone cobbled ground, its breath racing in the cold night air. Arrows streaked past us, one catching me in the shoulder, nicking the flesh. I was too focused on my target to care.

"Now!" I hollered, running my palm down the horse's neck. A stream of bright red hellfire erupted from the stallion's nostrils, scorching the skeleton barricade and sending the soulless creatures running for cover. Bursting through the flames, we hit clear air and raced past the lowering portcullis and into the open night. Scarcely believing our luck, I turned around to look at the dark castle and the red glow of flames silhouetting it. A figure appeared on the battlements overlooking the world below. We locked eyes, seemingly frozen in time. I had seen him in my most vivid of nightmares, experienced every nuance of his terror. I knew him well.

Death.

The black-cloaked master of darkness stood silently on the gantry, looking down. We were opposites in a war that spanned eons and had cost countless lives. Death could not believe the sheer impudence of this...*child*...and how she dared to defy his will. He was so close to the final victory now; nothing was standing in his way. The armies of Earth had turned on each other, and there was no sign of the Paladin. Just this infuriating girl who was messing up his well-laid plans. Grinding his teeth in anger, he swore to crush the callous engineer beneath his boot and tear the very life from her.

"Oh, he looks pissed," Naz mumbled, trying to force a tired smile.

"I'll deal with that bitch when the time comes. We gotta get back to the wall." I spurred the hell horse on and headed into the waiting arms of the black forest. There was no way Death was giving up that easily, and already I could hear the distant howling of lycans. He had summoned the lords of night to hunt us down. Our escape would be for nothing if we didn't make it back to the defenses before the pack took us down; but I didn't know how much further our brave stallion could take us. Three arrows were embedded in its rear haunches, jagged points sunk deep in his flesh.

"I'm sorry, I know you are hurting but we need a little more from you." The horse whinnied and stamped his hoof a few times but nuzzled up against my hand. "Thank you," I whispered as he turned and started running deeper into the forest. "Okay, keep a lookout for lycans," I said to the others, "and I'll do my best to get us home." The Manual had also been through hell and back. Some of his pages were scorched from the heat, but the little guy had a huge heart and bravely soldiered on. He climbed over me to check on Naz and take up watch. It wasn't long before we heard the first signs of howling behind us. I had read the lore of the night hunters in the Manual and knew of their legendary prowess. They never missed their target and were feared across the centuries. More ragged howls sounded up on the other side of the charging horse.

'*Classic half-moon formation. Catch us in a pincer movement,*' I thought, pushing the horse past his breaking point. It wasn't long before the Manual whistled and pointed. We spotted the gray wolf running beside us, flitting in and out between tree trunks flashing past, keeping his distance. The wolf was herding us, keeping us in line for the others to strike from behind. I tried veering off but knew we were boxed in, another wolf waiting for us to the left. Snarling and raving, the chasing pack closed in; the hell horse gasped for breath, red saliva dripping down his mouth. I glanced behind and saw three lycans appear on the misty gray path, their claws digging deep into the wet ground in their mad rush. Veering left and right, I tried keeping them off us, but we were losing this fight with each passing second. The hell horse was fading rapidly underneath me, and I knew it wouldn't last much longer.

"Come on, just a bit more…"

The lycans made their move, drawing up behind us. Rabid jaws snapped at my legs. Lashing out, I kicked one squarely in the jaw. This barely deterred it, only sending it falling back into the chasing pack. They knew our luck was almost up.

"Your side!" The Manual fended off an attack, chomping down on an outstretched paw. The wolf fought to shake off the book, howling in pain. "Let him go," I yelled, "he's slowing us down." The Manual let go, and the Lycan limped off to the side, nursing a gashed paw. Then, too late, I realized their plan. They'd tested our flanks for weakness, and now they would go for our most vulnerable spot.

Naz.

Quiet and helpless, she sat on the hell horse, seemingly oblivious to everything that was going on. The Lycans formed an arrow behind their leader, a snarling black brute of a wolf. We were royally fucked, and they knew it, relishing in their impending victory. I could not get anything more out of the horse, and we were alone in the forest, without any weapons to defend ourselves. In muted horror, I willed the horse forward, my hair lashing behind me in the wind. The brave little book held on for dear life, knowing the end was near, tears running down his spine. We could see the wall opening up in the distance, so close you could almost touch it, but it was a lifetime away.

And then, the soft splashing of paws on the muddy ground, nails digging into the earth. The lead lycan was running us down, its long red tongue hanging out in the wind. It smelled its prey, and it drove him wild. Strong legs stretching before him, he bounded across the earth, fangs glinting in the moonlight. As he launched himself, with wide-open jaws, Naz looked up at him, her face as calm as the first winter snow. She turned her head curiously and raised her open palm. The Lycan's eyes opened wide in horror, as if he had seen something that shook him to his very core. A memory centuries-old stirred deep within its canine brain, one that he thought he would never experience again. It fell to the ground, shielding his eyes and whining pathetically. The others stopped and milled around him, trying to make sense of it all. I didn't have time to process what was going on; all I could hear was their mournful howling. A sound that swept across the mist-covered forest and into the royal chamber of the dark castle itself. Death stood up from his throne and stared into the distance, blinking in disbelief.

It was not possible; it was just not possible.

We raced through the last stretch of the forest and hit the battlefield at maximum speed. Everything was ready, and the moment of truth had finally arrived. We stopped at the battlements and I jumped off the horse. "Help me get her off, quickly now." Ignoring my shoulder's screaming pain, I lifted the still form of my best friend down and laid her against the brick embattlements. "I'm going to get you help, you hear me? Just hold on for a bit longer." She simply stared at me blankly before closing her eyes. I turned to the Manual, cringing as my shoulder sang in agony. "I'm going to need you now, buddy. The control box is up there, I'll set the traps off while you call the shots. Keep them to the center where we're the strongest and watch for flanking. I don't know how long we're going to last, but, damn it, they are not taking us quietly."

We walked slowly up the steps as the night started to fade and dawn started breaking. Looking out over the battlefield and the waiting traps, I saw the monsters gathered at the forest line, where they were lit up by the morning sun. A natural hundred: orcs, common trolls, golems, lycans, hobgoblins, and witches lined up next to each other, banging their shields and brandishing weapons of war. Their calls of uninhibited bloodlust drifted towards us. As if in slow motion, they charged at us.

Outnumbered.

Outmatched.

Unbowed.

This is it, Michaela. Time to find your inner gangster. All on you now, girly.

CHAPTER 26

Somewhere on the other side of the wall

The first traps sprang into life as the incoming horde marched relentlessly forward, determined to crush the impudent pest who had embarrassed them so. Even from the wall, I could hear their heavy feet sloshing through the muck; foreign swear words flew about with unbridled gusto. "They're stuck in the tar traps—first salvo away." I pushed the levers on the control panel, and fire arrows flew into the early morning sky—orange fireflies streaking away in a graceful arc. I waited with bated breath, wondering if this idea was going to work. It was one thing taking down a single monster, but an entire legion? I needn't have worried. The fire arrows lit up the tar trenches in spectacular fashion, bathing the first line of monsters in a brilliant orange fireball. Their ragged screams ripped across the empty battlefield as they rag-dolled around and fell to the ground in smoldering heaps. It would not hold the rest for long, though; soon orcs and goblins were trampling over the smoking bodies. The Manual pulled my leg and pointed up at the sky. Dark shapes were rising above the marching horde.

"Witches," I mumbled under my breath, my fingers tapping lightly on the control panel levers. We had to get them closer; the net traps had a limited range. "Their spells only work at short distance. You ready to play gun dog, old buddy?" The Manual nodded and licked its chops. Already the monsters had cleared the tar traps and were wading through the hidden spike pits. A few of the charging pack, not looking where they were going, had plunged into the carefully prepared holes, skewering and killing them instantly.

'*Not enough…they're still coming. Have to stay focused.*' I turned my attention back to the squadron of witches coming down on us, hearing ancient curses fill the air as globes of dark energy formed in their hands. Still too far. Only had one shot at this. "Almost there…come to Mama." I waited until the last possible second, when the witches were almost on top of me. Shrieking and cackling in delight, they swooped down on their broomsticks, right into my trap.

"Now!" I pulled another set of levers, and three net traps sprang into life. The black nets went hurtling through the air, wrapping themselves around the flying crones, who crashed hopelessly into each other and tumbled to the ground. "Watch it." I pulled the Manual down as a witch streaked past us, blinded by a net around her face. She hit the wall behind us with a terrific crunch of bones.

"You okay?" I asked, pulling the book up. He nodded, dusting himself off angrily. "Okay, off you go, chief." The Manual bounded over the brick battlements and soon got stuck into the pack of writhing witches on the ground. The action was short and bloody, the book deciding not to mess around. He was quickly back by my side, picking his teeth with a straw.

"Sling traps next. We need to thin them out some more." The pack lumbered carelessly into the next line of defense, and I watched with grim pride as the ropes coiled cobra-like around thick ankles, one hurling an overzealous lycan far off into the distance. The heavier golems just shrugged them off and carried on marching forward. The Manual whistled and pointed to the far end of the battlefield. The lake left by the destroyed dam had worked perfectly, keeping the monsters from flanking me. The thick mud proved too much for the dark elf archers, who started floundering and then disappeared into the treacherous conditions. The few remaining ones tried to fight their way through, but I was ready for them. I pulled the control lever and flaming arrows were shot in their direction. They decided not to stick around for too long, scampering back as fast as they could to the forest's safety. I could bring the fight back to the center now, without having to worry about my flank.

Waves and waves of demonic creatures kept coming at us, though, and we were running out of traps and ideas. We were down to our last two lines of defense. We had lasted longer than I had ever dared dream, but time was not on our side. The ocean was about to break over us and wash us away.

"Spring traps! Hold on." I pulled the levers again to set them, but something went wrong. They were unresponsive—they would not click back. "The gears are stuck; we need to fix it manually. Come on." I charged down the steps. Naz still sat with her head buried in her knees. I wanted to comfort her, but the Manual pulled me away, pointing furiously at the monsters' column closing down on us.

"Stay here. I won't let you go." Hating myself for leaving her, I dragged myself away from Naz and ran for the spring traps, bounding over the uneven ground. Running as fast as my tired legs could catch me, I made it to the traps. The monsters were only a short distance away. "It has to be the gears," I shouted to the Manual. I bent down to the book and ran my hand over his cover, forcing a tired smile. "Just buy me some time, okay? I know we don't have much left, but I need five minutes to figure this out. Can you do that for me?" The Manual took my hand in his and clenched it tightly, nodding bravely. "Thank you," I whispered. "Let's work."

I grabbed my tools and scrambled for the furthest spring trap, where I started trying to figure out the blasted thing's issues. '*Think, Michaela, think!*' The rain must have jammed the gears; that had to be it. Meanwhile, the Manual had taken up position just in front of the traps and was cooly waiting for the charging pack of creatures. For centuries, he had been the assistant, but now it was time for him to take care of business. The book cricked its spine and went for the jugular of a brutish looking lizardman. Jaws snapped through the air as the paperbound warrior laid waste to any monster that dared get near him. Catching him out of the corner of my eye, I marveled at the sheer tenacity of my little friend.

"*Work the problem, Michaela.*' The calm, rational engineer side of me took over as I quickly, but carefully, worked my way through the list of potential problems. After a bit of muscle power, tinkering, and swear words directed at the gears, I soon realized that the wind-up chain had come loose. There was nothing to give the spring traps tension. Pulling with all my might, I managed to heave the chain back over one hook and onto the next.

The Manual was merrily bashing away at the monsters, but it soon ran into trouble. A golem had appeared from the mists, lumbering clumsily forward and pushing his stony body past the others. Fearlessly, the book went for the throat again. The golem's skin was too thick, and he swept the book away with the back of his hand. Nursing his sore teeth, the Manual looked up at the stony goliath and knew he had to try something different. He had to use the monster's size against him, had to buy me more time. Ducking and weaving like a professional boxer, the book stayed just out of reach of the golem's swinging fists. The monster swung wildly, knocking a nearby ghoul senseless. Chaos soon ensued as a schoolyard fight broke out, the creatures turning on each other. The Manual did whatever it could to egg the others on, riding on one's head, tapping another's shoulder, pinching here and there, and generally making mischief. Hanging on to the long ears of a dark elf that had been dragged into the unsightly mess, he looked up at me in expectation.

"Almost there, got the hang of it now." I was going like a certified bastard now, my hands seemingly taking on lives of their own. '*Check the gears, get the tension cable, check for unforeseen problems, keep going, girly.*' I was down to the last trap, but more monsters were coming; time was almost up. The last stubborn gear simply would not budge. The melee was dissipating as the monsters realized who the instigator of it all was.

"Ten seconds...just a little bit more...move, you bitch!" Finally, the gear released, and I waved to the book. "Let them come." Getting one last bite in on an errant orc, the Manual tucked ass and ran for safety. The mighty spring traps started working, thrashing back and forth. The sounds of cracking skulls and bones filled the air. Wave after wave crashed against the metal plates. At first, they held firm, but they soon started to give way, broken down by the pack of creatures. Grabbing the book, I turned and started running back to the battlements, hearing metal plates being pulled apart behind me. The tired and torn book looked up at me with resignation, knowing our luck was running out. I had one last trick up my sleeve, but it was insane, absolutely insane. We were going to need a miracle.

"Hail Mary time, buddy, fourth quarter and all those clichés. Trust me?" I asked as I ran, my sore feet stomping on the ground. Our resistance had only fueled the monsters' bloodlust, driving them into a rage-filled frenzy. The book in my arms raised a fist in defiance. "*There was no way this was going to work, girly. You've played your hand beautifully, but the house always wins in the end. You had to know that.*' Angrily, I quieted the voice in my head and kept running, ignoring the pain streaming through my spent body. The red glow of the morning sun was just appearing over the horizon. We made it to the battlements with the monsters only a hundred yards or so behind us. Lowering the book to the ground, I spoke to it through my racing breaths.

"I need one last thing from you. Pull off the material when I tell you, then run for cover; you hear me? Shut your eyes and don't look back, whatever you do." The book nodded, not entirely understanding what my last gambit was, but he knew he could trust this girl. She had somehow kept him alive through everything. I showed him the way and bounded up the steps.

There was one unused lever left, a bright red one with the words 'Fail safe—use only in the event of extreme danger.' I'd kept this one pretty close to my chest and never told the others about it. They would surely have stopped and told me I was wasting my time. Exhaling slowly, I pulled the lever and adjusted the angle. It came with a sinking feeling: I knew many of my traps would be destroyed in the process, but I was ass out of ideas, and there was nothing left to do. The Manual pulled off the trap's black material covers and stood back, shaking his head in wonder. He had only seen it once, many centuries ago, in Syracuse in 212 B.C. Smiling, the Manual thought back fondly to that fateful day when he stood next to his friend Archimedes and watched the Roman ships burn before their eyes. They had made a great partnership, and the book had helped the famed scientist a lot in those dark days. Now in 2018, they were about to light it up again.

Burning mirrors.

Were the angles right? Were the sun's rays strong enough? Did I time it all right? So many questions as I stood alone on the battlements, black hair fluttering in the morning wind. One wrong calculation and it would all be over; we'd be pulled apart by the pack and our limbs and pages scattered across the battlefield. The red glow intensified; legion after legion of skeletons and vampires bounded across the earth. The nightwalkers didn't seem to care about being caught in the daylight. Death had sent his best soldiers first, and somehow, we'd kept them back. Now the main army would sweep us away like dirt under a carpet. The Manual rejoined me and leaned its cover against my leg, its last energy spent. I picked him up in my arms and watched Naz slowly laboring up the steps. She looked at me with a mortally tired soul.

"I'm supposed to be the mad one." She cracked this joke before collapsing in my arms. Holding them both tight, I waited for the inevitable. Two hundred yards away, I could smell the stench on the creatures; I could hear the ragged howling and hissing below us. They knew we were trapped and had no place left to run.

"Don't look," I said solemnly, crouching down. The first rays of the golden sun appeared above the horizon, and the mirrors started heating up, turning white-hot.

A hundred yards.

Fifty.

Thirty.

Ten.

Now.

Pure energy erupted from the mirrors, sending a blast of brilliant sunlight right into the charging pack. It hit them like a hammer blow, tearing a jagged hole through their defenses. They barely had time to react; they just looked around in shock as the vampires exploded into dust and the skeletons' bones turned to jelly. Chaos and utter confusion broke out in the ranks as the monsters flailed about in the unforgiving heat. Those who tried to run were burnt to a crisp, making it only a few yards before the sunlight tore a hole through their bodies. One by one, the demons fell before the Archimedes' mirrors—they grasped at the skies, their flesh dripping, their bones vaporized in an instant. How could they be losing? This was simply not possible. How could one girl and a book, of all things, beat the very best Death could throw at them? Scores of warriors over the eons had fallen at their feet, all had had to submit eventually to Deaths' divine plan, but this *child* was resisting them? Inconceivable.

Our beautiful traps also perished in the solar onslaught, with only the metal ones remaining standing. All we had worked so hard for was burning away to nothingness. I didn't dare look up; instead, I held the other two tightly with everything I had left in me. The last mournful screams started to fade away, and I blindly reached out to pull the lever. Nothing could have remained standing; nothing could have been left alive in the light's overpowering glow. The mirrors tilted upwards and slowly began cooling down. It must have been a good minute or two later, but I finally opened my eyes and looked over the battlements.

Complete and utter destruction. The only signs that life once existed were the smoking carcasses of the once-mighty warriors below us. My traps were in flames, bathing the battlefield in pockets of crackling fires. Only a few metal traps remained standing, and they were in bad shape. A sense of melancholy washed over us as we looked out over the quiet theater of war. We noticed a solitary dark figure strolling past the fiery carnage, also looking at the destruction around him.

Death.

The reaper stood silently in the middle of the battlefield, trying to make sense of it all. When he saw the three of us on the battlements, his bony hands clenched in anger. I pointed at the skeleton, daring him to come at us again. Was that the very best he had? The worst he could do? I kept pointing, locked in time with the dark spirit, until he sighed, turned, and walked back to the forest. I sank to my knees, silently hugging the others tightly.

Then I let the pent-up emotions out. Tears ran down my cheeks and splashed the Manual's cover. Naz kept looking out into the distance blankly, not saying a word. There was a heavy weight on her shoulders, one she dared not speak of.

We had made it; we had finally made it.

Later that evening. Naz's house.

After patching up the hell horse as best we could, we bade it farewell and sent it on its way. The brave stallion had carried us to freedom and now deserved its freedom. It could roam the fields of the other side of the wall for the rest of his life, in peace.

It had been an uncomfortable trip back to Naz's house; we didn't speak a word. I knew Naz was hurting, not so much physically as mentally. She had been to hell and back, and it was showing. Her once bright and bubbly face was tired and ashen as she stared straight ahead of her. There was so much I wanted to share and tell her, but the words simply wouldn't come. It should have been a time of great jubilation—I mean we had just pulled off the most significant upset victory in history—but none of us felt like celebrating. There was a cold distance between us. When we got to her house, I walked with her back to her still open window. Luckily, Naz's mother was used to the teenager locking herself in her room for an entire day. She stood looking with melancholy at the window. I grasped her shoulder, and she looked back. Sadness was etched in her eyes, the sadness of one who'd seen horrors beyond those any other human had ever witnessed.

"Naz…" But I never got further. She shrugged my hand off and climbed through the window, closing it behind her. I stood there for what felt like an eternity, not saying a word and holding the sleeping Manual in my arms. Biting my lip, I fought to hold back the tears. There was nothing to do but turn around and walk away. She had been through a terrible time and just needed time to recover; maybe soon Naz would be back to her old self. But deep inside, I knew that was a lie. My friend had changed; she would never be the same again.

As soon as I made it back to the workshop, I went to bed, my head hitting the pillow hard. Didn't even bother changing out of my dirty and bloody clothes. As my eyelids started to droop, I thought back to my encounter with Death and the burning battlefield around us. I knew it wasn't over, not by a long shot. We had defied the Horseman, and retribution was coming. God knows what he had in store for us next.

The house always wins in the end.

Always.

CHAPTER 27

Somewhere in Middle America

It was hard getting back into the normal swing of things. I had just stared down Death and all his minions, and somehow pulled a victory out of my ass at the very last second, but wasn't that Calculus homework something? I struggled to concentrate the whole day, going through the motions at school and trying my best to keep it together. My mind wandered back to the events of a few days earlier, replaying everything. Part of me wondered why we couldn't pull it off again. What was stopping us from defying the reaper—holding out against impossible odds until the Paladin makes his appearance? Everything would be okay again when this supposed hero would take over and lead an army against the darkness. Inside, I knew I was bluffing myself, that the hourglass's time was rapidly running out. We had kept but a tiny fraction of Death's armies at bay, and we'd caught the fucker with his proverbial black pants around his ankles. It wouldn't take him long to conjure more demons from the pits, it was only a matter of time He would not make the same mistake of underestimating us again, and I knew he would bring his whole army next time to wipe us out. It was a humiliation he would not endure a second time.

Lying back on my chair in chemistry class with the Manual over my face, barely hearing the teacher's droning in the foreground, I was scheming up new trap designs. If there was even the slightest chance of pulling out another stunning upset, well, then I had to take it. The bell rang, and the rest of the students filed out, but I remained seated. I was in no mood to socialize and even less to explain the bruises and wounds all over my body. Truth be told, my whole body felt like it was on fire. It had been a mission just to get up in the morning and go through the motions. But the litany of black and blue marks I saw in the mirror wasn't my only worry.

Naz.

Since the incident at the wall, she has not been the same, and we had barely spoken a word at all. I often saw her at school, but she moved like a shadow through the crowd, ignoring the usual jibes and jeers from the inmates. There was a terrible weight on her shoulders; it pulled her down with each labored step she took. I tried catching up with her one break time, but she dropped her head and shuffled past me, never even making eye contact. I knew she had been to hell and back in the castle and had been inches away from being broken by the shadow, but there was clearly something else bothering her. It broke my heart to see my friend like this, but there was nothing I could do.

Then came yesterday's incident in the girls' locker room. The Dolls were up to their usual tricks, cornering Naz just after gym class. I could hear kicking and screaming as I raced around the corner and grabbed the first Doll behind the collar and flung her against the metal lockers. I dropped the second one with a right cross to the face, her whore-red lipstick mixing with streaks of blood. Thank goodness I had left the Manual sleeping in the library, or who knows what would have happened? The fight was over quickly, and the Dolls beat a fast retreat, wisely choosing not to screw with the unstable looking girl with the long black hair.

"Are you okay, sweetie?" I asked Naz, pulling her up as she dabbed at a busted lip with her hijab. It was strange; through the whole fight, she never cried out for help or tried to fight back. It was almost as if she had quietly accepted her fate. It didn't make sense to me, Naz pushed me angrily away, gritting her teeth and turning her head.

"Why won't you leave me alone?" Behind the hijab, her eyes were blazing in anger. "I never asked you to save me, white girl, so why the fuck are you still here?" All her emotions came out as I looked on.

"Naz…please." I tried calming her down but to no avail. She wiped away a tear and pushed past me, never looking back. There was nothing left to say; a horrid silence fell over the girls' locker room. A solitary figure stood there fighting to hold back the tears and realizing she was losing her best friend. I was truly alone now.

I waited that afternoon after school to see if she would show up, but there was no one in our usual spot. Glumly, I headed home, ignoring the worried looks from the Manual in my arms. The strain of the last few days had started to show, and he was morose and cranky most of the time. It couldn't have been easy for him, though; after centuries of war and dealing with male testosterone, taking on a teenage girl's issues must have seemed like scaling Everest.

I knew I had to carry on. I had to fix the remaining traps and get them back into working condition again. And if Naz didn't want to help me anymore, well then so be it. I spent the rest of the afternoon working out plans and schematics. The wooden traps were cinders now and beyond saving, but I was sure the metal traps could be brought back online with a bit of TLC. If I could hold the line for a bit longer, I could even think of replacing the wooden traps in the back. They didn't need to last long, just until the Paladin arrived. Surely, having heard of the commotion, he would soon come running.

'*Hold out for a few more days, and everything will be okay.*' It would be a herculean task to repair all the traps and get the materials myself from the hardware store. Well, what fucking option did I have? My supposed best friend had gone off the deep end, and here I was, a girl alone against the apocalypse. It wasn't fair, I thought, angrily pulling the papers off the table and watching them tumble to the ground. The Manual slowly got up and started gathering the schematics piece by piece, handing them to me again. I wanted to be angry at the little book, but how could I? Through all this, his faith and friendship had kept me upright and pointed in the right direction. Whenever I felt my spirits drop, he was there to pick me up again.

"Thank you," I smiled, picking the book up and hugging him tightly. I knew my faithful companion would be by my side until the bitter end. "Let's work." Skimming through the tattered pages, I saw an old diagram for a glue trap. It was one of my earliest sketches, one I had rejected, but somehow I liked the look of it now. If it worked, it would be an epic 'fuck you' to Death and all his nasties. But I was going to need to get the barrels first, which meant a trip back to school.

"You up for it, little buddy?" I asked the Manual as I poured over the schematics. The thought kept ticking over in my mind that it wasn't about destroying the monsters; it was about keeping them at bay until the Paladin arrived. The timeframe was a huge gamble, but I had to go for it and keep my faith in him. The Manual looked up worriedly at me, sighed, and slowly flipped through its pages, taking out a faded yellow envelope that was pasted to the last page. Tugging at my pant leg, he held it out to me.

"What's this?" I asked, turning it over in my hand. Just as I was about to tear it open, the book stopped me, waving its cover.

"It's for later? Okay, I understand." Perplexed about what could be inside it, I carefully placed it into my pocket and turned my focus back to the plans on the table. A worried look crossed the book's cover as it quietly turned and walked away. He didn't want to do it, but desperate times called for desperate measures.

Just after ten that evening, I got dressed and headed out to the truck. The winter weather was growing colder by the day, and I knew we were in for a bitterly cold season. Loading the Manual in, I started the truck and headed out. Even though all was quiet outside and nary a soul was moving, there was evil in the air, a foreboding feeling of dread that sent shivers running down my spine. The End Time was near, but I did my best to keep it from my mind. I had other things to focus on for the time being. About half an hour later, I pulled the truck up to the gates of the school. Luckily, they were too cheap to spend money on security guards.

"Stay close, you hear?" Pulling my gray hoodie tighter around me, I quickly picked the gate's lock. Kid's stuff. The place gave me the creeps at the best of times, but it was even worse in the dark. There were shadows around every corner of the eerily quiet corridors. Somewhere deep in the bowels of the cold, brick building I could just make out a dripping tap.

"Janitor's office is in the basement, just past the library. Shouldn't have a problem getting there, but keep an ear out for trouble." The Manual and I were making good progress, and I knew exactly where to break in. There was a side door by the chemistry lab that was never locked. Perfect. Quickly, we moved through the empty school building and down the stairs at the far end. A TV was blaring in the distance, and soon the sounds of an Eastern European woman getting porked became louder and louder. The Manual gave me a disgusted look.

"Two-liter hand cream. El Heffe is not coming up for air any time soon. Let's go." Effortlessly we slipped past the very preoccupied janitor, not daring to look at the smut that was keeping him so busy.

"Storage closet. No alarms inside. Easy work." I eased the door open carefully, so as not to make any noise. Peering into the semi-gloom, I saw what I wanted—two barrels of industrial-strength glue. God knows what they used the stuff for, and I swear it must have been around since the Vietnam War. Either way, it would suit my nefarious purposes perfectly. Commandeering a hand-truck, I shuffled two barrels onto it and tied it down with some nearby rope.

"Grab me a few packets of nails and a few metal rods, there on that table over there," I said to the Manual. Couldn't hurt to stock up on supplies while I was here. Having procured what we needed, we set off back down the corridor, tiptoeing past the janitor. It took some effort to get the barrels up the steps, but we soon cleared that obstacle. "We should come back more often; he has a good supply going there," I said merrily to the Manual as I carted the barrels down the corridors and out the unlocked door. I doubted the janitor would miss them, and it was for a good cause. The night air was bitterly cold; I picked up the pace, eager to put that blasted place in my rearview mirrors. There was still so much to do, and I didn't want to waste any more time.

"Let's cut across the football field, much quicker that way." The place was deserted, with evening practice having ended hours ago. The cold grass crunched under my feet. I'd barely made it across the halfway line with the trolley when I heard a familiar voice echoing up from the empty bleachers.

"You're wasting your time," Naz said sadly. She crossed her arms in front of her, quietly stood up, and walked over to us.

"Hey, book, how you doing?" She fist-bumped the Manual then turned her attention back to me. We stared coldly at each other, wisps of cold air escaping our mouths.

"What are you doing here, Naz? Aren't you grounded?" I asked as she eyed the barrels of glue.

"Can't get into worse trouble now, can I? My parents are even talking of sending me to Malaysia to go live with an aunt—said it would do me good to get away from all this Western garbage." Naz dug her hands deeper into her pockets and shied away from me. "As for what I'm doing here well, I am trying to save you from yourself."

"What do you mean?" I asked, already not liking the tone of her voice.

"You can't stop him; you know that, right? Death was always going to win in the end."

"I don't have to stop him; I just need to keep him busy. That's all." I replied, my voice tinged in frost.

"You are delusional, white girl, fucking delusional. You are putting all your hopes on this so-called Paladin showing up and saving the day. Is that right?"

"It's all I've got left, and if I don't do it, then who? Tell me who." The anger was growing in my voice with every passing moment. "This is the way it's always been. The engineer paves the way for the hero to show up and to restore the balance. There's nothing left but this, and I am the only one that can do it."

"And if I told you that you should run? Run as far as your legs can carry you?" She was face to face with me now, and I could see the fear in her eyes. A deathly fear that took the heart of me in that instant.

"I can't…" I whispered the words under my breath, knowing that it was my fate in life.

"Then you are going to die, Michaela, do you fucking understand the words coming out of my mouth? There is nothing but your bloody and broken corpse waiting for you out there. Is that what you want?" Naz shoved me hard against the chest, fighting to keep the tears back.

"Don't touch me again." I shoved her back, sending the hijabi tumbling to the ground. She leaped to her feet and swung wildly, clocking me across the face. The Manual tried pulling us apart but to no avail. We rolled around on the icy cold grass, kicking and biting with reckless abandon. Naz grabbed me by the collar.

Her open palm pulled back, then she thought better of it and let me go in disgust.

"It could have been anyone else on this God-forsaken planet, but it just had to be you, right? You had to play savior of earth, stand toe to toe with the Grim Reaper himself. And what do I get? Seeing my best friend torn to pieces by those animals. Until there is nothing left of her."

"I don't know what happened to you out there, Naz, but this is not how to do it." I dabbed the back of my hand against a busted lip, feeling the metallic taste of blood on my tongue.

"There is no other way, don't you understand that? The shadow tried to tear my soul out, take everything that I was inside, and I saw things, horrors beyond your belief." She pulled her hijab up and showed a black scar on her throat.

"Naz…" I tried reaching out to her, but she pushed me away angrily.

"This is my pain, and I will carry it for the rest of my life, so don't pretend you understand." She lowered her hijab and glowered at me furiously. "I saw Death's heart, felt that vile abomination beating inside me, pumping pitch-black blood. I know how all this ends, and you have to listen to me, Michaela, there is no version where we come out on the other side alive."

I paused for a moment and lowered my head. "Then what would you have me do?"

Her anger dissipated and was replaced with something akin to sympathy. "Run, girly, run as fast as you can, and don't you dare look back." Sorrow was eating her alive, and Naz fought like a demon to keep her emotions in check, biting her lip until blood began to trickle over it.

"I can't. I'll hold the line till the Paladin arrives. Please understand—this is what I have to do." My own words pierced my heart like an icy dagger.

"Then we are both dead," Naz said dejectedly, looking off into the distance. The moon had slowly turned from a pale white to a scarlet red. A sure sign that Death was ready to play his final hand.

"It doesn't need to be like this. Come with me, and we can hold the line like old times." Even as I said the words, I realized how hollow they sounded.

Naz forced a tired smile and gripped my shoulder tightly. "Allah wills that I walk a different path, and there is no turning back now." Naz brushed away a tear, turned and walked away.

"Naz…"

She stopped and looked back at me one last time. "In the words of the Heartbreak Kid: I'm sorry, I love you."

I stood on that cold and empty football field, watching as my friend ambled away. There was so much I still wanted to say to her, but the words would just not come out. A sisterhood had broken on that painfully sad night as we went our separate paths, never to see each other again.

The Manual tugged me on the leg, wiping tears off his cover and pointing at the blood moon above. I nodded solemnly, taking a deep breath and gathering myself again. We were in the endgame, and there were only hours left till Death made his final march against the wall. Pushing the creaky trolley across the football field, I felt the magnitude of what was waiting for us start to sink in. The final battle was upon us, and I had never felt so alone in my life. I would have given anything for Naz to be by my side.

Girl alone.
One last gambit to play
Till the bitter end.

CHAPTER 28

Somewhere in Middle America

It was with a heavy heart that I loaded the barrels into the back of the truck. I didn't want to think about what was going through Naz's mind but, damn it hurt, it hurt me down to the very core. Maybe I should have gone after her, but once she had made up her mind, there was no changing it. I just hoped she'd come to her senses and quickly. The Manual sat quietly next to me, looking pensively into the distance. He didn't want to show it, but Naz's departure had also affected him severely. I had never seen him so down; I reached over and ran my fingers over his pages.

"It's going to be okay, buddy. It's going to be okay." Maybe it was a lie, but I didn't have anything else left. I had to dig deep now. The book sat stoically, locked in his thoughts. The further we drove, the more we noticed people coming out into the street. The news of the blood moon had quickly spread through town, and everyone was coming to see the strange phenomenon. This was going to complicate matters, but I had no choice. I had to get the supplies from home and get to the wall, pronto. Luckily, everyone was too preoccupied with staring up at the sky to notice me slipping past them in the truck. Once we had cleared the first throng, we made good time back to the workshop. There was none to waste. The book and I got down to work with all haste. Every bit of scrap metal and wood we could pile on to the overloaded truck bed was packed in and strapped down.

"Make sure you pack in the extra box of screws and nails and check the fuel gauge on the cutting torch," I shouted at the book across the room, cramming a couple of homemade spikes onto the pile. I was working tirelessly, a desperate woman fighting for each precious second. "Have you got everything? We need to get going." I didn't know how much time I had left before Death launched his next assault. Days? Hours? All I knew was the window was rapidly closing, and I had to be ready before it finally slammed shut. The book came running with a box of iron caltrops, just the thing to puncture the most stubborn of monster's claws. With one last check of the inventory, I lifted the Manual into the truck and cast my eyes back to the stripped workshop. Everything of use had been taken, and only empty shelves remained behind. It was like I had found it at the beginning, and it seemed bereft of life now. I could almost see three ghosts, Naz, the book, and me, working late into the night, dreaming up and building new and improved traps to keep the darkness back.

'*Don't think about her. It's only going to hurt more.*' Biting my lip, I climbed into the truck and started her up. Even with the cold feeling running through my body, I couldn't help but think that maybe one day, somewhere far in the future, another engineer could make use of this secret space. To carry on the fight against the darkness and hold the line for just another day. The Manual nudged me gently in the ribs, perhaps understanding what was going through my mind. I looked at him and smiled.

"You're right. Let's go." Easing the truck out of the garage, I refocused on the battle ahead and steeled myself for what was coming. Already it was a struggle getting to the wall; the streets were jammed packed with people. Panicked voices were ringing out in the night, town folk were marching almost hypnotically towards the wall. Though they couldn't see it, they must have sensed the immense energy radiating from its direction—like moths to the flame.

A hand thumped loudly on the hood of the car, bringing me back to reality. It was a local cop trying to bring order to the rising chaos. My heart sank to my shoes as he looked wild-eyed at me. My hand gripped the shift tightly. I was ready to gun the engine and make a run for it. Damn the law—I would face the consequences later on. Just as his hand closed on the door handle, a shattering of glass caught his attention. A group of locals had smashed a storefront window and were busy carrying out TVs and stereos. Seizing my chance, I quickly slipped away in the chaos and eased my way through the crowd. The usual graveyard silence of the train tracks was gone. It was packed with people of all ages. The scarlet moon had turned an ominous shade of black and was sending panic through the crowd. I recognized the faces; I had grown up with them. Even the freaks and mouth breathers were standing in awe, looking up at the night sky. I saw some of the Jocks and Dolls as well, and I felt sorry for them; they didn't understand what was going on and what horrors lay beyond the wall. They had put me through hell, but even they didn't deserve what would be unleashed on them should I fail in my mission. Their eyes turned to me sitting in the truck. Cold fear gripped them tightly.

'Just let me through. I need to get through.' I didn't want to hurt them, but I had to reach the other side of the wall at any cost. Hands started rocking the car back and forth. Like a rabid pack of hyenas, they set onto the back of the truck, hands wrenching wooden poles and metal struts free.

"Stop that! Leave it alone!" Scrambling out of the truck, I ran to stop the mob ransacking my precious supplies. "You fools! You don't understand!" A flying fist struck me, sending me crashing to the ground. Wiping the blood from my mouth, I fought banshee-like to stop the mob, but there were too many of them, all hellbound to get a weapon in hand. Kicking and screaming with all my might, I tried to get my supplies back, but it was a lost cause. A two-by-four clipped me across the head and I saw stars. I felt the Manual dragging me away, snarling at anyone stupid enough to come near him. The mob had utterly lost its mind, was tearing the truck to pieces. I sank to my knees, watching with cold detachment as the truck went up in flames. There was nothing left. All my supplies, all my traps were destroyed in that moment of madness. I had nothing to keep back the darkness now; we were completely defenseless. I wanted to scream at them, scream till my lungs burst, but there was nothing left in me, just the cold shock that all my plans had gone up in smoke and everything I had gambled was burning before my eyes.

'I'm sorry, Daddy, I've failed you.' All his hard work and belief in me...gone. I felt sick to my stomach. And then, in my lowest

of low moments, I felt a solitary figure standing next to me. Through all this, the Manual had remained by my side. My friend pulled me up out of the mud and pulled me away from the raging mob. A red mist had descended on the crowd, and in their hysteria, they didn't notice me slowly walking away. A single tear ran down my face; there was nothing left but the raw, exposed nerve of my immense pain. I just wanted to help them, couldn't the fools understand that? And now they'd ruined everything. All hope was truly lost.

With heavy hearts, we passed through the wall, leaving the mob behind. All was quiet again, but I knew we were not alone. A red glow lit up the skies over the distant forest. Death had called up his reinforcements. The legion of the damned was waiting impatiently, dark figures silhouetted against a fiery backdrop. They were frothing at the mouth, ready to tear apart the insolent girl who had delayed their long-awaited final victory. Fireballs flashed across the heavens. Dragons. Death had even summoned a pack of dragons to his cause.

"Guess we got his attention, now," I said with a crooked grin, shaking my head in disbelief. There wasn't a need for lights out here; the monsters had turned the forest into a raging inferno, bathing the battlefield in an ominous red glow. Slowly, we walked past the still battlements and through the battlefield. There was precious little left. A few ramshackle metal traps stood useless. I didn't have any supplies left to repair them, and time had run out. I just knew that Death would make his move at first light. As soon as the sun rose, he would finally destroy any presence I ever had on this earth. I ran my hand over a still spring trap, feeling the cold metal under my hand and seeing the broken parts hanging loosely. A sense of finality came over me there in the early morning hours.

'*You had to know you could never win this battle, Michaela. Your job was always to hold out and wait for the Paladin.*' My inner voice echoed through my head. '*You did more than anyone could have expected from you, and there is no shame in defeat now.*' The pep talk didn't raise my spirits. I kicked a piece of charred wood away, hearing it clattering off into the distance. There, amid the broken wreckage of the battlefield, among all the traps and my dreams of achieving the impossible, I sank to my knees in the mud. The Manual stood silently next to me, his heart breaking with mine. Even though a wave of sadness washed over him, there was also an odd sense of pride in him. He had stood side-by-side with some of the greatest minds this planet has ever seen, but none matched this girl's courage. The Manual knew the end was near, but he'd decided, in his bookish ways, that this was one hell of a way to go out. He snuggled under my arm and looked up at me.

I said nothing, instead smiling tiredly at the brave creature as we listened to the growing chanting and howling of the monsters in the distance. As the night faded and the stars started to dim, I could sense their bloodlust growing. They were only waiting for his call. Death was out there, watching me, studying this most unusual of adversaries. For the first time in history, a new sensation was slowly creeping through this skeletal body, and he did not like it one little bit. And yes, it did bring the slightest of smiles to my face.

He was hesitating.

Dawn finally broke over the battlefield, and the sun peered

meekly through the thick cover of cloud. Any hope of using the Archimedes Mirrors again quickly faded away. It was a most unusual scene that greeted the morning. A single, solitary girl on her knees in the cold mud with a book by her side versus an overwhelming force of monsters and demons in the distance. Cold steel swords were drawn, arrows were nocked, and wickedly sharp fangs dripped with saliva.

A thousand against one. Good odds for any girl.

Impatiently, the soulless horde waited for their master's command. Straining at the leash, they did not have to wait long. The Lord of the Night effortlessly moved through the damned scores, past their waving banners and crude armor. Taking up a position next to the catapults and ballistae, he gazed out over the battlefield, eyes narrowing ever so slightly. There were no visible traps, no defenses waiting to slow down his army—just a field of mangled parts and a girl right in the middle of it. The resistance had finally crumbled, and Death gloated under his black cape. Raising his bony hand, he sneered and sent the horde charging.

This ended now.

My long black hair hung loosely down to my shoulders and my head was bowed as I felt the earth shaking at the monsters' charge. It was strangely peaceful, and I allowed myself to savor the cold morning air on my face. I could almost hear the world around me, breathing in and out. The strangest of sensations, being entirely at peace yet knowing the end was close now. And then I felt a gentle hand on my shoulder.

"I always said your stubbornness would kill you in the end."

I looked up through a tired, tear-stained face to see Naz and the hell horse standing over me. She grasped my hand and pulled me up. The moment was locked in time as we hugged tightly, unwilling to let each other go.

"Naz…" I began but could not finish the sentence, too overcome with emotion at seeing my best friend again.

"You never turn your back on a tag team partner," she replied, beaming brightly before glancing over the incoming wave of monsters. "You ready to work, girly?" Naz asked. She reached into my top pocket and took out the letter the Manual had given me. With shaking hands, I opened it and read the simple yet eloquent words. I looked at Naz again, my heart breaking as I realized what needed to be done.

"There has to be another way…" I said quietly.

"This is how it has to be," Naz replied sadly, wiping a tear from my eye. "Now, let's take these bitches to Squealtown, shall we?" The old fire was burning in her eyes again as I nodded and grinned wickedly.

Last play.

Hail Mary.

CHAPTER 29

Somewhere on the other side of the wall

I kept staring in the distance, seeing my best friend riding away gracefully on top of the hell horse, her hijab blowing in the wind. I could have tried to stop her and whatever she had planned, but somehow I knew I had to let her go. For all the insanity she brought into my life, she always had a plan. She just needed someone to believe in her. Wiping a tear away, I looked down again at the letter, my eyes slowly moving over the elegant writing. Seemingly oblivious to the tremendous force marching down on me, I ran my fingers over the paper.

Hey, girly. I'm going to need something from you now, so bear with me, okay? I need you not to be angry with me. Sorry if I broke your heart the other night, but if there was a chance of one of us coming out of this mess alive, well, I had to take it. I wanted you to run, run as far as you could possibly go. A part of me hoped that you would find your bliss somewhere out there in the world and grow old, have grandkids, and all that Hollywood bullshit. Maybe live a full life before Death finally caught up with you. However, you were always too stubborn to listen, so here's the plan. One final kick to the nuts before the curtain falls.

There was nothing left for me now but the dark path ahead. Stroking the hell horse's main, I kept talking to it, urging it to run faster than its pitch-black legs had ever taken it. I could hear the roaring of dragons and the clinking and clanking of war machines rolling over the earth. Death had been overconfident in his final victory. Drawing his entire army together to smash through the wall, he had left the slightest of gaps in his defense, giving me a chance to slip through. I was praying to Allah that none of the monsters would notice me, and by his divine guidance, I managed to break their lines. I knew what I had to do and where my journey would end.

Right back at the dark castle.

You are probably planning my demise in great detail at the moment, but in my defense, the Manual helped me out a bit here. Please don't be angry at him; he was just trying to help. You had to know we could never win this fight; we were outnumbered and outgunned right from the beginning. I mean, we were taking on fricken' Death and every messed-up asshole in his arsenal. However, I learned something vital from you, and that is to stand up to a bully. No matter how big or scary they seem, you plant your feet and woman-up to whatever stands before you. You gave me this courage, Michaela, and I will always be grateful to you. Now, before this turns into a terrible rom-com and I get all soppy here (You are so dead if you tell anybody, I'll kick your ass, woman, when we meet again), now comes the time we play our final hand.

Destroy the Aurora crystal, girly, and, hell, let's see what happens.

The forest was quiet and devoid of life, with not a soul in sight. We wound our way through the forest, my hand gently guiding the horse back home. He whinnied a few times, remembering the harsh treatment he'd suffered under his masters' hands in the dark castle. Nevertheless, I think he knew that what he was doing was important and so sped down the dirt path. Was I scared? You bet your candy ass I was. But since the shadow had tortured me at the castle, I knew what needed to be done. Not that it wasn't going to suck major wang, but I guess it was time I stepped up. Trying to push the thought to the back of my mind, I hunkered down on the horse and kept pushing him faster and faster down the path. Had to be on time and hope beyond hope that Michaela could stall them just long enough.

The ancients, those around long before man even knew what war was, included a failsafe in the crystal. Maybe they knew that one day man's armies would fall in their fight against the darkness. They never said what would happen afterward, it's just a blank, but I guess we make our own fate. So this is it. You send that crystal sky high and don't you dare hesitate, do you hear me? Believe in me as I believed in you, my friend. The Manual has the details, so just follow his lead and, yeah, let's open this circus for business. Oh, and one more thing. I might have accidentally, on purpose, started the angry mob you saw on the other side of the wall. I hope they didn't hurt you, but they needed some gentle nudges in the right direction. Please forgive me, but it's part of the plan, you just got to trust my ass. Okay, girly, this is where I wrap things up now. Thank you for giving me courage and heart, but most of all, thank you for being my friend. With Allah's blessing, we'll see each other soon.

Fi Amaan Allah
Your partner in crime,
Naz

I pulled up to the dark castle and looked around. Like the forest, it was deadly quiet and empty of any signs of life. Every demon and monster had joined the final push on Michaela. Allowing myself the briefest moment to take it all in, I thought back to the last time I was a guest at this house of horrors. However, that was in the past now, and my path was clear. Climbing off the hell horse, I stroked his head and felt him nuzzle my neck.

"Thank you for this. Now go." I closed my eyes and turned away, every step taking me closer to my fate. There was no sense in hiding anymore. I was going to stroll through the front door like a badass and hope to high hell there wasn't some dark elf left behind on sick leave or some shit like that. Gathering all my courage, I walked up the main road and stopped beneath the open drawbridge. It was enormous, extraordinary, like the whole thing would come crashing down on my head at any second.

'*Ovaries of steel. Let's do this, baby.*' I gave myself a little pep talk and stepped over the threshold, half expecting a volley of arrows to greet me. But nothing happened; the place was entirely deserted. Thrown-over carts and darkened buildings lay before me, and it was almost ridiculously quiet. Glancing into the barracks, I saw that they had emptied the place of every weapon and shield they could lay their hands on. Talk about overkill, all this for one little girl and her book. Pussies.

Refocusing, I headed to the royal court, leftover torches guiding my way. I didn't need to know how I could feel the black heart far below, pulling me closer, like a siren song of death. Even the royal court was abandoned and quiet. The servants must have either joined their master on the front lines or were hiding far away. It didn't matter. The way I was feeling at the moment, I would have gone right through all of them. Deeper into the embrace of the castle's bowels I went, feeling the heart's presence with every passing moment. I think it knew I was close now, but to hell with it. It was too late to turn around, and I would look like a complete and utter tit if I tucked tail and ran. I could already hear Michaela asking me just what the exact hell I was doing back at the battlefield. No, I had to keep moving.

Soon I reached the dungeon and opened the oaken doors. Bastards didn't even bother to lock it before leaving. Even the prisoners were gone; Allah knows where they were taken or if they were still alive. A part of me was relieved; I didn't want their blood on my hands. As I reached the final door, I saw a glinting of metal in the corner. The jailer must have left his knife behind in a hurry. Could be handy, I thought, pocketing the blade.

For just a moment, my hand hesitated on the cold steel of the door handle. This was it, the point of no return. I knew what lay beyond and there was a part of me that was terrified. I remembered the shadow trying to rip my soul from my body, the impossible agony, the screams tearing through the stone corridors, becoming one with the dark heart, pure hatred coursing through it, evil incarnate. I had never experienced something so utterly devoid of hope or light. It was a void of chaos and emptiness.

'*Come on, Nazmirrah, what would Warrior say if he could see you now?*' Yes, I knew it was childish and stupid believing in a made-up character, but I always went to that when life got rough. When they first broke my nose or stuffed me into a locker, just for being Muslim and different, I remember sitting in the locker's dark, musty confines and imagining myself at the Royal Rumble 1997, seeing Shawn beating Sid. I hummed his theme song for what must have been hours till they let me out. Wrestling was always my refuge, and I suddenly felt humiliated, like I had let my heroes down.

I marched through the door with a defiant push, and instantly I sensed the black heart knew who had come knocking. The heart stood before me, pumping wildly in the center of the room. Flashing a brilliant smile, I twirled the knife between my fingers, savoring this moment of revenge. Even in its final moments, the heart would not repent or beg for forgiveness; it spouted pure hatred in a language older than time. As I lunged forward, knife in hand, I stopped and stared at the abomination. Cocking my head to the side, I looked up at the second-story balcony. A wicked thought crossed my mind. As I stepped back and slowly walked up the steps, I could feel the heart frantically calling to anything out there to come to help it. But it was in vain; the vile creature was alone.

Calmly, I climbed up on the railing and looked at the knife before tossing it away. I didn't need it. The heart pumped wildly below me as an inner peace came over me. Standing on the little wooden rail, I finally knew what my purpose in life was, and at that moment I embraced my ending.

"My name is Nazmirrah Shah, and my path is clear. *Allaahummak-fineehim bimaa shi'ta.* I am the Paladin!" Leaping off the balcony, I did a flying elbow that Savage would have been proud of. In perfect motion, I plunged into the heart, my elbow hitting it in its blackest core. The heart screamed in agony, thrashing about wildly before its core gave way, and it imploded in a haze of pure, white light. A shock wave ripped through the dark castle, sending bolts of fire rushing through the corridors. In an instant, the entire building was in flames. The castle started to crumble, bricks and stones crashing to the ground. Wooden beams cracked, and walls toppled, crushing anything below it to dust. Nothing on earth could contain the pure energy rippling through the once demonic structure. Light poured out of the windows and shot up into the sky in a mesmerizing beam of light.

We stood alone on the battlefield, Death's entire army surrounding us. Dragons were swooping overhead and the creatures of the night stared at me with bloodlust. There was nowhere to run anymore. They could have torn us apart in an instant, but they seemed to be waiting for their master. But just then, a couple of orcs decided to punish me. Armored fists from one came crashing into my skull, heavy boots breaking ribs. Crawling on the ground, with blood flowing from my mouth, I watched in silent horror as another ripped the Manual to shreds. The brave little book fought valiantly but was soon overpowered—pages fluttered through the air as the orc crushed his spine. Its cover was trampled into the mud. I watched my little protector die before my eyes. An orc grabbed me by the shoulders and flung me to the ground, driving the air from my lungs. Sword drawn, he was ready to deliver the coup de grâce when a dark voice sounded up behind him.

"Enough!" The Lord of Darkness appeared, the monsters parting way to let him through. His bony visage was locked in a horrifying smile; Death was savoring every moment of his long-awaited triumph. Lifting my bloody chin with a bony finger, the skeleton sneered at me.

"Whatever made you think you could beat me?" I gazed into his soulless eyes and laughed softly, spitting out a gob of bright red blood.

"There were three of us," I said quietly.

Death spun around and saw the column of light shooting into the sky in the distance. He screamed in terror, feeling the heart exploding and dying. He stumbled backward, trying to make sense of it all. Falling to his knees, gasping for air, he could not believe what had happened. How could this girl, this nobody beat him? How?

Panic ensued among the army; they charged forward in a blind panic, ready to destroy me. I saw them coming between swollen eyelids, rage etched on their faces. Had to fight back the darkness for just a bit longer.

They were too late. I felt the first claws plunge through me.

With my last remaining bit of energy, I slammed my fist into the ground.

'*Cero Miedo, Paladin, may you run forever my friend. I love you.*'

Epilogue

The pain was gone. I couldn't feel the jagged claws sticking out of my back. No, there was just…warmth. An incredible warmth surrounded me as my soul connected with the Aurora crystal below. Two incredible forces of nature became one: energy coursing through my veins and bolts of lightning dancing across my fingertips. My eyes were turning bright white, my blood-stained black hair undulated in the wind and floated two feet above the ground. A strange realization washed over me. This was always the plan, the final gambit. Nobody could beat Death, not even the greatest warriors in history. The Aurora crystal was not just an incredible source of energy; it was a bomb. One that was going to turn the Reaper's world into ashes. The multitude of monsters around me faded away into the light, forgotten phantoms frozen in time. My hand was glowing in a golden haze, streams of ethereal energy streaking around it as I lifted it before my eyes and stared at it. All this energy, all this power at my disposal: I was in control now. But it never crossed my mind to use it for dark purposes. No, it was not a weapon of destruction, but of salvation. Maybe it was a fool's hope, but I knew the power inside me could give the people I loved a chance. Buy them a few precious days more.

'*Don't hesitate, Michaela. Do it.*' I felt my inner voice calmly talking to me, urging me gently. Then I felt his presence again.

Death was standing in front of me, swirls of stygian darkness wrapped around him. Hissing angrily, he lowered his hood and pointed at me across the great divide between us. "You're a fool, Michaela Jones. That power is beyond your understanding and control. It will corrupt and destroy you eventually. Better warriors, titans among men, have fallen before its seduction— Hannibal, Caesar, Alexander, countless others. They all succumbed in the end, reduced to whimpering mortals before my feet. What makes you different? Answer me!" He was screaming; the skeleton's infamous calm was shattered. I lowered my head and smiled. Not the vain smile of one with the world at her feet but of a simple human at peace with herself.

"That's where you are wrong. I am not a warrior nor a god trying to change the world. I am just a girl." I closed my eyes and the ball of energy inside me exploded, blanketing the battlefield in brilliant white light. Monsters were swirling through the air, their eyes wide in shock. Dragons were crashing to the ground, flames dying inside them. Machines of war shattered before my eyes. Battlements turned to dust, and in one final act, just as the light started to fade, the wall itself began to shimmer and collapse. All became quiet as the last vestiges of the great wall that had for so long kept Death and his armies at bay, that had divided the mortal world from the great beyond, came down to the ground in a cascade of ethereal blocks. The light faded from me, and I too drifted back to the ground. Breathing deeply, I knew my end was near. The injuries were too grave; the light was taking the last bit of life from me. I spied an old lawn chair on the ground. Blood dripping from the gash in my back, I stumbled over to it and sat down.

I felt the cold plastic through my torn gray shirt. Closing my eyes, I listened to the world around me. It was quiet now, the only noise the rustling of the far-off trees and the erratic fluttering of broken flags before me. A drop of scarlet blood hung precariously from my lips, seemingly undecided if it should stay or go before dropping sadly to the ground. With mortally tired eyes, I looked over the battlefield. The myriad of damaged traps, the heaps of broken bones and the slightest twitching and painful moaning of the odd orc were the only indication of the epic ass-kicking fiesta that took place here only a few minutes ago.

The shadow walked up to me and stared out from under his black cape. It had gone so well for him, destroying any resistance that dared stand in his way with callous ease, spreading his darkness subtly through the land and gathering power as he went, and yet he could not get the better of a little girl somewhere deep in the heart of America. It was pissing off Death something terrible. He looked down, raising his bony eyebrow at the sight of the impudent child and shook his head in disbelief. I looked the Horseman straight in the face, fire dancing in my black eyes; I smiled crookedly and spat out a blood-stained tooth.

"Bitch," Death said in a gravely, demonic voice. So there we were locked as if in time, two foes standing face to skull. Neither of us willing to give an inch.

"You are simply delaying the inevitable. In the end, I always win." Death looked around the battlefield and sneered at me. "So you've destroyed a few of my soldiers, I can easily raise an army of the damned again, this is nothing. You hear me? This is nothing. You have not beaten me."

I smiled for the last time and jerked my thumb backward. "Not me, them." Death looked up in amazement. The entire town stood there looking at him and his decimated army, all with their cell phones out. The news had already started to spread like wildfire on social media, and it would not be long before the entire world knew what was going on. From here to goddamn China, everybody would see the images of Death standing over a now still figure in a little plastic chair.

I had put the son of a bitch on display for the whole world to see.

With one final act of defiance, I blew him a kiss and closed my eyes for the last time. A rough pair of hands picked me up and carried me away from the battlefield. I was safe in my father's arms again, as the other two Horsemen watched on silently. I could hear his voice whispering to me.

"His heart is destroyed. We have a chance against Death now. Rest softly, Pumpkin; you've done your part." War pushed the bloodstained hair from my eyes and cupped my face tenderly. I was home at last.

So passed Michaela Jones, last of the great engineers. Her legend spread far and wide, and she became a symbol of the resistance. The elders told many a tale of how she and the fearless Paladin, with the heart of a lion, lit the match that started the fight against the forces of evil on that cold winter's day. Not through hatred and malice but through an indestructible will and hearts that would not give up. They tell of how two smalltown girls stood up to the Lord of Darkness and refused to back down.

It was a light in the great war of our time; they gave us hope that one day, perhaps, we could win this most impossible of battles.

A battle that started on a lonely battlefield.

Somewhere in a little town in Middle America.

The End.

What's Next From The Author?

Follow John Murray McKay

www.facebook.com/NDaysSeries/

www.goodreads.com/author/show/7480193.John_Murray_McKay

ABOUT THE AUTHOR

John Murray McKay is a parts unknown writer specializing in the genres of fantasy, historical and science fiction. He started off in writing by penning the long running web series "Man on an Island." that ran for multiple years. He finds his inspiration in the works of authors like Clive Cussler and in film makers like Quentin Tarantino. His critically acclaimed debut novel 'The N Days' took him in the dark heart of a post apocalyptic USA and now he returns back to the Red, White and Blue with his second series 'The Venom Protocols'. By day, he plies his trade as an English and Social Science teacher at a local primary school. John resides in Pretoria, South Africa but hopes to move to the United States of America soon to further his career as an author. He has a dog, two rescue cat and a beard that he currently takes care of.

CHECK OUT OTHER WORKS
FROM *CORVUS QUILL PRESS LLC*

9 781734 334197